About the Author

Cheryl had always wanted to write, so when her two children left home to pursue their own careers and with their encouragement, that's exactly what she did! After many years of living abroad, Cheryl has now moved back to the UK and is working on her second book.

To
Katherine
Best wishes
Cheryl x

Dedication

The book is dedicated to: Firstly, my children, Natalie and Garry for believing in me. My parents – Mum, for your blunt, yet honest opinions. I hope you like it. Dad – for such good advice and never-ending encouragement, to all my family and friends (you all know who you are) for listening to me endlessly going on about my characters and storylines. THANK YOU!

Cheryl Baily Clarke

ALONE

AUSTIN MACAULEY
PUBLISHERS LTD.

A CIP catalogue record for this title is available from the British Library.

ISBN 978 1 78455 031 8

www.austinmacauley.com

First Published (2014)
Austin Macauley Publishers Ltd.
25 Canada Square
Canary Wharf
London
E14 5LB

Printed and bound in Great Britain

Prologue

Sometimes it's okay to be alone, to feel totally alone. It isn't an easy place to find oneself, but with time the loneliness becomes almost a friend. You find out exactly who you are, what you really want, and also, what you don't. For if we never know what it is to be alone, we will never appreciate each moment when we are not.

Chapter 1

I honestly believed that today, the day we were taking our son, the youngest of our three children off to university, was the start of 'us'. The 'us' we used to be before we became parents, before life generally got in the way of who we used to be. I naively thought we would pick up from where we left off; the day our eldest child, Louise was born, twenty-four years ago, followed by the birth of Isobelle, two years later and then our son.

The day had started off the way it should have. It was a little stressful helping James pack his belongings up to take with him to university and I felt very stressed thinking about my baby leaving the nest. Of course, this is from my perspective, a mum's perspective. My husband, Simon, seemed to be taking it all in his stride. Whereas, I, took a long hard glance at James in his room, trying desperately to capture the moments in my mind so that I could replay them at a later date. Simon ate breakfast and read the newspaper with hardly a word spoken. As the time came for us to load up the car and leave the house, I heard him saying something to our son about 'keeping his head down,' but that was it.

I stood there, thinking, 'where's the hug? Where's the praise? Where is the dad who used to say the right thing at the right time?' I suppose I was so wrapped up in my own thoughts and emotions, I just let it go.

James and I stood in our bright, sunny hallway and hugged; one of those tight, can hardly breathe kind of hugs that you need when words just aren't enough. I stayed there for as long as he would let me. Wrapped up in his arms, I felt small and fragile, finding it hard to believe that my little boy, who now towered above me, was leaving home. It seemed like only yesterday that he would run to greet me after school, desperate for cuddles.

I held back my tears because I was so proud of him. I was so happy that he had got a place in the university of his choice. I felt that this was how life was supposed to be and that all of us: Simon, Louise, Isobelle James and I were exactly where we were meant to be.

I think it was on the drive to the university that I first felt it. 'It'. Something. I didn't know exactly what the 'it' was, but it didn't feel nice. The three of us sat in the car on our journey in silence. What little conversation there was, came from James and me. Simon just drove. I found myself trying to remember the last time Simon and I had actually had a conversation, a real conversation about something other than work, the children, what we were having for lunch or dinner. I looked at him and realised we were drifting away from each other. It almost took my breath away and I sighed deeply. He took his eyes off the road for a moment and turned to look at me. A frown crossed his forehead and his eyes narrowed, but he said nothing. He didn't ask me what the sigh was for.

"You okay Mum?" James asked, leaning forward, his hand touching my shoulder.

"Yes darling," I assured him. "I was just thinking how much I'm going to miss you, that's all."

"I'm an hour away, don't forget that. Just an hour." He gently squeezed my shoulder as if to reinforce his words. "No tears seeing me off, you hear!"

I turned to look at my handsome boy and smiled. His brown eyes were sparkling as he grinned back at me. He had a beautiful infectious smile that had made him popular with everyone who knew him. His chocolate brown hair fell down into his eyes and he swept it back, running his fingers through it.

"No tears. I promise," I said, putting my hand on top of his.

Still, Simon stayed silent. Now the silence was beginning to deafen me. A strong force almost, as though he was doing it on purpose. Suddenly, the smell of leather from the interior of his new car hit me and bile rose up into my throat. I swallowed hard. The feeling I'd had earlier rushed over me, almost like a knot in the pit of my stomach, and this time I just couldn't push it away. I wanted to speak, to say something that would break through the rigid wall that was appearing in front of me; brick by brick, cementing the frosty atmosphere that seemed to come from nowhere. I tried to speak, but couldn't.

I couldn't speak to my own husband.

I studied him closely. His dark hair now peppered with grey. Isn't that how we describe a man's hair when they're turning grey? And why does it make a man look more dignified, when it makes a woman just look older? His olive skin, still tanned from the summer sun, and the lines at the corner of his eyes, hinting just a little at the tell-tale signs of aging, but somehow enhancing his features.

He was still handsome now, at the age of forty-seven. He was slender and tall. His brown eyes lighter in colour now, but still they sparkled. He didn't seem to laugh any more now, as I sat here thinking about it. Maybe his job as a lawyer had taken its toll, maybe it was just life in general, but I still found him extremely attractive…maybe I needed to show it more.

As we drove through the entrance, to the tree-lined lane that took us to the Halls. my mind wandered back to why we were there and I wanted to be sick. The feeling of dread was so great, I felt as if I was being suffocated. As soon as Simon pulled the car over, I leapt out and took a deep breath, hoping the air would take away the queasiness. I inhaled and exhaled slowly, trying to calm my breathing.

The sun was shining and it was one of my favourite times of the year. I adored those Indian summers and I started to feel a little calmer.

James and Simon were already out of the car and taking the luggage and boxes out of the boot. The Halls were lovely, we had visited them in the summer and they were just as welcoming today as they had been then. People were milling about on the campus; mum's hugging their offspring within an inch of their lives, father's carrying suitcases and other belongings up the stairs to the main entrance, students, recognizing one another from the open day, waving and shouting in sheer excitement.

"Room 201 was it?" Simon asked, already walking towards the steps carrying as much as he could.

James nodded to his father and looking at me said, "a man of few words, my father."

"I'm sorry James. I don't understand him at all," I said.

"Probably best not to try, and anyway, it's a bit too late for that now." He held out his arms to me and I laughed as I rested my head on his shoulder.

I snuggled into him for one last time and it dawned on me that even my son could see things weren't right. Unlike me, he'd obviously been far more aware of his father's shortcomings. Unravelling myself from his safe and loving arms, I took two small boxes from the car and James struggled with the last of the cases. Together, we made our way to his room. I felt so mad at Simon for not even waiting for us. We found him already there, standing in the corridor outside James's room chatting to some other parents, smiling away at them as if he was Mr. Chatty. James shot me a glance and I knew exactly what it meant. Simon had no problems talking to strangers just, it would appear, to us.

We all came to life in the hallway of rooms 200 to 220, and I wondered if any of the others were playing a role as we were. I wondered if, they too, had travelled in a silence so unbearable it made you want to weep. I watched my husband and I resented his charming easy manner. I had the urge to scream at him, I don't know what it was I wanted to scream, or which words would have come out if I'd opened my mouth. So I stayed quiet. Smiling, playing my role of dutiful wife who stood back whilst the perfect husband shone, as always. He should have been called Peter. Peter Perfect.

When the time came to say our goodbyes, I was prepared. James had already met the people staying next to and opposite his room and they'd made arrangements to go out and eat at the local pub. I felt content. He was more than ready to face the real world now. All those years of being there, nurturing him, it was done.

The question was, was I ready? Was I ready to face my empty nest?

Settling back into the car, I felt nervous to be alone with Simon. We buckled up and drove back down the beautiful driveway and exited the campus.

I forced myself to speak. "He seems settled already, doesn't he?" I said.

"He'll be fine," came the short response.

"Yes I know, it's just...well, you know," I said, not finding the right words.

"No. I don't know! It's just what?" He seemed irritated by me.

"James, being our last one. Leaving for the big wide world." I paused, turning in my seat to face him. "It's our last one. Gone."

"Oh for God's sake, Jen!" He blurted out. "You were the same over Louise, our first to go. Then it was Izzie...'oh what will I do without my girl?' Now it's James...our LAST one!" He mimicked me in a hurtful, sarcastic voice.

I stared at him in complete disbelief. His mocking voice ringing in my ears. I wanted to cry. Cry or hit him, I couldn't decide which. I sat there, trying to figure out where on earth all this was coming from. I sat speechless. Not once did he look at me. I half expected him to laugh and put a reassuring hand on my leg, but no. Nothing. Just the silence that now seemed to be our new friend. A friend I was quickly tiring of.

I timed the journey home. One hour and five minutes in complete and utter silence. I didn't know what to do. We'd always been so busy wrapped up in the lives of our children or his job, or something – anything - that somehow the conversation had just flowed. Now that I thought about it, it was mainly me that did all the talking. I couldn't even remember the last time we'd been alone together, truly alone.

As we turned into our gravelled driveway and headed up to the house, I felt determined to make an effort. To break this awkwardness that had entered, uninvited, into our lives.

I got out of the car and looked up at our beautiful double-fronted house. How I loved our home with its large black door partly hidden from view in the archway of the stone porch. Taking the keys from my bag, I unlocked the front door and walked into the hallway. The sun shone in from the back garden into the kitchen and through the glass double doors, flooding the hall with light. I put my bag and keys on the hall table and went into the kitchen. I looked out onto the south facing rear garden through the French windows and I immediately felt better. I was home now and felt safe.

It was nearly one o'clock and I decided to make a prawn salad for our lunch with my special homemade cocktail sauce and fresh crusty bread, planning that we would eat in the garden as it was still warm enough to sit outside. I'd open a bottle of Pinot and maybe then we would relax more with each other. Maybe we'd even spend the afternoon in bed. I couldn't remember the last time we'd made love in the afternoon and I set about preparing the salad and decided I'd have a glass of wine before lunch, just to get me in the mood. As I was unscrewing the bottle, Simon appeared in the kitchen doorway.

"Okay," he said, "I'll be off then. I'm not sure what time I'll be back, so don't wait for me tonight." He had already changed into his suit and turned to leave.

"Simon," I called out, and he stopped and turned around.

"What?" he asked, in that irritated tone again, rattling his keys.

"I'm making us lunch. I didn't think you'd be going into work today."

"Why? Because our precious baby boy has left home?" he sneered. "I've got meetings back-to-back this afternoon and someone has to earn the money to pay for all of this!"

"What does that mean?" I asked, flabbergasted. "Simon, we need to talk. Please, stay and eat with me."

"You know what Jen, get a grip. In fact, get a bloody life!"

With that he was gone, out of the door. I stood motionless, listening as he started up the car and heard the wheels moving on the gravel. I couldn't understand it. I stood there for some minutes, four maybe five. I slumped down at the kitchen table, in complete despair.

My first instinct was to call Anna, my closest friend. However, the urge to have a glass of wine was greater. I poured myself a large glass and stood looking out onto the garden. Our beautiful garden. I stared at the table and chairs where I'd imagined Simon and I would have sat eating our salad, drinking wine. I actually laughed out loud as I realised that my plans that afternoon had included sex! The last time we'd been together was after our annual barbecue that we'd had on my birthday.

We'd both drank far too much and if I was being honest, the details were a little sketchy. What the hell had just happened? I stood trying to figure out things in my mind, taking large gulps of wine in an attempt to help and take the edge off it all.

A phone ringing snapped me out of my thoughts and I ran up the stairs to our bedroom, following the sound of Simon's mobile, rushing before whoever it was hung up. He'd left it on our bed. I checked who was calling before answering. It was Simon's secretary, Jean.

"Hello Jean," I said, a little breathless from running up the stairs. "Simon's left his phone here."

"Oh hello Jennifer," she sounded pleased to hear my voice. "I'm so sorry to disturb you. I know Simon's not coming in to the office today, but I just wanted to ask him something. If I could just speak with him for one minute, I promise I won't keep him. I know James went off today and he said you'd be spending the day together."

Confusion filled my already confused mind. "I'm sorry Jean, he's not here at the moment. Can I take a message?"

"Oh no, not to worry Jennifer, it's nothing that can't wait until Monday morning. I just thought if I could talk to him for a moment…Anyway, enjoy the rest of your day together! Bye bye now," she said, cheerfully and hung up.

I flopped onto the bed and lay back. I could hear my heart beating fast and it felt as if it was rising up into my throat, choking me. The tears came now, quickly. Where could Simon be? I sniffed and looked at his phone. There was a message. A text message. I took a deep sobbing breath, for I knew, I just knew this was the 'something' I'd sensed all day. I pressed the unlock key and then 'open' to view the message. My heart almost stopped.

"Where are you my darling? I'm here and waiting AND I've ordered my second glass of wine. Hurry my love…I miss you xxx

The message came from someone called Sarah. Sarah West. Sent at 14:05. I looked at the clock on my bedside table. It was almost three o'clock. My hands shook so much that I dropped the phone and it fell onto my chest. I left it there for several minutes. I had a choice. I ignore the text, the call from Jean and wait for his explanation, or I snoop. Go through all his messages and calls. I had to make the right decision because I knew deep down inside of me, that this choice would change my life. Forever.

Chapter 2

I lay on our bed for about ten minutes, just sobbing. Eventually, exhausted from crying I picked up the phone and looked at it. How had our marriage come to this? Twenty-five years we had been married and it never occurred to me that Simon would have an affair. I took a deep breath and unlocked the phone again. Shaking, I selected the 'inbox'.

I noticed as I went through the list, several messages from our daughter, Louise. I found this a little odd as she wasn't the best at keeping in regular contact. There were also some texts from me. I opened them up even though I knew their content. It felt safe to open mine. No surprises. Just the usual mundane stuff about dinner, and what James's movements would have been on that particular day. How boring they must have seemed to him when he had Sarah bloody West waiting for him intoxicated with alcohol.

My mind was racing...maybe I'd got it all wrong. Maybe she was just a work colleague. Or a client, or maybe just a friend he'd chosen not to tell me about. Truth was, I knew she was none of these things. I knew she was his lover. Then, underneath my last message sent two days ago, informing my pig of a husband that his dinner would be ready for him at seven, there they were, message after message from stupid Sarah West. I suddenly gathered myself, maybe it was simply the adrenalin rushing through me, but I sat up and propped myself up with the pillows as if snuggling down to read a good book.

Wed. 21/09/11@ 07:25 Darling...I miss you already.
Last night was amazing! I can
still smell you on my pillow.
Call me. Xxx

BASTARD!!!!!!!

Wed. 21/09/11 @ 09:30 You make me smile. Thanks
for the call. You've got me desperate
for you. Xxx

SLUT!!!!!!!!

Wed. 21/09/11@ 12:30 Richard wants me to work through
lunch, darling. He's out, so pop in
bring me a sandwich ☺ tuna salad
no mayo....you KNOW what I like X

BITCH!!!!!! No mayonnaise? Obviously needs to watch
her weight!!!!

As I scrolled down the numerous messages from Sarah
West, it dawned on me that maybe he'd been seeing her in
June when we'd celebrated my forty-fifth birthday and our
wedding anniversary...I opened random texts, ignoring the
words now, just checking the dates....August 24, August 21,
August 17,....it became clear that she'd text him almost every
day, so I kept scrolling through them, so many of them. June
30...June 15 and then, there it was, Friday 03 June 2011.

Fri. 03/06/11 @ 19:22 Good luck my darling with this
evening.
I know it's gonna be difficult, but just
smile & think of me. Remember last
night, remember one day all this will
be in your past....the future is 'us'
Just you & me. I love you Si xxx

By now, the feeling of dread had switched to one of
complete and utter anger. With each heartbeat thumping in my
ears, I felt a renewed energy. My hands were literally shaking.
I closed the inbox and opened up the sent messages box. Sarah
West's name filled the screen, scrolling down it became
obvious he'd deleted all messages he'd sent to me or anyone

else. Just those he'd lovingly sent to Sarah West remained. I continued to scroll and randomly opened a message.

> Wed. 21/12/11 @ 20:08 Missing you already my darling.
> Just got home. All family gathering! I
> Hope you packed my extra special
> gift & open it on Christmas day as
> we planned. I'll text you every day
> & call you on 25th as promised. Safe
> flight my darling. All my love Si x

I frantically tried to remember Christmas Day. At what point did he leave us all to call Sarah 'stupid' West? I couldn't recall a specific moment. And the message she'd sent on my birthday played around and around in my head!! Her words 'I know it will be difficult'. Had life with me been so awful? I doubt he told her that we'd made love that night and that nobody would ever have guessed he was in the middle of this fully blown affair.

I couldn't face any more. Not yet. It was now five o'clock. Two hours I'd been here on our bed, in our bedroom. I shook my head as if this would clear the past two hours out of my mind. What was I going to do? I had to devise a plan of action.

I went downstairs into the study and taking a piece of paper, I scribbled down her name. As if I was going to forget her name. Thoughts raced through my mind. Should I call her and ask to speak to Simon? That would spoil their afternoon of fun. Shock them both. No, I had to keep this close to my chest. Play it cool. Take my time. I held all the power now. That's the way I wanted to keep it.

****

So that was that. Plan of action: play it cool. I thought it best to carry on with my usual routine, preparing and cooking dinner. For my husband, Peter Perfect. The bastard. Without James, my life now seemed almost meaningless and now it was just going to be Simon and me! I felt physically sick at the thought of it all. What was I going to do?

'DO nothing', I told myself quickly. Stick to the plan. Give him enough rope to hang himself. As I peeled the vegetables, I thought about how I was going to question him about his day at 'the office'. It even crossed my mind to write down a list of questions and ask him one by one, keeping it hidden on my lap throughout dinner. Watching him sweat, watching him squirm. MI5 could use a woman like me…I'd be great! But what should I do with his phone?

I decided that the most important thing to do was approach the subject breezily, in a carefree, nonchalant manner. Throwing things into the conversation gradually as though it really wasn't that important to me. 'Oh by the way, darling, you left your phone on the bed,' I'd say matter-of-factly. Or 'by the way, work called for you…' and I'd let my voice trail off, all the while watching his reaction.

As I basted the chicken, I sat on the sofa in the family room and sipped my second (large) glass of Pinot that day. Six thirty-five. He'd be home just before seven. I was ready, just as I always was. (It should be me having the affair with the tediousness of my life).

Dinner was in the oven. I was prepared. I closed my eyes and took a series of deep breaths. PLAY. IT. COOL. I repeated over and over in my head. Whatever tomorrow brings, the important thing is, to gather as much information from him over dinner and take it from there. Saying nothing, not giving the game away was vital.

I had started to lose my cool around ten minutes after seven. Where was he? I picked up the home phone and called his mobile twice. This was all part of the plan. I left a voicemail after the second call asking him where he was. Then I realised I'd already spoken to Jean earlier on his mobile and he'd see this from the received calls. Damn. My plan was already falling apart. MI5 wouldn't want me after all.

I started to plate up our dinner. As I poured the gravy over the meat and vegetables, I heard the key in the front door. It was seven thirty. He was here. This was it. I must be calm, stay calm. I listened as he walked into the hallway and throw his keys on the hall table. I shuddered at the sound. Carefully and slowly, my hands starting to shake again, I placed the pan of gravy back onto the hob. His feet moved onto the wooden floor of the kitchen. His mobile caught my eye on the kitchen windowsill where I'd placed it earlier. Without thinking, I picked it up and turned to look at him. He was just stood there, loosening his tie.

My plan went completely out of the window as I brought my arm back and threw his phone at his head! It was as if time had stopped. Everything appeared to be in slow motion. I saw the expression on his face as the phone flew through the air. He was horrified and panicking but didn't have time to duck down very far before it struck him with force in the middle of his forehead.

"You're late, you bastard!" I screamed at him.

"What the hell are you doing? Have you gone out of your mind?" He yelled back at me, checking his head for blood. BABY!!

'You know exactly what's going on. Pig!" I was out of control. "Had a nice afternoon have you?" He was kneeling down picking up the pieces of phone that lay scattered across the kitchen floor. "Well?" I continued, "I'm waiting!"

"You're mad!" he shouted, a look of hatred crossing his face.

"Damn right I'm mad. Telling me you were going to the office when all the time you were…" I stopped short of saying he was with her. Tears rolled down my flushed hot cheeks.

"All the time I was what?" he asked, a horrible sarcastic tone in his voice as he carried on retrieving bits of phone and putting them in a pile on the table.

"You know exactly what, Simon! You didn't even go into the office."

"Did I say I was going into the office?" He frowned at me, waiting for my answer. I couldn't speak. "No," he continued when it was clear I didn't have a reply. "I didn't! What I said was that I had meetings all afternoon. They were my words if I remember correctly."

"Well you're late." I snapped, recalling his exact words were 'back-to-back meetings,' and I knew who's back he was talking about.

"I also told you I'd be late back tonight. In fact, I told you not to wait for me!" He stood up and scratching his head, tried to put his phone back together.

He was back in control, not that he'd ever lost it (so much for my plan and so much for playing it cool.). A lump was beginning to appear on his forehead. I pulled out one of the chairs and slumped into it. I had to say something. I remembered the feeling I'd had this morning in the car. We had to try and sort this out. We couldn't ignore what was going on.

"I know," I said quietly, wiping the tears from my face with my hands.

"You know what, Jen?" he asked, not even looking up.

"About Sarah. Sarah West." I sat there waiting for his reaction. None came. "Did you hear what I said?" I asked, desperation rising in my throat. "I know all about your little affair with Sarah West!"

"Yes," he said, emotionless. "I heard you."

"And?"

"And what?"

"Oh my God." I stood up in disbelief. I wanted to hit him. Right in the middle of his big fat forehead.

"I really can't deal with this right now," he said, gathering up the wreckage that was once his phone and the lifeline to his sordid little affair. I reached over and knocked them out of his hand and the pieces went crashing back onto the floor.

We stood there face-to-face, for what seemed like an eternity. I honestly didn't know how he was going to react. This wasn't a situation we'd been in before. I looked at him, urging him from inside my heart to hold me, to tell me he was sorry, and that it was all going to be okay. He'd made a terrible mistake.

Finally, he spoke. "I can't do this any more." He started to walk away and I grabbed him by the arm. He stopped looking down at my hands, not making eye contact he said, "leave me alone, Jen." And he pulled away.

He went upstairs and I stood motionless listening, my breathing was rapid and I felt like I was going to fall. I knew this wasn't just some affair. I had never in all the years I'd known him, seen Simon behave in this way. I was scared and my heart ached. It went silent upstairs and I just stood there.

I stood in my beautiful, bespoke kitchen, afraid of what was going to happen. I had never felt so alone in all my life.

Chapter 3

Simon didn't come down all evening. I could hear movements from upstairs. I half expected him to appear with a suitcase packed and ready to leave our home as well as our marriage.

I stayed downstairs. Kept my distance. I put our dinners aside and wrapped them in foil. Why? Did I really think that he'd come and eat with me after everything that had just happened? I thought back to this afternoon and what he'd said as he left for his little rendezvous with Sarah slutty West. He told me to 'get a life. Get a bloody life…'or words to that effect. He'd always been moody if things didn't go to plan, or should I say 'his' way, but he had never spoken to me like that before. Why had I let that go? I sighed, pouring myself another large glass of wine. I think this was my fourth glass. I was losing count and I didn't care.

It was now close to ten o'clock. I looked over from where I was sat in the open-plan family room to the kitchen and the two plates sat on top of the worktop. I walked over and took the foil off one of the perfectly laid out dinners, perfectly cold now. This was my life! Preparing and dishing up beautifully arranged, lovingly prepared food. I didn't need to 'get a life'. I had a life…until some woman came along. I tried to visualize what she must look like.

Young? Obviously! And thin. WITHOUT A DOUBT! And that was all I could come up with. Young and thin. The two things I certainly no longer was. I picked up the plate and threw it into the bin, followed by the other one. Normally I hated throwing food away, but today wasn't a normal day. I looked at my designer plates sat in the bin and closed the shiny stainless steel lid. That would only leave me now with six dinner plates to my expensive dinner service…I laughed out loud and snorted. I surprised myself, I had never snorted before. Maybe this was the start of a new me. Somehow, this wasn't a good start. An overweight, old and snorting me.

Tomorrow, I told myself was a new day and was going to be a new start of the new me, but without the snorting.

I picked the plates out of the bin and put them into the dishwasher. I downed the remains of the wine in my glass. Usually, I was a 'one glass of wine with dinner' kind of a woman and I'd sip it. Now it appeared I was in danger of becoming a snorting alcoholic. This amused me no end and I found myself laughing hysterically. For about five minutes, I continued to giggle to myself, then I heard a noise from upstairs. I stopped laughing and looked up at the ceiling, grabbing onto the kitchen table for balance as I swayed.

Then I realised the noise was coming from directly above the kitchen, from the guest room. Simon, the cheating bastard, was in the guest room. I unlocked the French doors that led into the garden and looked up in the direction of the guest window. A light was on. I came back to earth with a woozy thud! He had moved out of our bedroom.

There was a nip in the air now. September, and the nights had certainly begun to draw in. I popped back inside for a throw off one of the sofas and threw it over my shoulders. Switching on the outside lights, I stepped back into the night. It felt so peaceful, and walking up the steps to the raised patio where the cast iron table and chairs took centre place I sat down. To the right, were the garden sofa and armchairs where we'd always sit with coffee, after eating on warm summer nights. I looked up at the house, our family home. A tear ran down my face as it occurred to me that I could lose all of it, and I had absolutely no idea what I was going to do.

****

I woke the next morning, at seven, to the alarm ringing on my bedside table. I looked to my right, and the empty pillow brought the memories of yesterday flooding back. Ouch, my head hurt! I headed into our en-suite for some tablets and caught sight of myself in the bathroom mirror. This didn't help me. My blonde shoulder-length hair was in need of brushing after a restless night, and was now greying rapidly – I looked old. No wonder Simon was leaving me.

Was he leaving me? I contemplated this as I leaned over the basin and stared at my reflection. He might not be leaving me. He was having an affair, but it might just be a fling, just a fling and nothing more. I couldn't believe that I was being so blasé about the whole thing. I ran my fingers through my hair, trying to flatten the sticking up bits, swallowed two tablets and prepared to do battle. Well, a talk at least, with Simon, my husband. I had dropped the word 'bastard' for now.

Crossing the landing, to the opposite side of the house, I knocked gently on the door of the guest room. I slowly opened the door. Simon was already up and he'd left the bed unmade. This irritated me. When you're having an affair, and breaking someone's heart, the least you could do was to make the bloody bed. BASTARD!

I checked the guest bathroom, not there. With some urgency, I rushed downstairs into the kitchen, expecting to see him sat at the kitchen table reading the paper. No sign.

"Simon!" I shouted, coming back in to the hall. The newspaper was still on the floor in the hall, but pushed to one side, presumably from when he'd opened the door to leave.

I stood there, breathing heavily. His keys had gone from the hall table, and with a heavy heart, I looked through the living room window from where you could see the driveway. His car had gone. He had actually gone. I raced back upstairs to our bedroom and into the dressing room, frantically opening his closet doors. Everything was still there. So, not gone for good yet then.

Again, I caught a glimpse of myself. I walked over to the dressing table, which sat nestled neatly under the window. The blind was open at the window, and the sun was shining through. I didn't like what I saw. The light hit each crack and line on my face, magnifying them. I was tired, so tired and it showed. I went to the shower and did something I hadn't done in a long time. I took off my dressing gown, and pulled my nightdress over my head and facing the full-length mirror I made myself stare at my naked body. Now, I remembered why I avoided it at all costs.

I just stood there, looking at my sad reflection. I turned sideways. I was horrified if I didn't pull my stomach in, I looked about three months pregnant. I breathed in, but the result wasn't much better. I felt sick at the sight of myself and a slight sense of shame. How had I not noticed what I looked like before now? Of course I'd noticed...why had I avoided mirrors everyday? Why then, hadn't I done something about it? Why had I let myself turn into THIS? I was forty-five, but felt more like sixty-five. I looked at my drooping breasts and my orange-peel legs. Turning around, I studied my bottom. Everything had drooped, and the sun seemed to shine just that little bit stronger, as if to intensify every bit of cellulite and any stretch marks that I'd kept well hidden under my clothes.

My ankles, I decided, were the only saving grace of a body well and truly past its sell-by date! I reached over and closed the bathroom blind and it hit the windowsill with a thud. I slid down the tiled wall, and watched my face become distorted as I let out a yell before breaking down and crying my eyes out.

Eventually, I managed to pull myself up off the floor, and turned on the shower. All the energy had drained from my body and I wondered if all this would translate into a dramatic weight loss. I stepped inside the glass cubicle and let the water rush over me. I washed and conditioned my hair, and finally after I'd had my fill of the warm water, I reached out, and grabbed a fluffy towel from the wall mounted radiator, and wrapped it around my head.

As I dried my hideous form, thoughts turned to what I was going to do. I tried to think clearly, but my head was in turmoil. Parts of last night's conversation kept running through my thoughts. Flashes of her text messages darted in and out of my brain. Was this how it felt to go mad?

It took all my strength to dress and dry my hair. Once downstairs, I checked my mobile to see if Simon had called me. There was a message from Anna, reminding me about her 'farewell to summer' barbecue, and asking me to confirm I was still doing the salads.

Oh God. What will I say to Anna? I'm such a private person; I never really confide in her about Simon and me, which is why I didn't call her yesterday, when I could probably have done with talking to a friend. Plus, there really wasn't ever much to tell. Whereas Anna on the other hand, let the whole world know about her life.

Anna had been my best friend all the way through high school. We were each other's bridesmaids. She had married Tim Bradley, a banker, and they had two boys together. David was now twenty-two and John was seventeen. Making myself a coffee, I suddenly realised just what a high maintenance friend she actually was – as a friend and a wife! Here I was, in my darkest hour, and instead of turning to her for solace, I was worrying about what she would think?

I decided, now, wasn't the right time to call or answer her text. Not until I knew what I was going to do, because SHE would want to know WHAT I was going to do, and then she would spend half of the conversation disagreeing with me.

So, I did the next best thing: I called Simon. It went straight to voicemail. It was only after my fifth attempt and fourth hysterical message, that I realised his phone wasn't working after I'd smashed it into bits last night.

It was almost nine-thirty. I couldn't face breakfast, but I wanted a coffee, but not here in the house. I'd never been one to sit alone in a coffee shop, but decided that today I was going to do something different. I grabbed my keys and hopped into my car, heading into town. As I drove up the quaint high street into town, full of familiar shops, a new place caught my eye. It was a little coffee shop called 'Cozy', painted black, with a sign outside in burnt orange, with stainless steel lettering. It did indeed look inviting, and I parked up in a space just a little further up.

It was buzzing inside, with people chatting away at lovely little black tables, with stainless steel chairs, and carrying on the orange theme with cups and accessories. It had a lovely feel to it, and I was glad I'd made the decision to come out. I got into the queue, nervously eyeing up the room for a vacant table. There was just one left in the window. There were three people in front of me; an elderly couple that I felt sure wouldn't be taking out, and a pretty, slim young woman behind them. She was frantically searching through her oversized bag, and muttering under her breath. I could hear her mobile phone ringing, and as she finally found it, the caller must have hung up as the ringing stopped.

"Aaargh," she let out a moan, "bloody bag!" She looked at me, smiling, her small button nose scrunching up. I gave her a half-grin back. I didn't want to get into a conversation, not today. Normally, I'd smile and agree with her, but I'd come here to 'Cozy' for some quiet.

"Don't you hate it when that happens?" She continued, waiting for a response. "You can guarantee, I'll put it back in my bag and they'll call again." She didn't seem to mind having a one-way conversation at all. "I should pop it in here," she said, showing me a nifty side compartment designed especially for mobiles. "Oh well, never mind."

It was her turn to order, and I watched as the couple headed towards the table in the window. Damn! Just my luck, I'd really fancied sitting there and watching the world go by. Now, I feared, a table would come available and the pretty woman would insist I sit with her. Not today, I wanted to be alone with my thoughts. I didn't want to make small talk about the weather or the latest fashion in designer handbags.

Inside my head, I started to repeat a mantra of 'please be a take-out, please be a take-out' as I checked out the list on the board of the different coffee's available. I just wanted a basic cappuccino as I didn't even recognize what half of them were! The woman ordered a tall, skinny latte, and I watched as she handed over her money and took her coffee from the counter. I was just about to order mine when her phone started to ring again, and as she turned to leave, she miscalculated and bumped straight into me, spilling her skinny bloody latte all over me. I was drenched and it was hot!

"Oh my God!' she cried out. "I'm so sorry."

I burst out crying, tears pouring down my face and I heard the most awful wailing sound coming from my mouth; a sound I'd never heard before, or ever wanted to hear again.

After a lot of patting me down with cloths and serviettes to mop up my tears, everything calmed down. People had finally stopped glaring at me with expressions of horror on their faces, and gone back to their own chitchat. The lady behind the counter, Gill, apparently, was very apologetic, and as soon as a table became available, settled me down in a nice, quiet corner with a cappuccino and a vanilla muffin on the house. Just what I needed when I was hoping to lose weight!

"Now then," Gill said, "you just take your time. If you need anything else, just call me over, okay?" She gave me a sympathetic smile, and I nodded feeling pathetic and scanned the room to make sure no one I knew had witnessed what had happened. The cause of my outburst was hovering by the door, I could tell she didn't know whether to make a quick getaway or come over to me.

'Go away, go away, GO AWAY!' I repeated in my head, my second mantra of the day so far. She obviously didn't get my mantra as she started to walk gingerly over towards me.

"Again, I'm so sorry." She looked so guilty, I immediately felt bad for her. "I don't know what to say. I…"

"It's okay," I said, beckoning her to sit down at my table. "I'm just having a really bad day and…"

"And I made it considerably worse." She smiled at me, showing off a perfect set of white teeth.

"Well, you could say that," I replied, trying hard to smile back, and suddenly becoming aware that, as well as a good pair of ankles, I too had nice teeth. "Actually, I feel a little better after our little episode, believe it or not."

"Oh I believe you. I'm a great believer in letting it all out. I'm Jade by the way, Jade Christie."

"Jennifer Aagar," I said, as we shook hands, "pleased to meet you, Jade."

"Really?" She giggled and then suddenly let out a gasp, which made me jump a little. "I've just had a great idea. I'm going to give you a whole new look, a makeover!"

"Oh," I said, sitting back in my chair feeling very deflated. She'd just this minute met me and decided that I needed a new look. Strangers looked at me and wanted to give me makeovers! Did I really look that bad, even when fully clothed? Could my day get any worse? Why hadn't I just stayed at home, boiled the kettle and had an instant coffee in the safety of my own kitchen?

"Oh no, that came out wrong...don't look like that." She went on, "let me explain. I own the salon around the corner, the one on Corden's Lane. Do you know it?" From the blank expression on my face, she could see that I didn't. She went on to explain that it was called 'Jade's' (what else?), and that she had just set up a business there a few months ago. "We do everything there: hair, beauty treatments, everything! I would like to offer you one of our pamper packages, on the house!"

"Jade, that's very kind, but really there's no need."

"But I want to. Please, won't you let me? It will make me feel better." She gave me such a kind, caring glance that I couldn't refuse. "Great! I'd have worried about you forever if you hadn't accepted."

'Forever' seemed like a very long time and a huge exaggeration, but somehow when Jade said it, you somehow felt it was true.

She left me with my coffee and muffin, and I actually felt my spirits had lifted by meeting her. We'd talked about our options for my hair, but she'd thought I'd look good with a blonde bob and highlights. She gave me her business card and told me to call that afternoon with dates when I was available. She told me to 'block at least four hours of my day'. Gosh, that's serious pampering, and I didn't mention that I was free any day, every day for the foreseeable future. When I asked her why she was being so kind, she had told me that people didn't usually cry over spilt coffee!!

Chapter 4

After arriving home from my morning at Cozy's, I set about planning my pamper day. With James now at university, my time was my own. After all those years of my day being mapped out around the children, it felt strange to have time on my hands. I was going to have to get used to it.

I checked the home phone, no messages. Simon hadn't called to say he was sorry for everything. So, I called the salon. I spoke to Fria, who booked me in for next Saturday morning at ten o'clock. She informed me that she'd been expecting my call and that Jade would be doing my haircut, I had a consultation with Maxime, for my colour, and that Belinda B (apparently there were two Belinda's), would be doing my facial and full body treatments. FULL BODY TREATMENTS. I pulled my stomach in just at the thought of someone seeing my body, let alone touching it. I came off the phone feeling very special. As though I actually mattered. I smiled to myself at the thought of turning up at Anna's barbecue, on Saturday evening, looking fabulous. Simon would soon see he'd made a mistake. He'd see my new look and beg for my forgiveness. The phone rang and brought me straight back down to earth.

"Hello?"

"Jen." It was Simon.

"Oh, hi," I said, quietly. My heart was pounding as I had no idea what he was about to say.

"Look, I think it's best if I move out for a while."

"What?" I asked, not believing what I was hearing. "What do you mean for a while? How long's a while?"

"I don't know."

"You don't know!"

"No," he said, and there was silence.

"Simon!"

"I'm still here," he muttered, but we both knew he really wasn't.

"I thought you'd gone," I replied, ironically.

"You'd have heard the tone if I'd hung up," he explained, and I suddenly thought how irritating his voice was, how irritating he was!

"Don't you think we should talk about things?"

"I can't talk to you when you're like this."

"Like what?!" I yelled, proving his point.

"Well, like this!"

If this had been a tennis match, it would be fifteen love right now.

"Simon," I said, calmly, "I have just discovered that you're having an affair. How do you expect me to be?"

Fifteen all.

"I really can't deal with all of this right now, Jen. What with work and everything…it's all a bit too much for me."

I was gobsmacked. "Work AND everything?"

"Yes."

"And, the everything being…" I cut off and stopped myself from pointing out that the 'everything' was his slutty little girlfriend. "Her I suppose!"

"You see?" he went on in a very condescending tone.

"Oh yes Simon, I see. You can't face me or come home because you'd much rather stay with your slutty little bitch at her place, her whorehouse." I tried not to, but it was impossible not to vent. Impossible not to use words and expressions I don't think I'd ever heard come out of my mouth in my life so far. "And who could blame you? I'm sure it's been so difficult to come home for all these years to your fat, old boring wife!"

Unsurprisingly, he hung up. I immediately called the office, but Jean told me he was not to be disturbed. It struck me that maybe Jean knew. Maybe everyone knew. I thought back to yesterday and the messages on his phone. Louise. Did she know? Is that what she'd been texting him about? Lou wasn't one for a lot of communication, not like Isobelle who was never off the phone. Why hadn't I looked at her messages as well as slutty Sarah's? The painful doubts and thoughts started all over again and ran riot in my head.

How could he have done this to me?

Soon enough it was six o'clock in the evening and no one was coming home, I didn't need to cook dinner for anyone. I couldn't face eating alone and I'd sat all afternoon watching daytime television until I couldn't watch any more. I set the house alarm and went upstairs, closed the curtains and curled up in bed. No tears came, there were no more left to cry. I just lay there, my eyes wide open, hoping sleep would come soon and give me some relief.

Sleep did eventually come and I woke at ten o'clock the next morning. I'd had a restless night and remembered looking at the clock a few times during the night, but just lay there. I couldn't believe it was ten, but like my mother had once said, if you slept in, it's because your body needed sleep. I smiled as I thought about my parents.

They were travelling the world together and hadn't been home for years now. They had always been free spirits and it hadn't come as a surprise to any of us when they announced they were selling up and leaving suburbia. Considering how laid-back my parents and my childhood had been, it was unusual that I have always been a little uptight. Aunt Rose, my mother's older sister, had never agreed with their lifestyle.

"A child needs boundaries," she would tell my mother. "You can't let a small person make all their own decisions."

"Jenny's fine," my mother would reply. "She's got a wise, old head on her shoulders."

"Is it any wonder? Somebody in your household needs one!" said Aunt Rose.

Aunt Rose was the complete opposite to my mum. Whereas mum dressed in long flowing skirts and sandals, no make-up and long dark flowing curls, Aunt Rose was blonde, sophisticated and always dressed up to the nines. She owned her own fashion business and had never married or had children of her own. Mum always described her as 'the ambitious one'. And that was a true description of her.

She'd started off working as a sales assistant in 'Trundells', a large department store in town. After six months she was running the floor of ladies fashion and within two years she was promoted to head buyer. She would tell me that none of it was down to luck, but pure drive and ambition.

"Jennifer,' she would say, never calling me Jen or Jenny. "I had to work twice as hard as the others, because I was beautiful. People didn't take me seriously at first and oh, the jealousy." She'd pause as if recalling those days. "Anyway, I didn't need friends. I'll never forget their faces when I designed my first collection and got my own label. They were green with envy. Green!! Which is why most of the designs were in that very colour?" And she would laugh out loud. She had such a wicked sense of humour. She tried to make everyone believe she was emotionless, a hard businesswoman, but where her family were concerned, she had the softest, biggest heart you would ever find.

She had resigned from the department store soon after that and started up her own label 'Just Rose' and had never looked back. Her designs were so chic, she sold all over the world. She lived in the most beautiful cottage and drove a red sports car. At seventy years of age, she still wore sunglasses on her head, even on the dullest of days. Always immaculate, she lived life to the full in the very next village to me. She sold her company five years ago for a small fortune and spent her days volunteering her services to help the 'old folk'.

I decided to call her. "Aunt Rose, it's me Jennifer." I tried to sound cheerful.

"Darling," she sang out, happy to hear my voice. "How are you? Oh it's so lovely to hear from you."

"I was just thinking of you and so I thought I'd give you a call to see how you are."

"That's so kind, my darling. Now, tell me. Did James get off okay to university? I didn't want to call in case you were all teary. I know it would just irritate that husband of yours."

"He did just fine." I laughed, knowing that she hated tears and fuss as much as Simon did. "He settled in very quickly."

"Of course he did! You did a good job there, my dear. Please don't tell me you've called the poor boy a hundred times since he left."

It occurred to me that I hadn't even thought about calling him. "No, not once," I replied, truthfully.

"Well, that's good to know. You don't want to embarrass the boy in front of his new pals. Louise and Isobelle, they're okay?"

"Yes, they're both fine, last I heard..." My voice trailed off.

"Jennifer?" She could sense something. "Everything alright with you?"

"Yes, everything's fine," I lied.

"That's two fine's. What's happened my dear?" Her voice as always, was soft and caring. "Jennifer?"

"I'm fine, honestly I am. Just feeling the effects of an empty nest, that's all."

"No, that's not it. A person who says they're fine, usually isn't. What is it? Is it that buffoon of a husband?" She had never thought Simon good enough for me. She knew from my silence that it was. "What has the fool done?"

"Aunt Rose..." I began, but I couldn't find any words.

"Right," she said, sternly. "What are your plans for today?"

"I haven't got any."

"That settles it then. Put something nice on and get to mine for twelve. I'm taking you for lunch somewhere fabulous."

"Oh, that's really kind of you, but I really don't feel like going out today."

"Well I do. I want to go to Haversham Park. My treat. I've been sat here since my car went into the garage on Friday and I'm so glad you called. Come on then, chop chop."

There was no point in arguing with her and she had hung up before I could protest any further. All of a sudden, people were hanging up on me. As I sat on the end of the bed, my mobile rang. It was Isobelle.

"Izzie, hello."

"Hey mum! You okay?" she asked, cheerfully.

"Yes darling, I'm fine." That word again. "And you?" I asked quickly, getting the subject off me. "It's early for you to be calling at the weekend. Everything okay?"

"Everything's perfect. I'm off to Paris next week with my boss, Clara. She's looking at some new designers and asked me to go with her. Can you believe it?" she asked, so excited.

"Yes, my love. I can believe it. Wait until I tell your Aunt Rose. Actually, I'm on my way over there, we're going out for lunch. We're going to Haversham Park."

"Blimey!" She giggled. "Let's hope she's paying then. Well give her my love. Is dad there? I'll have a quick word with him."

"No," I said immediately. "He's not in at the moment. Why don't you give him a call on his mobile, tell him your news."

"Okay, will do. I'll text you when I'm back from Paris. Love you!" And she hung up.

Did people not say goodbye any more?

As I was looking through my clothes, pondering what to wear, my mobile rang again. It was Louise. She'd just spoken to Izzie and was also very excited for her sister to be going off to Paris.

"What am I going to wear for lunch, Lou?" I asked, flicking through the hangers.

"What about your pale blue silk blouse and white linen trousers? You wore them for your birthday, you looked lovely."

"Oh yes…" I said, searching frantically through the rails. Perfect, I thought as I found it. Taking the trousers off the hanger, I laid my outfit on the bed. "Thanks for that darling, I didn't have a clue."

"Well, that's what eldest daughters are for. Probably the last chance you'll get to wear them, this Indian summer won't last long now."

"Very true," I agreed. "Anyway, you and Scott up to anything special today?"

"No, not much." She sounded vague. Scott was her childhood sweetheart and they'd been living together since they both left university. "What's Dad up to whilst you're out with Aunt Rose?" she asked, changing the subject.

"He's golfing. Maybe try his mobile."

"Okay, but I haven't been able to get him the last couple of days."

"Well, he did drop his phone the other evening, clumsy thing…" I said, my voice trailing off. "Did you want him for anything in particular?" I asked, very curious as to why she'd be calling Simon.

"No, no. Just wanted to talk to him about a case at work, that's all. Anyway, have a great lunch and I'll speak soon. Bye Mum."

"Bye Lou," I said pleased to at last have a 'goodbye' at the end of a phone conversation.

I looked at the outfit she'd suggested and my stomach churned as I remembered the last time I'd worn it. It was comfortable though and stylish too. As I fastened the trousers, I noticed they went on a little easier than in June and I realised I had lost a little weight after all.

Aunt Rose was waiting for me in her very apt rose garden, sat on the little white bench under her kitchen window, looking radiant, as always. Her soft grey hair and her steely blue eyes shone in the sunshine. She was wearing a platinum satin blouse with grey linen trousers with a coral shawl draped over her shoulders, with matching handbag and shoes. I got out of the car and walked up the garden path to give her a big hug.

"Oooh, that's a lovely hug," she said, her voice all muffled from being tucked away in my arms.

"That's from me, Lou and Izzie. They both called me after you...hey, you didn't put them up to it, did you?" I asked, releasing her from my hug.

She shook her head and smiled and I didn't know if she had or not.

"Don't you look beautiful, as always," I said, stepping back admiring her.

"Thank you, I do try." She winked as she stood up and followed me to the car. "Having said that, look at you. You look lovely."

"Really? I think I need to lose some weight to be honest."

"No, Jennifer. You look radiant. Really you do. Has he finally left you so as you can breathe?"

We both got into the car and I didn't answer her. I hadn't expected her to say something like that and I hadn't planned on telling her that Simon had left. What did she mean by that anyway? I said nothing. Aunt Rose had patience in abundance, so she wasn't going to dig. I knew it was just a matter of time until I caved in and told her. She'd always been there for me, all my life. I just didn't want her to feel disappointed in me.

We drove the rest of the way making small talk.

As I drove up to Haversham Park, we both commented on the beautiful flowers in the gardens at the front of the hotel. It was indeed a beautiful place. It was a grand, white building with acres of ground and quite breathtaking to look at. As we approached the entrance a handsome young man stepped towards the car. I pulled up and he opened the door for Aunt Rose and held out his hand to her. I jumped out of the car and handed him the keys for parking.

Once inside we were greeted by yet another good-looking man who led us into the 'summer room' at the back of the reception where they were serving lunch. It was such a delightful room, all glass windows and painted in delicate greens and pinks with white chairs and tables. Huge French windows opened up onto a little courtyard with more tables. A gentle breeze blew in through the room. It was a little like stepping back in time and I knew exactly why Aunt Rose loved to come here.

"Hello Ms Hutton," said a friendly voice and a young woman stood there dressed in a pretty flowery dress that matched the décor perfectly. "I see you have a reservation to lunch with us today, for two people," she continued, smiling. "Would you like to eat inside or would you prefer to dine in the courtyard today, take advantage of this beautiful weather?"

Aunt Rose looked at me. "The courtyard," I said and she led us out to a table surrounded by pots overflowing with flowers and in the partial shade of a tree. A waitress brought us over some menus and we ordered our lunch with two glasses of champagne. Aunt Rose adored champagne, ever since she'd tried it in France when she'd sold her first collection there, all those years ago.

"Cheers my darling," she said, raising her glass.

"Cheers," I said, as our glasses clinked together. "Mmmmm, this is just lovely."

"Now then," she said to me, putting her glass down and looking me directly in the eye. "Are you going to tell me what's going on?"

"There's really nothing to tell, everything's f…" I started to say 'fine' again and I stopped. "Everything's fabulous!"

"Ha!" she said sarcastically. "Fabulous?"

"Yes. Fabulous."

"Okay, okay. If you don't want to share with your old aunt that's just FINE!"

I looked at her for a second and wondered if I should tell her everything, but I wasn't ready to share what had happened with anyone, not just yet, so I simply said, "Good! Let's just enjoy this fabulous lunch and this wonderful sunshine, shall we?"

We both laughed out loud and that's exactly what we did!

Chapter 5

After our wonderful lunch, I dropped Aunt Rose off at her cottage and carried on home. I'd managed to get through the afternoon without discussing my arse of a husband. I really felt as if I'd achieved something. I'd listened to Aunt Rose's tales of what was happening at the bridge club and she'd had me in fits of laughter. I wished I had half of her zest for life. She had entertained me well, taking my mind off everything, but there was no fooling her. I knew that she knew things were anything but fine.

Letting myself into the house, it all came flooding back. No Simon, no James, no Louise and no Isobelle. Just me. I was all alone in this big house once full of happy memories, full of pain now. I threw my keys on to the hall table, flinching as they hit the solid oak surface. There in the late afternoon, the hall seemed dark and cold. I turned on the lamp and looked around me. What to do now? I went into the kitchen and opened the French windows, breathing in the air as the last bit of sunshine disappeared behind clouds.

Normally I'd be starting to prepare dinner. Simon would still be at the golf club and not due home until around six o'clock, whereupon we'd sit at the kitchen table and discuss his game and he'd retire to the living room to watch football or some other sports programme. We didn't tend to watch the same things on TV, so he'd stay in there and I'd sit here in the family room, watching something he thought was 'rubbish'.

No wonder he's been having an affair. I'm surprised I'm not having one! As I caught my reflection in the window, perhaps I wasn't that surprised. Feeling sufficiently miserable and fed-up, I decided to call Simon.

No answer. I rang again. His phone was obviously working again as it wasn't going straight to voicemail. I wish he'd pick up. I rang again. This was becoming ridiculous. I tried over and over again, becoming more and more agitated. Eventually, I lost count of how many times I called…I was on a mission. Then, on my last attempt it went straight to voicemail. I hung up immediately. He must have switched it off.

What had started off on my part as an attempt to talk and try to sort things out, was now a frantic, crazed need to hear his voice. I pressed re-dial and waited for his message greeting:

"Hello, you're through to the voicemail of Simon Aagar. I can't take your call at the moment, but leave me your name, contact number and the reason for your call and I'll get back to you as soon as I can. Thank you for calling…" BEEEEP.

"Yes Simon," I began, "it's me, Jen, your wife. You know my number obviously, so call me back. We need to talk about everything. There's things we need to sort out and I…" I was too slow. I ran out of time. I dialled again. Listened to his stupid message again. "Hello, you're through to the voicemail of Simon Aagar, blah, blah, blah…BEEEEEP. "Simon," I said, speaking quickly but not as polite or as controlled as my first message. "It's me again. We need to talk. I know you've turned your phone off you bastard." I couldn't help it. I was consumed with anger now. "Sorry to interrupt you, you're probably shagging the weekend away. No golf then? Call me!" I hung up, shaking.

I know I was within my rights to feel this way, but wasn't the anger part supposed to come further down the list of stages you go through when a spouse had an affair? I'm sure I'd read somewhere that I was supposed to grieve before getting mad. I must google it and I wrote on a post-it note as a reminder: 'google spouses affair, stages of…' I couldn't think of the right words, so I just wrote… 'shit stages of going through a shitty affair.'

Like I didn't have the time to do it now! Right now. Instead, I flicked on the TV in the family room, kicked off my shoes and put my feet up on the coffee table. Straight to movies and I caught the beginning of 'Family Man' starring Nicholas Cage. I cried my way through that, then switched to another channel and watched 'When Harry Met Sally'. I cried at that too.

By eight o'clock, puffy eyed and exhausted, I was all cried out. I looked at my phone, not one message or missed call from Simon. Amazingly though, after all the angst I'd felt since the morning we'd taken James to university and everything that had followed, deep inside I felt a slight relief that he hadn't called me back.

My mind must be playing tricks on me, because I felt as if he was away on a business trip or something, and enjoying those peaceful times alone, when you don't have to answer to anyone. Those lovely cherished moments.

Oh My God! Cherished moments!! Was I not grieving because in some way I was glad he'd gone? No, surely not. He was my husband and I loved him. I decided the best thing to do was to open a bottle of wine and wait for the grief to come, but in the meantime, just make the most of just being me. I was alone, by myself, but not lonely in a strange way.

I woke early the next morning. Signs of an inbuilt alarm I suppose. Sunday mornings I would usually get up and read the paper downstairs over a cup of coffee whilst Simon snoozed. It dawned on me what a bloody good life he had with me and, more importantly, what a great wife I was. I tossed and turned, unable to get back to sleep. Feeling the anger building up inside me again, I decided to get up.

It was another beautiful day and I was relieved. I loved opening the curtains and sunlight streaming in to the rooms. Once downstairs, I put the kettle on to make a much needed cup of coffee and it was then I noticed the empty bottle of wine on the kitchen table. My sudden need for coffee became clear.

I looked everywhere for my mobile phone. I even tried calling it with the home phone, but it seemed to be nowhere. Eventually, I found it on silent, stuffed down the side of the sofa. There was a missed call. With a feeling of what I think was excitement, I checked to see who had called.

It was Simon. He had called just after midnight. He hadn't left a voicemail. My heart was racing, the kind of rush you might get when you first start a relationship and are waiting for them to call. For me, this had become a distant memory. Is this how he'd felt when she called him? Probably.

I didn't want to return his call immediately. That would seem too desperate. The same feelings I'd experienced last night came back and I realised I felt quite comfortable on my own. I had actually enjoyed my day yesterday and my evening alone, watching what I wanted to watch, drinking what I wanted to drink without anyone passing judgement. Although, being my own judge, I had drunk far too much. What I had to ask myself was, what exactly was I going to say to him? I had no idea.

The home phone rang and I jumped. "Hello?" I said, a little unnerved.

"It's me." It was Simon.

"Oh." That's all I could say, oh.

"I really didn't appreciate your calls yesterday and I certainly didn't appreciate your message."

"Really?" I enquired sarcastically. I felt defiant, not like me at all.

"Yes, really!" He cleared his throat before continuing. "Now, I want you to give me some more space to think things over, to consider what options we have in light of our situation." He rambled on and on, as though he was in an office meeting, as if talking to some co-worker and one that he wasn't too happy with at that! "So, I'll let you stay in the family home for now; obviously you have no means of paying the bills, so I will continue to do so. I'll contact you in a month from now and maybe by then you will have calmed down. May I suggest that you start thinking about going back to work. I also think you should start looking for a solicitor." Then, silence. As if he had come to the end of a well rehearsed speech.

"Finished?" I asked in a nonchalant manner.

"Well, er yes, but..."

And before he could say anything else, I hung up! Just like that. I was trembling with anger, but at the same time felt elated. As though I could put on a pair of trainers and run for miles. I suppose it was the adrenaline pumping through my body. How dare he. HOW DARE HE! He was making decisions and not even discussing them with me! Me, the one he was in this fucking situation with!

And he wanted me to 'go back to work'. I hadn't worked since I got pregnant with Louise.

"Fuck, fuck, fuck!!" I screamed at the top of my voice. Never had I sworn like this in all my adult life. Sure, the odd curse through the years here and there, but 'FUCK!" I yelled and it felt good. I hated him.

It appeared that I was going through the stages list at an alarming rate. GOOD. I'd be over him in no time!

I felt suddenly hungry. I opened the fridge and the sausages I'd bought for Simon's fry up caught my eye. I grabbed them and three floury baps, making myself sandwiches, smothering them in tomato ketchup followed by a mug of hot tea. Bliss. When I finished I sat back, full to the brim and let out the most enormous burp.

I decided there and then, that this was a step too far.

I spent the rest of the day in the garden, pottering. I didn't have to make a Sunday roast as I was still stuffed from my breakfast. I sat at the garden table soaking up the last of the sunshine, sipping a glass of wine. I smiled to myself how organised I had always been.

SUNDAY: Roast dinner lovingly prepared for Simon's return from yet another game of golf.

MONDAY: I'd make my list for my big shop and pop off to the supermarket, stocking up. Then when I'd unpacked my shopping, I would put the washer on, dry everything and then iron. Simon would have a shirt ready and hanging for each day of the week.

TUESDAY: I cleaned the house. I didn't have a cleaner, much to the bewilderment of Anna, who couldn't live without one, apparently.

WEDNESDAY: I racked my brain for what I did on the other days…pottered about I suppose. It all seemed so very boring, but I had loved my life. Is that how Simon saw me? Boring? It was easy to see why he would look at me that way, being honest. Then along came a young, attractive woman who showed him some interest. It wasn't hard to understand why he'd strayed.

I poured myself another glass of wine. It helped take the edge off things. I surveyed the garden. We'd got it just as we wanted it over the years and it was full of happy memories of the children playing, the parties we'd thrown and just the enjoyment of sitting out in it. When the children were younger and in the holidays, we'd fill up a paddling pool and at the weekends, Anna and Tim would bring their boys David and John. We'd had a wonderful life, where had it all gone so wrong?

I wasn't the first wife to be dumped for a younger model once the children had grown up, and I certainly wouldn't be the last. Did the years of love and dedication count for nothing in a marriage nowadays? Why did these younger women want an older man anyway? Was I being naïve? Was it all about the money? Was that what Sarah Slutty West wanted, Simon's money? It certainly was an easier road to take than the one I took. Giving up my job with a local interior design firm to be a full-time mother, which I didn't regret in any way. Staying at home to take care of the family was to me a luxury. I'd felt so grateful that we could afford for me to do that and I had always appreciated Simon.

My mind wandered back to my birthday. Everyone had been there. Most people had arrived at around six in the evening. The weather had been glorious and we'd hired the local butcher, Bob, to do the barbecue. It had been a wonderful evening, everyone had said so. He had supplied waiters and waitresses to serve our guests with food and drinks, each champagne glass filled up the moment it had been empty. James had sorted out the music, choosing hits from the eighties and joking that it would remind me of my youth.

I'd worn the blouse and linen trousers that the girls helped me pick out especially for the occasion. They'd chosen earrings, a bracelet and shoes to match the pale blue silk blouse and I had felt great. Simon had even commented on how nice I looked. And all that time, he'd been texting her and she'd been wishing him 'good luck' on getting through the evening. Good luck to spend time with me, his family and all our friends...had I never known him throughout our married life?

That was it. That thought was the trigger that brought the grief. The tears came and I sat there, all alone, sobbing. Moments came where I just took deep breaths, followed by more tears, followed by more deep breaths.

Eventually, and another bottle of wine almost finished, I ran inside to the downstairs cloakroom to be sick. I sat there on the tiled floor for a long time. There I was, back at stage one on the list, grieving.

Simon probably wasn't ever going to come back to me, to our home, to our life. And then his words about letting me stay in the house for now suddenly hit me. He may as well have been sitting there on the floor with me and slapped me in the face.

Chapter 6

I did NOT have a good week. I didn't even do a BIG shop or even for that matter, a small shop. I spent most of the time in bed, crying. I would go in each of the children's rooms and just remember bedtimes of years gone by.

I stopped drinking wine in the hope I'd not feel quite so emotional, but it was no good. Emotional was how I felt. I'd spoken to James on Monday evening and he was having a ball during 'fresher's week'. He told me his Dad had called to see how he was settling in, which surprised us both. I pretended I knew, telling him it's why I hadn't been in touch. Somehow, I think he'd appreciated it. Louise called me on Tuesday during her lunch break. She sounded a little down, I think she was having problems with Scott or being a lawyer like her father, it could have been a case she was working on, but Lou was a private person and didn't talk about it. I called Izzie that evening to check that everything was going well in Paris. It was and Laura her boss, was showing her Paris by night.

I'd finally got around to calling Anna on Wednesday morning. It was such an effort, but I knew that in the afternoon she had the church ladies at her home and she wouldn't want to talk for too long — too busy making everything look perfect for the visitors.

"Anna Bradley," she said on picking up my call. This had always puzzled me. She could obviously see it was me who was calling. I felt slightly irritated (this was nothing new for me these days).

"Hi Anna, it's Jen."

"Jen! At last darling. You didn't respond to my text message about the salads. I was beginning to worry." But obviously not enough to pick up the phone and enquire how I was. Maybe she was only worried about the bloody salads!

"Sorry," I said, rather pathetically. "Not forgotten. How many do you want me to do?"

"Hmm, now then, let me see…" I could hear her going through the list of guests and counting. "About four, or maybe even five to be on the safe side?" Nearly everyone we invited is coming, so it's fabulous. I hope this weather holds. I checked the forecast and I think it's going to be okay until evening. Ugh, I told Tim he'd better organize a cover for the terrace."

"Great." Was all I could manage to say, really not caring about any of it."

"So, you and Simon will be here for shall we say, three? That way Si can help Tim with the last bits and bobs. Okay?"

"Yes, that's great. See you Saturday then."

I couldn't bring myself to tell her Simon wouldn't be there. She'd have given me the third degree. I'd just tell her he was working and hope that satisfied her. She would be very disappointed though as she always lit up when he was around. Normally very serious, she would almost turn into a giggling schoolgirl.

****

Today was Saturday, the day of the barbecue. More importantly, the day I had an appointment at 'Jades'. She had called me yesterday, just as I was having second thoughts about the whole makeover idea. She told me she was just checking her staff had made a good impression. I felt she had really called to check I wasn't backing out. It was just like the day I'd met her in the café, as if she could read me.

I checked the time. Eight a.m. I had to be there for nine. I sat on the edge of the bed and took a vitamin, the ones that were supposed to give you energy. I had bought them yesterday from a chemist in town. I hadn't been eating very well and I felt I should have a supplement to my non-existent eating plan. There was no need to wash my hair, or shower even, seeing as I was going to be pampered from head to toe. I washed myself quickly at the sink and cleaned my teeth. It was such an effort, everything felt like such hard work.

Like yesterday for example, when I nipped out for the pills, I had to lie on the sofa as soon as I got back home. It was a lack of food I'm sure and the fact that my marriage was over wasn't helping my energy levels. I would have to make an effort to start eating properly.

I arrived at the salon five minutes early. The reception was decorated in a dark charcoal with soft pink & lilac furnishings. It felt very chic, and the receptionist, a pretty young woman dressed in a perfectly matching lilac dress, sat behind a desk of black granite, which sparkled in the spotlights.

"Good morning," she almost sang as she looked up at me. "I'm Fria. I'm guessing you're Jennifer, Jennifer Aagar?" She smiled.

"Yes, that's me," I replied, as she came around from her desk towards me.

"Let me take your jacket for you," she said, helping me take it off.

"Oh!" I exclaimed, surprised by the hands-on service (what will I be like during the full body massage?). FULL.BODY.MASSAGE. Oh God! Nobody, including my husband had seen me naked in a very long time.

"Belinda B will escort you upstairs in just a minute. In the meantime, can I get you something to drink? Tea, coffee, water perhaps?"

I wanted to ask for a wine, but so early in the morning she would think I was joking.

"Definitely NOT a coffee!" Came a voice from a doorway behind reception. It was Jade.

She greeted me with a hug and a kiss as if we were old friends. She looked totally relaxed in a charcoal grey T-shirt with a sparkling, lilac 'J' embossed on the front of it and a pair of black flared trousers.

"So Jennifer," she said, a cheeky grin on her face. "Are you ready for some serious pampering?"

"I am." I lied. "And a coffee!" We both laughed and Fria looked slightly confused.

"Okay. Fria, a coffee for Mrs Aagar please, just a small one. She's in for a very long treatment and the last thing we want is her needing the loo." She winked at me as Fria tottered off into the back. "How are you doing?"

"Oh, not too bad thank you," I replied, not very convincingly.

"Well, whatever it is going on, enjoy the next few hours with us. Yes?"

"Yes, I will, Jade. I can't thank you enough for this, but I really would feel more comfortable if you'd let me pay…"

"Ah, ah, ah," she interrupted, "it's on me. I insist. Tell you what, you can treat me to a coffee one day. How about that?"

"You're so kind, Jade." I was genuinely touched.

"Sssshhhhh," she put her finger up to her lips, and looking around her she said, "let's keep it between the two of us, shall we?"

And with a wink, she was gone. Fria returned with my coffee and ushered me to a seating area with black leather sofa's and a glass table full of magazines and brochures of treatments etc. She explained to me that the salon was through the smoked glass doors behind her desk and the treatment rooms were upstairs.

It was such a lovely place and it felt special somehow. From the outside it looked small and the same as most of the hairdresser's in town, but it was so much bigger once you were inside.

A tall elegant lady, aged about thirty years old appeared from the stairway. She had dark hair, scraped off her face into a high ponytail. Her face was perfectly made up and she wore a pale pink beauticians coat with cropped sleeves and the 'J' logo on the pocket. I could see that Jade had put an awful lot of thought into everything in her salon, and she had got it just right.

"Good morning, Mrs Aagar. I'm Belinda. I'll be taking care of your treatments today."

"Hello. Please, call me Jen."

"Okay Jen," she smiled a perfect smile. "If you would like to follow me." And she led me up the stairs into one of the treatment rooms. The lights were dimmed and relaxing music played softly in the background. "Okay Jen," Belinda whispered, "I'm going to leave you to undress and I'll be back in five minutes. Just pop yourself under the cover on the bed when you're ready.

I started to quickly undress. The soft lighting and gentle music clashing with the panic I felt. I threw my jeans and shirt on a chair in the corner. I stood there in my underwear…why didn't I put on a prettier set? Oh no, it was a full body massage. Did I get under the cover naked? Even something as nice and relaxing as this was turning into a stressful situation. Aunt Rose had drilled into me on the day she bought me my first bra with matching panties, that it was important to always dress well underneath your clothes, as you never knew what the day ahead held, and matching underwear was a must and one last thing to worry about. Why hadn't I listened to her advice?

Leaving them on, I jumped onto the bed as the beautiful Belinda B came back into the room, making a mental note to buy some new, matching, underwear.

"I still have my underwear on!" I announced, immediately.

"That's fine," she whispered softly, "we're starting with the facial and I'll give you some paper panties before your body massage. Just relax."

Beautiful Belinda cleansed, toned and steamed my face and I felt myself starting to relax. Really relax for the first time in a very long time. She covered my eyes with goggles and turned on a bright light.

"Okay Jen, I'm going to neaten up your eyebrows for you," she said, and I nodded imagining how polished I was going to look at the barbecue. "And then I'll remove your moustache."

Moustache? REMOVE MY MOUSTACHE? Oh my God, I have a moustache! For how long had a moustache been loitering on my top lip? Had anyone else noticed it, or just Belinda with her extra strong light shining on my face?

Was my moustache the reason Simon was leaving me for Sarah West?

"Oh, I'm sorry. You must be very sensitive to your eyebrows being plucked, your eyes are watering," she said, wiping the tears away with a tissue. I didn't tell her I was actually crying over the fact I had a moustache.

Two hours later, I emerged from treatment room no.1 feeling amazing. I felt lighter and extremely relaxed, especially now I didn't have a moustache. Belinda had commented that I felt a little tense in my shoulders and I'd let out such a laugh that she had to ask why.

As she had exfoliated my body, I felt as if she was erasing the events of the past week. I didn't feel judged or pitied. In fact, I'm pretty sure Belinda had shut off to my tales of woe soon after I'd started talking. Not because she didn't care or that she was being rude, simply because I'm sure that she'd heard every tale there was to tell, there in the beauty room.

She led me back downstairs and with a final flash of her perfect white smile, she turned and headed back upstairs. Fria was waiting for me and led me immediately through the heavy glass doors into the salon. Seeing my reflection in one of the mirrors, I could see why she'd rushed me in, I would have scared off any waiting clients. She sat me down at one of the chairs and left me.

Suddenly, the most beautiful man appeared behind me. I normally wouldn't describe a man as beautiful, but he was. Tall, slim with dark thick hair swept to one side, we looked at each other through the mirror in front of me. I literally had to catch my breath, never had I seen anyone so perfect. I felt my neck begin to flush and continue into my cheeks as he swished a metallic grey cloak over my shoulders...it all seemed to happen in slow motion. Fastening it at the back he cocked his head to one side and tilting the opposite hip, resting a hand on it.

As he opened his mouth to speak, I imagined the softest, sexiest French accent to come out. "Now Jen, my darling," he said, in a soft feminine voice with a thick Newcastle accent, "let my hands work their magic on you. You're gonna love it!" He winked and explained he was going to prepare my colour.

My eyes followed him and settled on Jade, who was now standing behind my chair. "Wow!" I mouthed to her.

"Like a little piece of heaven, isn't he?" She giggled. "He's called Maxime."

We giggled like two schoolgirls and Jade went on to tell me what they thought would do with my hair. Maxime reappeared and set about colouring me.

When they had finished, I sat looking at myself. I had the most amazing shoulder-length, layered bob, blonde with highlights. It had taken years off my face. I couldn't stop smiling or touching it. Jade and Maxime stood admiring their work.

"Radiant," he said, clasping his hands in delight.

"Absolutely!" Jade agreed.

"I'm so glad you spilt coffee all over me!"

I walked out of Jade's Salon feeling like I'd never felt before. When Simon sees me, he won't want to leave me. Sarah West will be nothing more than a dirty little affair.

Chapter 7

I walked through the front door of my home to the now familiar sound of nothing. Absolutely nothing. I dropped my keys onto the hall table, and noticed the toll of throwing down keys had taken on the beautiful wooden surface. I stood in the hall for a moment and sighed. It had been a week since Simon had left and I still couldn't believe it…any of it. I caught my reflection in the mirror hanging above the table and I looked great. Before my blow dry, a lady called Greta had popped down from the beauty salon and applied my make-up. Nothing too heavy, quite natural tones, but she'd done a great job! I smiled at myself.

I suddenly became aware of the time. It was one thirty. That gave me just half an hour to get ready. I was supposed to be at Ann and Tim's for three o'clock. Mind you, I was supposed to be going there with Simon and that wasn't going to happen.

I went upstairs, not a clue what I was going to wear. Why hadn't I given it some thought during my treatments? However, rather than nervous, I felt an excitement within me. I went into the dressing room and started to rummage through the rails. There, at the very back was a summer dress I hadn't worn for years. My heart actually raced a little at the thought of being able to get into it. It was black and white with a halter neck and an a-line skirt. Timeless. I undressed and took it off the hanger.

Would it actually fit? A week ago, definitely not, but it's amazing what a cheating husband can do for weight loss. There were no zips or anything, so I just stepped into it and tied the two pieces of material at the back. I still had my tan from summer and I looked nice.

More than nice, I looked amazing!

******

I had matched a pair of slingback black wedges that Izzie had given me last summer, but I'd never worn before and they went perfectly with my dress. From my glass-fronted cupboard where I kept my handbags, I chose a red clutch. I found a pair of red drop earrings too. The splash of red was striking. That was it…I was ready to face the world again.

It struck me that if Simon hadn't left, or if I hadn't found out about his affair, I wouldn't look like this, let alone have worn what I was wearing. Suddenly, a wave of sadness came over me. To think that it had taken the worst event of my life so far, to make me take care of me.

Simon. Ugh! I decided I should call him. As his phone was always going straight to voicemail, I decided to call hers, Sarah's. Sarah West's. I had made a note of it from Simon's phone.

My heart raced. My neck flushed red and my hands were shaking as I pressed dial. It rang out three times, then…

"Hello?" Oh God. She picked up, it was her.

"Hello," I replied, my mouth dry. "Could I speak to Simon please?" I kept my voice soft and as polite as possible.

"Er, sure. Who's speaking?" she asked, nervously (I wanted to scream down the phone, "you know who it is you fucking whore, now put my bastard of a husband on the phone, now!" But I didn't).

"It's…." Oh God, do I say 'his wife' or just 'Jen'?

"Hello?" she said, with an impatient tone.

HOW RUDE! She had my husband captive and has the nerve to be impatient with me!

"Sorry Sarah," I said, surprising myself with how nice I was. "It's me, Jen. His wife" (when in doubt, go with both your options).

"Oh, I…I…" she stuttered, obviously a little surprised herself. I like hearing her uncertainty. It felt good.

"It's okay Sarah, I just want to speak to Simon about something. His mobile is going straight to voicemail and I have to discuss something. I'm sorry if I've shocked you."

"No, no, not at all. I understand." Damn it, she sounded quite nice too. This was NOT what I had wanted my husband's mistress to sound like. "Just a moment, Jen. I'll pass you on to him."

I could hear movement, as if she was going into another room. Probably the bedroom! I bet they'd been at it all morning. Her niceness made me madder now. This was a very confusing time!

Suddenly, I was aware of whispering voices, muffled as she'd probably covered the mouthpiece. Idiot! Why didn't she put me on hold...as if she'd read my mind, music began playing in my ears. Actually, I preferred the muffled whisperings. This was dreadful. Before I could think another thought, he came on.

"Hello." Ooo, he sounded quite miffed.

"Simon, hello. It's me."

"Yes, I know. What do you want?" He asked in a very condescending tone.

"It's about Anna and Tim's barbecue."

"What about it?" He actually sneered. I preferred talking to Sarah than to him!

"Well, obviously you won't be there and..."

"Obviously!" He cut in.

"Look," I bit back. "I just wanted to get our stories straight that's all."

"Why?"

"Why?" I repeated. "Well, because people are going to ask questions and I..."

"And you what?" He raised his voice to me and I could hear Sarah in the background telling him to calm down.

"If you'd just let me finish a sentence. I don't know what I'm going to say to them. It's been a week since you left and I...I just...I call your phone, it goes straight to voicemail..."

"Because you broke my phone! Anyway, I've changed my number." He was being very direct now, no emotion.

"Oh, and have you given your new number to our children?"

"Of course!"

"Simon, my God," I cried, "it's like you hate me!"

Silence. No response. I felt the tears start to prick the corners of my eyes. I blinked hard and gently wiped underneath my perfectly made-up lashes. I wasn't, I decided, going to cry.

"Okay," I said, breaking the cold silence. "We have to talk. This is ridiculous. You can't just ignore me. I'll just tell everyone that you're working."

"Tell them what the hell you like," he snapped, "I don't care!"

And just like that, he hung up. I stood there in my lavish dressing room, motionless. I had the urge to redial, but there was no point. I straightened my shoulders, ran my fingers through my perfectly styled hair and decided to leave for the barbecue.

I felt strong now. He wasn't worth it. And, tomorrow I would tell the children EVERYTHING!

******

As I drove to Anna's house, I couldn't help but reflect on the conversation — if you could call it that, with Simon. Where had all this hatred and anger come from? He hadn't so much as raised his voice to me during our marriage. And as for her, Sarah West, she seemed so bloody nice. I wanted her to be a complete and utter bitch. Not nice! I could possibly see why Simon had fallen for her. This was bad! If I couldn't stay mad at her, what would I do? Anyway, this was early days. I'm sure that if and when I meet her, I'll want to slap her in her young, pretty face. My hands gripped the steering wheel a little tighter.

I tried to conjure up in my mind what she must look like. Why hadn't I taken the opportunity to look at Simon's pictures on his phone when I'd had the chance? He was bound to have snapped her. Stupid, stupid, stupid!!

I arrived in Anna and Tim's road. There were already quite a few cars on the drive and so I decided to park outside. It was now three-thirty. I was late. I walked up the tree-lined driveway to their thatched cottage and knocked on the door. Through the open leaded windows, I could hear the chattering of voices. Then above them, I could hear Anna's voice announcing that she'd get the door.

She opened the door smiling. When she saw me, her smile disappeared.

"Hi!" I said, smiling and leaning in to kiss her.

"You're late!" she replied, giving me her cheek.

"Sorry Anna. You know what it's like."

"Do I?" she asked, looking me up and down, a look of puzzlement on her face. "Where are the salads?"

She peered over my shoulder, as if they'd be walking up the path behind me. Then she strained a little more and once again the huge smile was back. Pushing past me, I turned to see her greeting the Witherspoon's. "Darlings, come in, come in. You're a little early, no matter. Tim's in the garden, he'll see to your drinks."

"Hello Jen," Amelia Witherspoon said as she came towards me.

"Hi." I greeted her, actually pleased to see a friendly face.

"Wow!" she gasped. "You look amazing!!"

"I'll say she does," added Gregory, as he kissed me hello.

"Thank you, that's very kind," I said, a little taken aback at their enthusiasm.

We all turned to look at Anna, who had so far not mentioned my new look. There followed a very uncomfortable silence as we stood waiting for her to say something, anything. But she said nothing. The Witherspoons' smiled at me and carried on into the house.

I watched them and then turned back to Anna who was still standing in the driveway. "Salads?" she asked, but it was more of a statement than a question.

Before I could answer her, Bernard from 'The Kitchen' in town, walked up the path towards us carrying five boxes, each containing different, perfectly prepared salads.

I smiled at him and he asked me where I wanted them. Anna's horrified expression amused me. I hadn't told her in advance that I'd ordered them in rather than make them myself. Yesterday, when I'd been thinking what to do, I remembered the beautiful salads you could take out and so simply called them.

"Anna, where would you like Bernard to put the salads?"

"Follow me," she said, trying to sound as if she didn't care. She pushed past me once again, not even looking at me.

"Thank you so much," I said to him, "tell Heidi I'll pop in on Monday to set up."

"No problem Mrs Aagar," he said cheerfully.

Chapter 8

By five o'clock the party was in full swing. The day was beautiful and added to the good mood of everyone there. Champagne and gin and tonics were flowing freely. I was actually enjoying myself.

Everyone I'd spoken to had asked me where Simon was and they had accepted my story about him having a huge case on at work. I apologized to Tim immediately for Simon not being there to help out and he was fine about it, telling me not to worry from the top of a step ladder, as he'd put the finishing touches to the marquee. He had jumped down and given me the biggest of hugs, telling me how 'utterly gorgeous' I looked and what a fool Simon was for working when I'd obviously gone to so much trouble. We laughed and squeezed each other tightly. A much warmer greeting than I'd received from his wife.

Anna was still avoiding me like the plague. I sat myself down at one of the tables that offered some shade from an umbrella and sipped my glass of champagne. I looked over to where Anna was stood, talking loudly, telling a story to a group of our friends and laughing at something that had happened to Tim earlier that day. Poor Tim. She'd always made him the butt of her jokes.

Sitting there, I realised I didn't like her very much. I was usually too busy being told what to do at the 'farewell to summer' barbecues to even think about it. Today, I'd not received any instructions, so I wondered about catching up with people I hadn't seen since my birthday bash. Another thing, I wasn't in the shadow of Simon, who always took command of conversations.

People were so complimentary about me, and funnily enough about my salads. Anna took great pleasure from telling everyone they'd been 'ordered in by Jen'.

I couldn't help but wonder why Anna had not commented on my new hairstyle at least. And, why was she ignoring me completely? I hadn't done anything wrong. Okay, I'd arrived a little later than she'd asked, rather, told me to and I was Simon-less.

Then there was the matter of the salads, though I don't know why that should have annoyed her so much. It suddenly occurred to me that she hadn't even asked me anything about the absence of Simon. I squinted my eyes in her direction. Could she already know what's happened? Surely not! How would she know? She couldn't know…my mind was starting to race and I put my glass of bubbly on the table. It was time to stop drinking and time to eat something.

I made my way to the back of the house and to the barbecue area. Tim and about six or so other men were flipping steaks, burgers and sausages. On one part was a beautiful array of fish. It all smelt wonderful and I could feel my appetite begin to wake up. People were lining up with plates at the ready, chattering away.

I was about to take a plate, when Anna appeared. "Can I have a little word?" she whispered, grabbing my arm and leading me away and into the kitchen. "What's going on, Jen?" she asked, once we were inside.

I just looked at her, shell-shocked, I didn't know what to say.

"Well?" she snapped.

"What do you mean?" I asked, my words slurring a little.

"How much have you had to drink?"

"Three, maybe four champagnes. Why? What's the problem?"

"I think you've had enough!" she hissed, a smug look on her face.

"What?" I snapped back, struggling to understand her attitude.

"You heard me. I think you should stop now. I bet you haven't even eaten yet?"

"Excuse me, Anna!" I said, indignantly. "I was just about to when you dragged me in here!"

"And," she continued, "I have to ask. What is all this about?" And she gestured to me from top to toe.

"What's that supposed to mean?" I seethed.

"Well, look at you! New hair, losing all this weight...wearing wedges!" she said, with a hateful, sarcastic tone.

I looked down at my feet, my manicured toenails peeping out of the open-toed sandals, painted in dark red polish. They looked fabulous. I wasn't going to feel bad for looking good. I looked at her leather, low-heeled sandals that befitted an older woman.

"Izzie gave me the wedges. She thought they would look fantastic on me and she was right, thank you very much, Anna! What is wrong with YOU? You're being absolutely awful with me."

"And," she continued, as if not hearing a word I'd just said to her, "where the hell is Simon?"

I felt my eyes begin to fill up. She looked so angry and almost as if she could slap me. I was in such shock that my oldest friend could speak to me in this way. There was no way I was going to tell her anything, especially not here.

"I need another drink!" I said, and started to walk away.

"That's the LAST thing you need, lady!" she snapped.

I ignored her and walked out of the patio doors back into the garden. I was shaking with anger and struggling to balance in my wedges, but determined that she wasn't going to make me cry.

One of the young waiters who'd been hired to wait on us hand and foot passed by with a tray full of glasses, filled to the brim with champagne. I smiled at him and he stopped to offer me a glass. I took one and he moved on to the other guests. I took a large gulp and immediately felt better, calmer anyway. I looked behind me to see Anna heading towards the doors. I hurried towards a group gathered on the lawn.

"Hey!" Sam Heywood shouted as I snuggled into the circle. "Jen Aagar, look at you!" Everyone turned to look at me. "Wow!" He looked me up and down. "You look amazing, Jen!" His wife, Clara, nodded agreeing with him.

Everyone started to compliment me on how great I looked and I turned in the direction of the kitchen to see Anna, standing on the patio, shaking her head.

All these compliments and affirmations on how gorgeous I looked were indeed, great. But how bad must I have looked before? I couldn't help thinking again, that it was little wonder Simon had moved on to pastures new. I also wondered if they had noticed I'd had a moustache and felt a great relief that I was now moustache-free.

I stayed there in the Heywood feel-good group for some time. We all discussed where our children where and what was going on in our lives. As I chatted away about James and the girls, not one person mentioned Simon.

Several thoughts flashed through my mind:

Maybe nobody cared.

Maybe nobody actually liked him.

Maybe my new look made them forget him or

Maybe, everyone knew about Simon!

Maybe they'd all seen him out and about with Sarah West and that's why they didn't mention him.

I felt a little unbalanced all of a sudden. I shouldn't have taken a glass of champagne each time the boy had passed by. It wasn't compulsory to take one!! Everything became a little blurred. Voices seemed muffled and I couldn't make out the faces of the people I was talking to. That would explain why Anna and Tim too, hadn't asked me about him. They knew!

As if he'd read my mind, Tim appeared at my side and took me gently by the arm. He used the same tactic as his wife, but a little more discreet. I wondered if they'd had a plan of action that they'd been waiting to use at some point during the evening.

"Anna thinks I should take you home now, Jen" he whispered in my ear.

I pulled away in horror and looked at him in disbelief. "What?"

"Jen, let me take you home."

Some of the group looked over at us and were frowning. I decided that, despite the champagne giving me Dutch courage,

I would go peacefully. "Night, night folks," I said cheerfully. "Tim's my chauffeur for the night as Simon's working late…" My words trailed off as Tim led me away.

I don't think I'd fooled anyone. After holding myself perfectly for the whole afternoon, now they'd all wonder what was going on. I felt quite ridiculous and had to muster all my strength not to scream out loud about Sarah 'slutty' West and how she'd taken my husband away. I prayed that I could get outside without having a Tourette's-like outburst.

Once we were in the car, I looked across at Tim. He looked back at me and smiled a sad, nervous smile.

"You know don't you? Does everyone know?" He didn't answer me. He just sighed and continued to drive. "Tim," I said wearily, "I need to know."

He looked at me with such compassion that I started to cry. Not hysterically or loudly, just tears falling, silently.

"Jen," he whispered. "Don't cry."

I didn't respond and neither of us spoke during the journey to my house. Tim pulled up on the driveway and got out, coming round to my door and helping me out. I searched in my handbag for the key to the front door, when I had no luck he took the bag from me and found them immediately. When we got inside, I keyed in the alarm code and he turned on the hall lamp. He went through the house, closing curtains and blinds for me, checking doors and windows were locked. I stayed in the hallway, swaying and feeling so lost and so very alone.

"I'm sorry," he began, "I just don't know what to say…"

"How do you know?" I asked, interrupting him, not giving him a chance to think of something.

"Si called Anna," he said bluntly, and I looked at him, shocked. "He told her he'd moved out. Look, if you want my opinion, he's idiot, but…"

"Hang on," I cut in again. "Anna knew and didn't say anything." I thought for a moment. "When did Simon call her? How long has she known?"

"Look Jen," he continued awkwardly.

"HOW long?" I asked, and the firmness in my voice troubled him a little.

"Erm, Monday I think. She felt she'd been put in a very difficult situation."

"A difficult situation?" I raised my voice. "SHE felt in a difficult situation," I repeated slowly, emphasizing the words. "Let me get this straight, her best friend's husband leaves for another woman, a much younger woman," putting emphasize on the word younger. "And she doesn't even pick up the phone to see how I am? And why did she ask me why Simon hadn't turned up if she knew exactly why?"

"Jen, please. You have to try to understand."

"Understand?" I was screaming. "What is there to understand?"

"You have to try and see things from Anna's point of view. You know she's always had a soft spot for Si."

I looked at him in utter disbelief. He was defending Anna even though he knew she had a 'soft spot' for my husband, even though he knew her behaviour towards me was appalling.

"Get out!" I yelled at him, walking towards the door and opening it. "Get out!" I was like a woman possessed.

"Jen. Come on. Calm down." He put his hands on my arms gently and I shrugged them off.

"Just get out!" And I pushed him towards the door.

"Jen…" I heard him call out as I slammed the door on him.

I listened as he started up the car and I heard the tyres on the gravel. I slid down the door and cried and cried like I had never cried before.

Tomorrow, I decided, when I finally had no more tears to cry, tomorrow I would definitely tell the children. It was time they knew everything.

****

I woke in my bed with a headache at seven o'clock. Thoughts of yesterday rushed into my mind within seconds of opening my eyes. I just couldn't understand Anna's attitude towards me yesterday, and then the shock revelation that Simon had called her to let her know he'd left me. Why would he call her? Maybe he thought that she'd be there for me? Well, he'd got that wrong if that was his reasoning.

I couldn't get the thought out of my head that she wasn't the friend I had thought she was. She was a selfish, self-centred woman. I had always known Anna had that side to her, but I guess over the years I had learned to ignore it, learned what to say and what not to say to get through the social occasions. Poor Tim was even nervous of her. There is no way he believed what he was saying to me last night. He would have known deep down that there is no way I was going to understand how Anna could have ignored my situation.

My plan had been to call Louise, Isobelle and James today. It occurred to me during the early hours of the morning that if ANYONE should tell them, it should be Simon. I grabbed my robe from the end of the bed and felt the chill in the air (I'd taken to sleeping naked since Simon had left). I ran a brush quickly through my hair and it fell perfectly into place. It was then I heard a car on the driveway.

I ran to the front bedroom window. I couldn't believe it. There parking up was a black Jaguar. It was Simon's jaguar. He was here!

Chapter 9

I ran down the stairs, almost missing a couple of steps and grabbing the banister to stop myself from falling. That was all I need, him seeing me roll down the stairs landing at the bottom, my bathrobe agape. I made it down to the hall safely. I waited for the sound of the key in the door, but it didn't come.

I stood there, puzzled. Not knowing how to stand. Do I look shocked as he walks in, or should I be busy making some breakfast in the kitchen? No! That's exactly where he'd expect me to be. Before I could strike a pose, or decide which pose to strike and in which room, the doorbell rang. This threw me a little. I couldn't believe he'd actually rung the bell to his own home. Or was that the right and considerate thing to do and I should be happy he was being respectful? Or should I be furious that he'd moved on so quickly?

Furiously, I opened the front door. He was standing there in a pink (yes, pink!) shirt, the top two buttons open and a pair of pale blue jeans and white trainers. Simon had NEVER worn trainers in his life, nor a pink bloody shirt.

I had been waiting for this moment since he'd left. Imagined how it would be…wondered if he would beg me to take him back and to forgive him. However, none of this was how I'd imagined.

1.   He had rang the doorbell
2.   He was wearing a pink shirt, and
3.   He was wearing WHITE trainers.

We stood there in silence, me examining his new boyish look, him trying to figure out what was different about me. He had never been able to spot a new hairdo (not that there had been many to spot through the years) or a new outfit.

"Can I come in?" he asked, matter-of-factly.

"Yes," I replied, stepping aside, and opening my robe just a little at the bosom.

He walked towards the kitchen. "Not in there," I said, opening the double doors into the living room that overlooked the driveway. "We can talk in here."

If he was going to ring bells, I wasn't going to allow him into the heart of the family home. He followed me and sat down on the sofa. Interestingly, he hadn't chosen to sit in his favourite armchair. The curtains were still closed so I opened them allowing the light to flood in. I sat in the other armchair, opposite him. Neither of us spoke for a few minutes.

"Why did you call Anna?" I eventually asked.

"I don't know…" he started to say, looking down at his hands.

"I find it very odd. Did you ask her not to tell me you'd contacted her?

"No." He looked up at me, slightly frowning. "Why would I ask her not to tell you?"

"Because she didn't, so I presumed that's what had happened. She behaved very oddly towards me yesterday at the barbecue."

"You went then?"

"Yes of course. Didn't you think I would go on my own?"

"I haven't really given it much thought if I'm honest."

"No, I suppose you've been far too busy shagging your mistress to possibly wonder what I'm up to!"

"Oh, here we go." He stood up. "When did you start using the word shagging?"

"Oh, I don't know…let me think. Erm…when you started shagging! The truth hurts doesn't it, Simon?" I said bitterly.

He began to pace up and down. I was slightly relieved he hadn't made the decision to leave. I watched him and even though he had dressed in the vain attempt to look younger, he actually looked older. Maybe things with slutty Sarah West weren't as wonderful as he thought they would be and my heartbeat quickened slightly. Maybe he wanted to come home after all.

I decided to change tactics and be sweeter. "Look," I said, softly. "I'm sorry. Please, sit down."

He looked at me for a second and then turned towards the window. After a slight hesitation, he sat back down on the sofa.

"Shall I make us a coffee?" I smiled.

"Yeah, a coffee would be good. Thanks."

Good, we were talking again. I stood up and tightened the belt around my waist. He followed me rather sheepishly, into the kitchen. I put the kettle on and opened the blinds and curtains.

"I'd offer you toast or something, but I've nothing in," I said, rather matter-of-factly.

"That's not like you."

"No. I'm not really like 'me' any more."

"Have you cut your hair?" he asked, studying me as if trying to figure out just what it was that was different.

"Yes," I ran my fingers through it. "Had it done yesterday."

"Oh…" his voiced trailed off and he pulled a chair out at the kitchen table and sat down. He looked quite pathetic.

I made the coffees and joined him. "So," I asked, passing him his coffee. "Why are you here, Simon?"

"We need to sort things out."

"Obviously. Are you…are you coming home?" The words stuck in my throat. "Because you can, you know. Come home." I put my hand across the table and touched his. He immediately pulled away and I felt ridiculous. "Oh, I see. You're not here to make up then?"

"Jen, I know this is a shock for you and that you're hurting, but I love Sarah. I have for some time now."

I wanted to throw my mug of hot coffee over his head (exactly where the bruise was from the mobile phone incident), but I just sat there. I had to listen to what he had come to say, all of it. No matter how painful it was going to be, I needed to know everything. I wiped the tears that were starting to fall out of my eyes.

"Go on then. I'm listening," I sniffed.

He said nothing. Couldn't even look at me. Just sat there, staring into his coffee.

"How long?" I suddenly said, breaking the silence. He looked at me with a puzzled expression. Idiot! "How long have you been 'in love' with another woman?" My voice laced with sarcasm.

"Oh, I don't know…"

"Well, think!" I snapped. "And when was it, whilst we're on the subject, just when was it, you stopped loving me?"

He looked at me straight in the eyes and it made my stomach leap. That hadn't happened to me in a very long time. I loved his eyes, his dark brown eyes and long eyelashes. The wrinkles forming at the sides through years of laughter, the grey hairs starting to run through his chestnut brown hair. I loved him so much. Why didn't he love me any more? What had happened? What had changed? I knew I had to stay calm or he'd clam up again and leave me here without any answers.

"I'm sorry, Jen. I'm so, so sorry." I thought he was going to cry too, but he managed to hold any tears back. "I don't know when I stopped loving you…I don't remember exactly when it happened…it just did."

I felt sick and covered my mouth with my hands, but remained silent.

"I just didn't feel the same way about you any more. The kids were growing up and one by one they started to leave home. We just seemed to drift apart. You didn't seem interested in me. James and the girls were your priority. I started working later and later, and you stopped calling me to ask me to hurry home…"

Oh my God, he was making out that it was MY fault. MY FAULT! I took care of our children and then saw them through their teenage years into being young adults. My fault I'd given up ringing him at the office to see what time I should plate up dinner. And yet, I always had text him to tell him dinner was almost ready.

"Everything I did just seemed to be wrong," he continued muttering.

"Like what?" I had to ask.

"Oh, I don't know." He paused and almost seemed to be searching his memory for an occasion when he had felt like he'd been wrongly done by. I was fascinated at the way he was shaking his head, as if shuffling around thoughts and memories from a file inside his stupid fat head. Suddenly, he said, "Yes! Like that time last year when I bought you a Kindle for your birthday!" He was triumphant.

He looked so pleased with himself. My God! THIS was an example of why he'd shagged another woman, because I didn't like my Kindle! U.N.B.E.L.I.E.V.A.B.L.E!!

"What?" I yelled out.

"Yes. I thought really hard about that gift. Every holiday on the beach, the pages of your book flap about and I thought, with a Kindle you'd have none of that!"

He should start flogging them! He obviously cares so much for the bloody things. Our marriage had fallen apart over a fucking Kindle. I was crying over a man who felt let down over my reaction to a Kindle!!! I couldn't get over it.

"Seriously? A Kindle ruined our marriage?"

"No, no, no. It's just an example of what you're like. Nothing's ever good enough. Like the year I bought you a top of the range washer/dryer for Christmas. Cost me a fortune. But did you like them? No! Everyone could see the utter disappointment on your face."

It was little wonder Aunt Rose couldn't stand him! "Firstly Simon," I began, trying hard to push down the rage that was burning inside me. "I love, absolutely love the feeling I get when I turn a page of a book. I like the smell of the pages, the sound they make when I turn them. In fact, I love EVERYTHING about books and IF you knew anything about me at all, you'd have known that! Secondly, yes you're right, I was bitterly disappointed with the washer/dryer combo you got me at Christmas because I'd quite fancied, oh I don't know…a piece of jewellery!"

"You see what you're like?" he snapped back. "You're actually quite ungrateful?"

I was speechless. I could have gone on to remind him about all the lovely notes I used to pack inside his suitcase whenever he went away on business, telling him how amazing I thought he was and thanking him with all my heart for our wonderful lives which we wouldn't have without him, blah, blah, BLAH! I'd always tuck them inside the collar of one of the shirts that I'd lovingly washed, ironed and folded before packing them for him. He had never mentioned them to this day or even written one back, leaving it somewhere I'd find it after he'd gone. I could have mentioned it, but I couldn't be bothered.

"Can I ask you something, Simon?" I calmly asked.

"What?" Any traces of tenderness gone.

"Have you bought Sarah a Kindle?"

"What?"

"You heard me." I sat there, waiting for his answer.

"No. Why on earth would you ask me that?"

"Didn't think so! But I bet you've bought her flowers. Chocolates maybe? Jewellery? Or maybe, some sexy designer underwear?"

He stood up, pushing his coffee away from him.

"Ha!" I said, sarcastically. "I knew it!"

"You're being ridiculous."

"Am I? Am I really, Simon? Tell you what, why don't you try it? I'll give you the one you bought me, it's still in the box. Take it back with you and see if she sucks your dick tonight after you've given her a FUCKING Kindle!" Standing up, I screamed, "you never bought me underwear!"

"Because you're too fat!" he yelled back.

We both stopped shouting. We both knew he'd gone too far. I ran from the kitchen and upstairs, locking myself inside the en-suite. I slid onto the floor and realised that this was becoming a bad habit, sliding down walls, crying. I heard him running up the stairs after me and into our bedroom. He tried to open the bathroom door.

"Jen." He knocked on the door several times. "Jen. Please, open the door."

"Go away," I wailed. "Go back to your skinny little slut."

"Jen. Please, I'm sorry. I shouldn't have said that. It was cruel of me."

"But it's what you think," I sobbed.

"Jen…" His voice trailed off as I cried uncontrollably.

I yelled at him from behind the locked door, to take the suitcases from the loft and pack all his things. I just wanted him to go. I just wanted to be alone. Suddenly, I knew exactly how it felt to stop loving someone.

Chapter 10

Monday morning, I woke at eight o'clock and attempted to sit up in bed, but I couldn't. My head hurt and I flopped back onto my pillow. After Simon had left last night, taking all his clothes with him, as I had demanded, I had gone downstairs, opened a bottle of wine and drank the whole lot. I'd cried long and hard until there were no tears left to cry. Exhausted, I had dragged myself to bed around two in the morning.

As I lay there with my sore head, feeling extremely sorry for myself, I remembered a plan that I had made. It had come to me somewhere between glass number three or four. I was going to go to Simon's workplace and confront him and Sarah West. Finally, take a look at what she could give him that I no longer could. As I recalled the plan, I laughed out loud. But the more I thought about it, the more it made sense. Suddenly, thankfully, I had a purpose to my day.

I practically leapt out of bed. Holding my delicate head in my hands, I got into the shower and washed my hair. Whilst drying it I mentally chose what I would wear. You had to choose carefully when meeting your husband's lover. I had a very nice and very smart black 'Karen Millen' suit which I hadn't worn for years. I felt sure it would fit me now and I wanted to look business like. Simon worked in a huge, plush building where several different companies operated from, and I wanted to blend in easily once there.

I admired the way I'd dried my hair. Because of the excellent cut, it had been easy to do. I grabbed a silk cream camisole from right at the back of my underwear drawer. It would look perfect under my suit. I applied my make-up and checked the time. Nearly ten. I decided to have a little breakfast and a coffee before heading into the city. On my way out of the door, I took a silk black and cream scarf from the coat stand and wrapped it around my neck. One final check in the hall mirror and I was good to go.

The drive in would take me about an hour and then I would have to park. Simon would probably come down for lunch between twelve thirty and one o'clock. I would just have to wait around in reception. That was as far as my planning had gone. I didn't have a clue as to what I would do or say. I just knew that I had to try and get a look at her.

I was running late. As I was about to leave, Aunt Rose had called to talk to me about a new drawing group setting up in town. I had always loved drawing and painting when I was younger, but hadn't picked up a paintbrush in years. I couldn't exactly rush off the phone, but I neglected to tell her where I was going. I had yet to find the time to tell her what had happened with Simon, and she would certainly have talked me out of going to his office.

I didn't get off the phone until gone eleven and I was beginning to feel extremely flustered. Once I was on the motorway, I began to calm down and put on an Emili Sandé CD the children had bought me for my birthday. Her voice soothed me and I listened to the words and sang along. Then, I suddenly hit traffic and didn't move for around thirty minutes. It was now ten minutes before twelve and it would take me at least forty five minutes to reach the city, then find somewhere to park the car...why did nothing ever go to plan? It was after all, the most basic of plans.

There was nothing I could do about it. I would just have to accept that I probably wouldn't arrive there in time to 'hover' in reception, and that I ran the risk of bumping into them leaving or coming back from lunch.

I began to imagine what she looked like. Sarah West. In my head she was surely going to be beautiful, probably with a perfect figure. A size eight, I bet, no stretch marks from carrying Simon's offspring. I pictured her with long, flowing blonde hair, sun kissed highlights from the summer sun, wrinkle free, glowing complexion and I hated her.

Eventually, I parked up on the fifth floor of a nearby multi-storey car park. I made a mental note of the floor and space I'd parked up in. As I came down in the lift, I caught a glimpse of myself in the mirrors. I looked great. I felt great! Despite what was going on or where I was going, I felt really good.

It was such a shame that it had taken this; his affair, for me to look after me! Though, drinking a bottle of wine so as to numb the pain and hurt, wasn't exactly 'looking after myself'. But on the plus side, I had lost some weight and had a new, fresher look and that was at least, a start.

I turned left onto the high street and walked quickly towards Simon's offices. My heels made a very girlie sound on the pavement and got the attention of some builders working in the road. They even whistled and I was mortified. I ran a little to get past them.

Finally, I was there. I stood outside the revolving glass doors and took a deep breath. I attempted to hop inside, but timed it wrong and had to step back quickly as people were heading out. Then, someone pushed in front of me and I had to step in behind, which was a little awkward to say the least, so I turned away from them, facing the street. As the doors reached the point of getting out, I mistimed it and ended up having to go around again. My scarf got tangled in the sides and almost strangled me until it reached the street opening, where I was released to the horror of people waiting to get in…I was mortified.

When I finally reached reception, I had composed myself and stepped out like a true professional. I had the bright idea of pretending to be on my phone so that I didn't have to speak to the receptionist. As I smiled at her, I sat down on one of the bright red sofas. She soon became pre-occupied with an older gentleman in a pale grey suit. I kept my head down, waiting for a glimpse of Simon.

I checked my watch – almost one o'clock. I felt sure I'd see Simon soon. Ten minutes passed, no sign. The receptionist kept looking over at me, so I just kept pretending to be talking on my phone or reading messages.

I started to wonder if I should just go and forget about it, when I saw her. A young woman with long blonde hair, dressed in a chocolate brown trouser suit, with a satin duck-egg blue blouse underneath, coming out of the lift.

Oh God. She was beautiful. Petite and so slim. And worst of all, she had an aura about her; a presence that you felt when she appeared and it wasn't just me, other people had noticed her too. If this was her, how could poor old Simon have resisted? She was stunning.

"Sara," the receptionist called out, "have you got a moment?"

Oh, this was all I needed. The receptionist must have sussed me out and was about to warn her that I was lying in wait. Calm down, I told myself...how could she know who I was or who I was waiting for?

Stunning 'Sara' stopped in her delicate little tracks and smiling started to walk over to reception. Before she could get there, I jumped up and ran to her, blocking her view of the horrified receptionist and making her jump at the shock of me appearing in her way.

"Sarah," I said holding my hand out to her. "Are you waiting for Simon by any chance? I asked.

"Well, I..." she began, startled.

"Well, let me introduce myself." I interrupted her. "I know we've spoken on the phone, but it's not the same as meeting face-to-face, is it? I was on a roll.

She looked, I have to say, a little confused, but shook my hand anyway, mouth open. The receptionist had left her desk and was approaching us.

"Is everything okay here?" she asked, looking at Sarah for some reassurance.

"I don't know, I'm not sure..." she answered, trying to speak, but struggling to get her words out.

"Can I help you?" Kirsty, as her name badge read, asked me rather firmly.

"No, no, it's fine." I assured her with a confidence that must have come from the adrenalin that was pumping through my body. "I just wanted to introduce myself to the lovely Sarah West, that's all." I glared like a woman possessed into the beautiful blue, yet nearly popping out, eyes of my rival.

"Oh," Kirsty said, realizing what must have happened, and slightly relieved, announced, "Sarah's out with Simon for lunch...this is Sara, Sara Appleton."

"It is?" I asked, horrified and letting go of Sara Appleton's limp and clammy hand. "I'm sorry. I thought you were Sarah. Sarah West. S.s.s.orry. I'm so sorry, really, I..."

Now it was me who couldn't quite get my words out. I quickly retrieved my bag from the sofa, ignoring Kirsty's request as to whom she should say was looking for Sarah West. I waved at the pair (poor Sara Appleton still looking in a state of shock), and rushed as quickly as I could into the revolving doors, pushing in front of someone who was just about to enter before me and found myself back on the high street, short of breath and feeling as though I was about to have a heart attack.

I searched in my bag for my sunglasses. I didn't know which way to turn...I first went to my left, then to my right. As I put my sunglasses on, I saw them; Simon and Sarah across the road, heading towards me. I thought about running back inside but saw Sara and Kirsty still standing there, watching me and shaking their heads, so I bobbed into a shop doorway where I could watch the two lovebirds.

They were holding hands and laughing. She was almost as tall as Simon, who had always towered over me. She was wearing a tailored black jacket with a matching pencil skirt and white cotton blouse with black flat slip-on shoes, a leather satchel-type bag over her shoulder. She was nothing how I had imagined her. Her hair was brown and short. She had a slim boyish figure.

I just stood there watching them as they crossed the road and went inside, still holding hands. I peered in through the office windows of their building, and there, waiting for them at reception was Kirsty and Sara. I immediately walked away; the last thing I wanted was for them to turn around and see me glaring in at the windows. I stepped off the pavement and crossed over to the other side, making my way to the car park.

Inside the car, I sat back and let out a sigh of relief. Shaking my head, I tried to imagine what would have happened IF it had been Sarah West that I'd come face-to-face with. I looked up and felt as if someone had been watching over me, and I started to laugh, laughed out loud.

I started up the car and set off for home. It had been difficult to see them together, to see the 'other woman'. But I took an almost smug comfort in the fact that 'my Sara,' was by far, better looking than Simon's.

****

As I entered the house, the silence suddenly hit me. Now, after seeing Sarah in the flesh, the reality of the situation started to sink in. I headed for the kitchen, and opened the wine cooler and another bottle of wine. The quantity of wine was fast diminishing. It was early to be drinking, but these days it didn't make a difference what time of day or night was.

I poured a large glass and took it upstairs to the bedroom. I stripped off and throwing my clothes on the bed, changed into a pair of black velour pants and matching zip-up top; a Christmas gift from Isobelle last year that I'd never worn before, feeling they weren't really 'me'. Now, no longer knowing who 'me' was, they seemed perfect. I huddled downstairs in the family room, with just my glass of wine for company.

I had never in all my life felt so isolated. Somehow, I didn't mind the loneliness so much. I could do whatever I liked without having to think about anyone else. I knew the reality of it all would soon hit me, and hit me hard, but right now, being alone was exactly what I needed. However, there was someone I had to call. Someone so important to me, they would want to know what I was going through. Tomorrow, I would call the children, but now, I had to tell Aunt Rose.

Chapter 11

After an extremely restless night, I woke at seven o'clock. I lay there for a moment thinking over how Aunt Rose had reacted. Naturally, never being Simon's biggest fan, she ranted on about what a waste of space he was, before telling me I was to stay strong and that she was there for me whenever I needed her. She also assured me that if I took Simon back, she would still support my decision. I was relieved after telling her, and as always, she made me feel a little better.

I went downstairs and made myself a coffee, and sat at the kitchen table just staring into space. I had no newspaper to read any more as I'd cancelled the delivery; it was just another stark reminder of Simon not being here. I felt completely numb. It still amused me whenever I thought about the chaos and mistaken identity yesterday, but other than that, I felt emotionless.

The events of yesterday only made it clearer to me that my marriage was definitely over. After seeing Simon and Sarah together, looking so carefree and happy, looking like an actual couple, I knew Simon was never coming home, never.

It was time the children knew what was going on. But how were we going to tell them? Did I call them and give them the shocking news over the phone? Surely, that would be too devastating.

After several coffees and a couple of hours later, I decided I needed to speak to Simon. This was the LAST thing I wanted to do, but needs must. This was as much his mess as mine. As I dialled the office number, I prayed he hadn't sussed out it was me in reception yesterday.

"Good morning. You're through to Simon Aagar's office. How may I help you?" a very cheery receptionist asked.

I asked if she could put me through to Simon, announcing that it was Mrs Aagar on the phone. She asked me to hold before putting me through. She was very pleasant, but I couldn't help thinking that she too would know about Simon's affair. It felt as though I was waiting for an eternity to be 'put through'.

I envisaged Simon making up some feasible excuse for not speaking to me. I could feel my blood beginning to boil. My patience was well and truly running out, then he came on the line. This threw me for a moment and I realised I had to stop imagining the worst and concentrate on actual happenings, and stay in the moment.

"Hello?" he said again. "Jen?"

"Hi."

There was a mutual silence. Two people who had been together for all this time, found themselves struggling to get past the formalities of 'hello'. I didn't know where to begin. I'd called, hoping we'd both be reasonable, but prepared for a fight. However, suddenly, all I felt was sadness.

"Are you okay?" he asked, and it took me a little by surprise. He sounded gentle, sympathetic. After the last few weeks of his bizarre and sometimes almost aggressive attitude, it took my breath away. How the hell did we end up here?

"Yes, I'm okay. How are you?"

"Okay, I guess," he replied. So, we had both discovered we were 'okay'.

"I suppose you're wondering why I'm calling. I've been doing a lot of thinking and I really feel the children need to know what's happened."

Again, I was met with a long silence. What was he thinking? Was he going to tell me he had made a mistake…had he changed his mind? My mind was racing. What if he did say he was coming home? Did I want him home? It was as if I'd erased yesterday and the loved-up couple out of my memory.

Finally, he spoke. "I think you're right."

It still hurt to hear him agreeing with me and telling our children would make it a reality for sure. "Alright then. Have you any ideas of how we should approach it?" I had already thought of a few of my own, but thought I'd ask.

"Not really."

"I don't think the phone is a good way to go about it, do you?"

"Probably not."

"Maybe if I got them home at the weekend? We could maybe tell them together," I suggested.

"That could be a little awkward."

"Awkward?" I repeated in disbelief.

"Well yes. You, me and the kids…"

"Have you any better ideas?" I tried to keep my composure but he was really getting on my nerves. I was beginning to think she was welcome to him!

"No, not really. I guess it has to be done."

"Yes Simon," I said sadly. "It does."

We arranged that I would invite them all home for the weekend, and on Saturday, he would come over around 6 o'clock in the evening. They would just suppose he was golfing and everything would seem normal. Then, together we would shatter their worlds.

I couldn't believe that I was starting to accept the situation. How could it be? A month ago, I was in a marriage with a man I loved so much. Now, it seemed I was letting him go without much of a fight. Maybe I was in a state of denial and maybe I was hoping he would change his mind at some point, but whenever I tried to analyse my feelings, I hit a brick wall. I couldn't decipher any of it.

All I knew was that I felt alone, so very, very alone.

Later that evening, I set about calling them, one by one. Louise first.

"Oh hey Mum," she said brightly. "How are you?"

'Fine darling, everything's just fine." I lied. I told her why I'd called and hoped she'd be free to come home.

"What's the occasion?" she enquired, after telling me she was able to make it.

"I just thought it would be nice for us all to get together."

"I suppose you've called your eldest child first?" she giggled.

She knew me so well and had the ability to unnerve me at times. She had always been a daddy's girl and my mind went back to the day I'd seen all the texts she'd sent to Simon's phone. Being close to her Dad, it would seem plausible, but Louise wasn't the greatest of communicators. It just wasn't in her nature.

"So you'll get here for lunch?" I asked.

"Sure, sounds good. Do you want me to arrange it with Izzie and James for you?"

"You don't mind?" I was slightly relieved. James could well have sensed something was wrong, and Izzie would have probably quizzed me until I told her all over the phone, ruining everything.

"Of course not. Okay, see you Saturday then." And we said our goodbyes.

I sat quietly at the kitchen table for a good ten minutes. I loved my eldest daughter dearly, but she was always such a closed book. Normally in the six years since she'd left home, Louise had been a nightmare to pin down for a reunion. I found myself thinking about those messages again and wishing I'd read them and then I wouldn't be torturing myself as to whether she knew about the affair. What if he'd confided in our eldest daughter? This thought horrified me and I pushed it to the back of my mind.

I ran my hands over the top of the pine table that we'd had since the children were little. Even when we had the kitchen redone, I kept the table. It was full of all the little marks made over the years. How those years had flown by. I ached inside at the thought of Lou, Izzie and James and the memories of them growing up. How I wished I could step back in time and relive those precious times.

The light glowing from the wine cooler caught my eye. It's contents held the only thing that would take the edge of the pain and loneliness; help me to block out what I was really feeling. Drinking alone was becoming a very familiar way of life for me since my husband had left me. For the moment at least, the only comfort I could find was there inside that fridge.

There was nothing I could do, except open a new bottle and let it ease my sorrow at least for tonight.

Chapter 12

The next few days passed without event. The evenings came and went. The nights were drawing in now, though I found comfort in this as it enabled me to close the curtains and snuggle down on the sofa, cosy in my dressing gown, earlier and earlier. Each evening around seven p.m. I would settle down accompanied of course, by a bottle of wine. Friday night, I started at six and began some preparations for the weekend ahead.

Saturday morning my alarm went off, though I needn't have bothered setting it. I'd been awake since three o'clock. Now, it was a struggle to get up. Now, I could actually sleep. I had no choice however, but to get up and prepare for today.

It was a beautiful morning and it felt as if the sun didn't want to let me down. I made a coffee and sat in the family room, looking at the view and contemplating what today would bring. I was going to make a nice roast dinner, give them something filling to eat, as, come tomorrow, they probably wouldn't have an appetite. Yesterday, I had stocked up the fridge and replenished the wine. I didn't want any of them to think I'd been hitting the bottle a little harder these days.

I took a shower and washed my hair. I wanted to look my best. I had already chosen what I would wear tonight, a sage green linen shirt dress, belted at the waist. I'd not worn it for years, but now since my weight loss, it fit perfectly and looked very stylish.

Looking at myself in the mirror, I realised I looked better than I had in years. I was slimmer, healthier and definitely younger looking. The new hairstyle helped enormously and I wondered what the children would think. Deep down, I wondered what Simon would think. After everything he'd done, I still wanted him to notice me.

Louise, Izzie and James arrived late morning. As they got out of the car I knocked on the living room window and waved. By the time I opened the door they were already stood there, overnight bags in hand.

"Hi Mum," Louise said, hugging me and planting a quick kiss on my cheek.

Izzie followed behind her. "Oooo, I've missed you!" she said, throwing her arms around me and squeezing me tightly.

"Me too, I've missed you." I took her face in my hand and kissed her forehead.

With a huge, wonderful grin James said, "Come on you two, let me in."

"Come here you," I said, holding him tightly. "It's so lovely to have you all home."

James picked up the girls' bags and took them upstairs whilst they went into the kitchen and Izzie filled up the kettle. The house felt as it should at last and I smiled to myself as I heard a thud from upstairs as James dropped the luggage.

"I'm starved!" he said, joining us. "What's for lunch Mum?"

"For God's sake, it's only just gone eleven!" said a disgruntled Louise.

"That's okay," I began, checking my watch. "we're not eating dinner until your Dad gets here, so we can have lunch now." None of them asked any questions, so they obviously presumed he was playing golf.

We decided we'd celebrate us all being together with a good old-fashioned fry-up. For the first time in a long time, I was suddenly ravenous. Having my children here had energized me once again and as I sat there watching them, my heart sank at the thought of breaking our sad news to them later on.

I sat back when we'd finished eating and listened to their chitchat. Louise, ever the organiser, took the plates and put them in the dishwasher. She then set about cleaning the hob and tidying away. She had always been the neat one out of the three of them. This carried through to her appearance also. She was wearing a crisp white shirt with dark blue jeans and a smart pair of black leather ankle boots, her long dark hair tied back. She wore a pair of silver hooped earrings and this was her casual look. She was so striking with her dark hair and eyes, so self-assured, yet somehow never seemed to relax.

My thoughts were broken by Izzie laughing. She had such a loud, infectious laugh that you couldn't help but smile. She was the total opposite of Louise. Izzie was fair skinned with long, wavy blonde hair and blue eyes. Everyone said the day she was born, that she took after Aunt Rose, and they were right. She was extremely vivacious and put everyone at ease. She had graduated last year from art school, but landed a job weeks later as a P.A. to a top fashion buyer in London. She was perfectly suited to the role and had gone on to win numerous awards for best employee. She had met so many rich and famous people in the past year, but none of it had phased her, as long as everyone was pleased with her work, it didn't matter who they were.

I watched her laughing and joking with James. They were so close and I wished that Louise could join in with them more. Somehow, I think she felt that being the eldest she should be the sensible one.

"Need any help, sis?" Izzie asked, leaning back in her chair. She winked at me, already knowing the answer.

"No, no. It's all good thanks. You just stay there. In fact," she continued looking out of the window, "why don't you all go and sit outside and I'll make us all some coffee."

"Great idea!" James said. "Any cake to go with that?"

"Go on you two," I replied. "I'll bring some out." Izzie and James took themselves into the garden. I stood watching them, a huge grin on my face. My cheeks actually ached. It had after all been a while.

"So," I began, turning to Louise who was still scurrying around the kitchen. "How's Scott?" No answer was forthcoming. She was attacking a mark on the hob with such vigour, I was afraid she'd injure her wrist. "Lou," I said, taking her hand. "Everything okay?"

"Yes, yes. Everything's fine. I'm fine. Scott's fine." She pulled her hand away from mine, avoiding eye contact, she repeated, "everything's just fine."

I recalled my recent conversation with Aunt Rose, so I knew probably 'everything' was not fine. I wanted so badly to dig a little deeper, but I knew there was simply no point. Louise had made it clear she didn't want to discuss Scott. Something didn't feel right, but I knew when to leave well alone.

So that's exactly what I did. I took the coconut cake that I'd baked yesterday from its tin and placed it on a cake plate, grabbed four side plates and asked Louise to bring out the coffees when she was ready.

The four of us spent a lovely, relaxing afternoon in the garden. It was warm and there was a gentle breeze blowing, reminding us that soon, summer would be over. I didn't think about Simon or Sarah West or the last few weeks. I was happy and content to have my children around me. They made me happy. They made me feel good about myself. Something that struck me was, not once did they ask me about their Dad, not once. It also struck me how I hadn't missed him…maybe he had felt pushed out and maybe that explained his reaction towards me the day James left for university. I pushed the maybes out of my mind.

"You look really well, Mum," Izzie commented. "I thought your boy leaving home would have pushed you over the edge." She laughed and cocked her head to one side, studying me.

"Yeah," James agreed. "I noticed when I walked in. There's something different about you, Mum."

"Well, thank you, that's very kind of you both to say so." I smiled, feeling a little uneasy in case the conversation went any further.

"And you haven't been bombarding us with phone calls either. I thought we'd have more than ever, with you all alone every day in this big house. No one to fuss over except Dad." Izzie nudged James and winked at him.

"Leave her alone!" Louise snapped. "She looks so bloody great because she's probably got her life back after all these years instead of being stuck at home looking after all of us. Just ignore them, Mum. I think it's been the best thing to happen to you, us all letting you get on with your own life."

"Lou, it's okay, darling. They were only pulling my leg. And yes, I suppose I'm trying not to crowd you all, cut the apron strings and all that..."

"You know we appreciate everything, don't you, Mum?" James said, in a serious tone.

"Of course we do. You're the best Mum ever," Izzie added, glancing at Lou for approval.

At three thirty we made our way back into the house. James and Izzie wanted to shower and change before dinner. Louise began the washing of dishes ritual again and I started to prepare dinner.

"You go and get ready if you like," I suggested. "Dad's not coming until six, so plenty of time. Have a lie down if you like, relax a little."

"Is there anyone else coming to this dinner?" Izzie asked.

"Like who?" I asked, slightly taken aback.

"Oh I don't know...Aunt Rose? Anna and Tim perhaps?"

"No. Just us." A fear of dread washed over me.

"Then there's really no need to get changed. Is there?"

"No, of course not. Not if you don't want to. You look lovely. I just thought..." I was beginning to blab.

"Mum," she interrupted, "I'm fine like this." That word again. "I'm going to stay here and help you with dinner." She smiled at me. "Okay?"

"Okay. Thank you darling, that's lovely." She looked into my eyes and for a moment there was such a feeling of tenderness, it overwhelmed me and I thought I might cry.

I managed to control my emotions and we passed the time talking about everyday things, me trying not to think too much about those texts I'd seen on Simon's phone from Louise. I couldn't help it, I felt troubled. I looked at the time. Five o'clock. Simon would be here in an hour. We were all so happy. Why had he done this to us? He would arrive and our lives, their lives, would be changed forever. A wave of anger rushed over me. I needed a bloody drink.

"Lou darling," I said, breezily. "Do me a favour, open a bottle of wine from the cooler."

"Which one do you want?" she asked, looking inside.

"Oh, I don't mind really," I pretended. "Pinot Grigio? That would be nice."

She opened a bottle and poured us both a large glass, I felt quite relieved that she was joining me. "Cheers," she said, and our glasses clinked together.

"Cheers my darling."

"I love you, Mum." Taking me by surprise as she hugged me.

"I love you too, Lou," I said, rubbing her back. "You okay here if I go and freshen up?"

"Yep, knock yourself out."

"Oh, I hope not." I smiled, taking my glass of wine with me.

When I came downstairs, Louise, Isobelle and James were sat in the family room watching TV. The girls were drinking wine and James had a bottle of larger. Louise had set the table for dinner and it looked beautiful. I walked in and the sound of my shoes against the floor, a pair of brown leather open-toed sandals with a heel, that matched the belt around my dress, made them turn around to look at me.

"Wow Mum!" Izzie gasped. "You look amazing."

"Thank you, Izzie." I felt a little self-conscious.

"Really lovely Mum," James agreed.

"You look absolutely stunning," Louise said, walking towards me. "Dad won't know what hit him."

"Thank you. That's very kind of you all."

"Talking of Dad," James said, walking through the open double doors into the living room, "I think he's here."

We all followed him to the window and could hear the crunch of gravel as he parked his car up. I swear my heart stopped. I felt like a teenager again. I obviously looked as good as I felt and maybe Simon would see me and change his mind. Maybe there was no need for any of this, maybe we could be a happy family again and I pushed away the realization that we had been a family unit all day, happy and without him.

"Hey!" James called out. "Who's the hottie with Dad?"

I stood frozen. Izzie rushed forward to look. Louise froze, as I did, on the spot, and it was then it hit me. She did know! I ran, followed by Louise, to take a look at the 'hottie' Simon had in tow.

I couldn't believe my eyes…he had brought Sarah West to our home!

Chapter 13

Time seemed to stand still as the four of us stood looking out of the window. Sarah was dressed in beige Capri pants teamed with a black cotton three-quarter length sleeved shirt and flat black ballet pumps. Simon was in a grey checked shirt open-necked and almost matching beige trousers. Pinky and Perky came to mind and if I wasn't so bloody furious I could have laughed. Simon took Sarah's hand and they headed to the front door.

"What's going on Mum?" Izzie asked, turning to look at me with a look of complete shock on her face. "Who's that with Dad?"

"And why the hell is he holding her hand?" James demanded.

Before I could give anyone any kind of explanation, Louise was heading into the hallway. I quickly followed her, a feeling of dread overwhelming me. She opened the front door before I could reach her, just as Simon was putting his key into the lock and he almost fell into the hall.

"Lou darling," he said smiling and attempting to hug her.

"Don't you Lou darling me!" she yelled, and Izzie and James appeared, astonishment and horror etched on their faces. "What the hell are you doing bringing HER here?"

"Jen! You haven't said anything? You've had all day and you've said nothing!" he said, turning the whole situation onto me.

"And don't even try to blame any of this on Mum," Louise continued, "get her out of my sight before I do something I'll regret!" she screamed, becoming hysterical. James came towards her to take control of the situation. He put himself between Simon and Louise.

We all stood there in silence for a moment. I looked at Sarah West, who had taken a step back and was now back in the driveway. She looked scared and also a little vulnerable.

"Will someone explain what the hell is going on here," Izzie cried out. "Who is she, Dad? I don't understand." She bit her top lip, trying to hold back the tears.

"Dad?" James asked, calmly.

"I'll tell you EXACTLY what's going on!" Louise screamed, hatred filling her eyes. "He's screwing that slut! Has been for months." Her eyes were wide open and she was breathing heavily. "You promised me. Swore to me you'd stopped."

Simon ran both hands through his hair and rubbed his eyes hard as if attempting to make the whole thing disappear. I looked at Louise who was now sobbing.

"So, you knew?" I asked as gently as I could. "I'm so, so sorry."

"You've nothing to be sorry for. It's him who should be apologizing," she seethed.

"Right," James said firmly. "Can we all just calm down and come inside. We obviously need to talk." We all stepped a little back and Simon came inside, followed by Sarah West, bold as bloody brass and obviously finding some courage. "Not you! You wait outside."

"Yes!" Louise yelled, "you are not welcome in our home. Do you hear me? You're not welcome here!"

"Look darling," Simon began, taking Sarah's hand. "Here are the keys to the car. I won't be long." She snatched the keys from him and walked out. Turning his attention to Louise he said, "there is no need to talk to Sarah in that manner. None of this is her fault."

I stepped back as he passed me and went into the living room, followed by Izzie. James closed the front door and put a hand on my shoulder. He turned to Louise and took her with him into the room. I stood there for a moment feeling such helplessness. I had to face the fact that Simon wasn't going to come back. He hadn't even noticed me, let alone what I was wearing. I wanted to know how Louise had found out. The poor girl had been carrying this with her and said nothing. It must have been eating her up inside.

They were all seated by the time I went in the room. Izzie and Simon seated on the larger sofa, and James and Louise on the two-seater. I sat in the armchair. None of us spoke for some time. It was as if none of us wanted to be the first to speak, because we all knew, once we started there would be no going back and nothing was ever going to be the same again. So I began.

"The reason I asked you all here this weekend was to let you all know what was going on…I didn't think telling you over the phone was the right thing to do, so…" I paused, wondering if anyone wanted to say something, but for now they were happy to let me continue. Each one of them looked at me directly, the children hungry for information, Simon sitting there, a blank expression on his face. "So, I asked your Dad to come over at six so that you'd think he was golfing as normal. I wanted to keep everything as normal as possible for as long as possible. Louise, I had no idea you knew." I gave her a sympathetic glance. "I've only known myself for a few weeks. If I'm really honest, I hoped today wouldn't be necessary and that your Dad might have changed his mind." Did I? Did I really think he would come back? "I certainly didn't think for one moment he would bring her here."

"Her?" Simon suddenly found his voice. "She has a name. It's Sarah. And, why the hell did you think I'd change my mind? You knew we were having this meeting today to tell them I'd left. It was your bloody idea?"

"I just thought maybe you would have come to your senses that's all." I stuttered a little. "I…I…I just hoped you'd see us all together and realise you'd made a mistake." I could feel my bottom lip start to quiver. Izzie rushed over to me and sitting on the arm of the chair, put her arms around me.

"Oh, here we go," Simon snarled. "Turn on the water works."

"Dad!" James said, getting to his feet. "Don't speak to Mum like that. What on earth has got into you?"

"Sarah bloody West!" Louise blurted out. "That's what's got into him!"

Silence fell upon the room once more as we all tried to take in what was happening. Our family had never had a moment like this before. We'd always been united. Not perfect, but almost. As I looked at Simon now, he seemed like a complete stranger to me. Someone I'd shared most of my adult life with, but suddenly I felt as if I just didn't know him at all.

"So, that's it then?" James asked, breaking the stony silence. "You're leaving Mum?"

"He's already left," I added quietly.

"Mum," Izzie said, squeezing my hand tightly, "you shouldn't have gone through all of this alone. You should have called us."

"I just didn't want to upset you all. I didn't know if your Dad was going through a…" I tried to find the right word, "a stage."

"Oh, like a midlife crisis?" Simon butted in, sarcastically. "Give me some credit!"

"You're pathetic!" Louise blurted out. "Have you seen her? Have you? She's not much older than me! It's disgusting. You're disgusting!"

"When did you find out?" James asked her.

"After Christmas, some time around then," she replied, calming down a little.

"How? How did you find out?" Izzie chipped in.

"I was out with friends and we'd decided to try out 'The Bold' restaurant in town. It was just opening and Jessie's boyfriend worked there. It's when I was still home for the holidays. You remember, Mum?" she asked me.

"Yes," I nodded. "It's the new restaurant inside 'The Cavendish Hotel'."

"That's right…" she said.

"Look," Simon said standing up. "We don't need to go into all this now."

"Oh I see," Louise interrupted. "Mum doesn't know any of this. Okay…" she nodded knowingly.

"Carry on, Lou," James insisted.

"Well, to cut a long story short, we were going through the foyer of the hotel when Dad comes down the stairs with HER on his arm. They were kissing and laughing, completely oblivious that I was stood there, watching!"

"Simon!" I cried out in disbelief. "What's happened to you?" I was horrified that all this had gone on and I was only just hearing about it. Louise had been trying to protect me, obviously, but at what cost to her?

"Sarah fucking West happened!" Louise snapped.

"No!" Simon said, a deep anger in his voice. "Your mother happened. You don't know what it's been like for me?"

We all looked at him, not quite believing our ears. The children looked as shocked as I felt. What had I done to him that was so awful? People had affairs, they got into ruts and they got bored. I wasn't naive. I knew all that. But, where on earth was his anger coming from?

"Okay Simon," I said, pulling myself together. "Tell us. What has it been like for you?"

"Yeah, Dad," James added. "Tell us how awful it's been having everything been done for you so you could build your career. Play golf every weekend."

"That's right," Simon continued in a self-pitying voice. "Take your Mother's side as always."

"Simon, for God's sake!" I stood up. "If it's so bloody terrible for you here, just go. Get out!"

"You said we had to sit down and talk…" he started to say.

"That was before I realised what an ungrateful pig you are. Go on! Get back to your little hussy in the car. I can't bare to look at you for a second longer!" I walked out and went into the kitchen just as the oven timer went off for the Coq-au-vin.

I could hear them all talking over one another and the front door opening and then slamming shut. I put the casserole dish on the side and turned to see the three of them: Louise, Isobelle and James standing there in the kitchen doorway, looking at me with such sadness and sympathy that I couldn't help myself. I just broke down.

Chapter 14

The next morning, I woke to the sound of someone moving around on the landing. It suddenly all came flooding back to me that the children were there. I felt an enormous sense of relief and then sadness, recalling the events of yesterday. I wished they could stay forever and that everything could go back to the way it was before. Then, from nowhere I realised I wouldn't want to go back.

Simon was a selfish, spoilt man and I'd been so busy trying to make his world perfect I'd forgotten about my own. I'd turned into a dowdy, downtrodden housewife and it was my own fault. I couldn't blame him for that. But the deceit, all the lies, for that, I would never forgive him.

After he had left the house last night, driven off to his new life with Sarah West, we'd all sat down to dinner. We didn't think we could eat, but we did. We ate and we washed it down with wine. We listened as Louise described again how she'd seen Simon and Sarah at 'The Cavendish Hotel' and how she'd watched them sitting at a corner table, kissing and holding hands over dinner, how she'd not mentioned it to anyone, not even Scott. Luckily, Scott had already left for home, so that evening, she'd been with friends who didn't know Simon. Louise had approached Simon when he'd returned home the following evening and we all recalled how we thought he'd been on a business trip. It amazed me to think he hadn't even considered that he could have been seen by a number of people, business colleagues, close friends, let alone his own daughter.

She explained to us that he had promised her it was over and that he'd been a fool. He had begged Louise not to say anything. She had genuinely believed her Father. She had even kept in regular contact with him by text messages and phone calls so that he always had her at the back of his mind, just in case he thought of straying again. She truly believed that he loved her so much, that he would keep his word. She felt totally betrayed and I could certainly empathize with that. She had presumed, especially after he'd arranged my birthday and anniversary party for all our friends and family, that all was back to normal. She said that she felt awful for trusting him and not confiding in me.

I had to tell her over and over again, it was not for her to feel responsible for any of it, and that telling me wouldn't have helped anyway. I felt so sorry for her and I knew this was probably going to have far reaching consequences for her in the future.

Izzie cried a lot. She couldn't believe that this had happened to our family. She kept saying again and again how I'd been an amazing Mother and wife and that Simon was an idiot. She actually made us laugh over her comments about Sarah. She thought that from the back, she looked like a boy and that people seeing them together would think Simon was gay. It was wrong to laugh and a little cruel, but laugh we did.

James was more reserved in his opinions. He listened and nodded a lot, but for the most of the evening, he was quiet. I wondered if he felt guilty for calling his Father's mistress, his bit-on-the-side a 'hottie'. He needn't have felt bad, he couldn't have known, but somehow I thought it inappropriate to bring it up. I felt James had put up a bit of a wall...I could feel his distance and it unnerved me a little.

We had all gone to bed around midnight. I actually slept well. Probably my best night's sleep since all this had begun. I plumped up my pillows and sat up in bed. How I loved my bedroom...loved waking up to the familiar comforts it offered. I sighed as I realised I probably wouldn't be waking up in it forever. realised that Simon would want to sell the house and set up a new home with missie!

I thought back to yesterday and the expression on her face. Part of me felt sorry for her and I couldn't understand why. Why would I feel sorry for the woman who had taken my husband away from me, the woman who had stolen the Father of my children? And then it struck me why. It wasn't her fault. Of course, I'm sure she'd known he was married, but who knew what Simon had told her. No, this whole thing was down to him!

I threw back the covers and grabbed my robe. I wanted to get downstairs before they woke up, wanted to open the curtains and blinds, get the kettle on, make everything seem as normal as possible. It's what I did, what I'd always done.

As I got downstairs, I saw I wasn't the first one up. The alarm had been turned off and light was streaming in through the living room and into the hallway. The glass doors to the kitchen were closed and I could see Louise washing the crystal wine glasses from last night. She had scraped her hair back into a high ponytail and was wearing a pale pink cotton dressing gown.

"Good morning, sweetheart," I said, walking into the kitchen. "You didn't need to do that."

"You know me Mum, I like to keep busy." She smiled, leaning over to kiss me on my cheek.

"Coffee?" I asked, reaching for the kettle, and she nodded and leaned back as I reached over, filling it with water. "Did you manage to get some sleep?"

"Surprisingly, yes. I slept quite well."

"Me too. I think it was because you were all here."

"Oh Mum,' she began, taking off the yellow rubber gloves and placing them neatly on the side. "You've been here all alone. How have you coped?"

"Rather well. I'm as shocked as you," I said, seeing a surprised look on her face. "You just have to get on with things. To be honest with you Lou," I continued, pulling out a chair and sitting down at the table, "I think that until last night I believed he was coming home."

She nodded and joined me, sitting opposite. "I'm sure you did."

"It's why I had the make-over, changed my hair, dressed up last night…I honestly thought he'd take one look and come home. Foolish of me I suppose."

"Mum, no!" She got up and made our coffees. "Not at all. You look wonderful, better than ever…your hair's amazing. Takes years off you. No, if you ask me, he's the foolish one.

He's taken you for granted for all these years. He'll have such a wake-up call living with her. She won't have a hot meal waiting for him every night when he gets home from work, or on Saturday evenings when he finally returns from a game of golf. IF he's still allowed to play golf that is!"

I laughed out loud, she was probably right. Sarah West and I came from different generations. Though I have to say, I had always enjoyed taking care of Simon. He worked hard to provide for us all and I had appreciated everything he did. I'd just been blind, not noticed how we'd let things slide. My mind went back to the day we had taken James to university and how I'd visualized Simon and I starting again. It was going to be a new phase of our lives, the two of us, together.

How wrong could I have been?

"And, how the hell you didn't hit her I'll never know," Louise continued, bringing me back to reality. "What the hell does he see in her? She's hardly a sex bomb for God's sake. Izzie's right, she looks like a boy!"

"Beauty's in the eye of the beholder, Lou. After all, your brother thought she was a 'hottie'." At last I'd got it out in the open.

"Yeah, only because she was young." Her words hung in the air and I could feel her kicking herself mentally for saying it. "You're way too nice, Mum. You've let Dad get away with so much crap."

"What do you mean?" I asked, frowning.

"Oh Mum. He's so spoilt. If he came in from work in a bad mood and hardly bothered to speak, you just let it go. I know I've always been close to Dad, but the way he treated you, ugh, sometimes I just wanted to slap him."

'Lou!" I wasn't used to hearing her talk this way about Simon. "He worked so hard, some days he was worn out. I really didn't mind."

"Well you should have! I remember whenever Tim and Anna came round, he was always so charming. I used to think what a pity he can't fuss over you a little more."

"Gosh, I didn't realize."

"You were perfect in every way! I know you're comparing yourself to her, but what has she done so far? Nothing? Has she had three children, brought them up whilst her husband lives out the life of his dreams? Given up her own ambitions in order to put the needs of her family first? No! You've always put us first Mum, always. Now you need to take care of you. You deserve to do what you want to."

"Like what, Lou? I asked, feeling vulnerable.

"What would you like to do?"

"I have no idea." I was blank. Out of ideas.

"What about painting? Aunt Rose always said you should have carried on."

"But I haven't painted in years."

"Well, now you can. Think about it. This is your time now. You show Dad and that, that slut of his that you're going to be just fine. Please Mum, don't let this define who you are." Louise begged.

Isobelle appeared, followed by a very sleepy looking James. They both kissed the top of my head and Louise got up and we all had a family hug.

"What's for breakfast?" James asked, and we all fell about laughing.

After a light breakfast, we got dressed and later ate lunch in the garden. It was still warm, but you could feel autumn approaching now. We all sat there reminiscing over happy times we'd spent in our beautiful home; things that had happened as they'd been growing up, remembering when each one of them had left for university and how I'd cried. I didn't dare mention that this house was not going to be in our family for much longer and from the way they were talking, I knew the thought hadn't crossed their minds. The next thing would be the divorce. I wondered if we could use just the one lawyer, Anthony Bailey from Simon's company, Dalton & Co. We'd known Anthony for many years. Simon would certainly want to use him. This was going to be so hard.

Aware of my mood changing, I insisted they all pack up and head home so that they could settle down before work and university tomorrow. Despite everything, they were in good spirits and I didn't want to dampen them. Whatever happened, we knew the four of us were there for each other. I just hoped, for Simon's sake that they could get used to this new situation. The last thing I wanted, was for them to lose their relationship with their Dad.

I waved them off, smiling, and James commented on how it was the first time I'd said goodbye without shedding a tear. He was right too. I didn't, not one. As I closed the door behind them, I felt a new sense of freedom wash over me. Louise was right, I'd done everything I could possibly have done as a wife and Mum and now it was time for me!

Chapter 15

Three weeks had passed since the children had been to stay. I'd contacted Simon the next day and told him to make amends with them, sooner rather than later, and especially with Louise. I told him how saddened I was that he'd let her be dragged into this situation. He hadn't said much and the distance between us now was immense. It truly was as if the past twenty-five years had never happened, we had literally become strangers.

He told me he intended to sell our house, the family home, as he wanted to buy something for him and Sarah. I wasn't surprised. Nothing Simon did these days surprised me any more. He said he was going to be fair and that Tony was going to look after the divorce for him. After much deliberation, we decided that Tony could handle it for both of us and I agreed to settle on a percentage of his pension.

Aunt Rose had wanted me to fight for more, but I no longer had the energy for fighting. I wanted everything to be done as quickly as possible. I wasn't greedy, and I knew Simon was never coming back, so what was the point. I wanted him out of my life.

Aunt Rose had instructed me to fight hard for the house, reminding me that it had been our family home, the place where I'd raised each of the children. I pointed out to her that although it was going to be a massive wrench to leave our home, the memories were sometimes too painful...I needed to escape them, not hang on to them. And anyway, I would never forget my children growing up in each room of the house, but the memories were always going to be inside my mind, forever.

Autumn was well and truly upon us. The leaves had turned to beautiful shades of orange and reds. The air felt crisp and the nights were drawing in. Each evening around five o'clock I would close the curtains and change into my dressing gown. I looked forward to blocking out the world outside my door. I wasn't crying any more, but I felt very alone. I was numb.

Invitations came from friends to go for dinner or out for drinks. Messages of shock and sympathy flashed on the answering machine, but I didn't want to go anywhere or speak to anyone. Aunt Rose had called regularly, even inviting me to join her on a cruise she was going on in the New Year, but I declined. Louise, Isobelle and James would take it in turns to call and they regularly sent comforting text messages to my phone.

My biggest shock though, was Anna, my supposed best friend of the past twenty-four years. We had met when I was pregnant with Louise and she with her eldest, David. We had hit it off straight away and Simon got on well with her husband, Tim. So that was that. We spent lots of time together over the following years: dinners, family day's out, birthdays, Christmas's and numerous New Year's had been spent together. I couldn't explain her coldness towards me, or the fact that she hadn't contacted me once since her barbecue. I wasn't one for confrontation and the thought of picking up the phone and asking for an explanation made me shudder. No, that problem could be swiftly swept under the carpet for now.

It was ten o'clock in the evening and I turned off the television and lights, set the house alarm and made my way up to bed. The following day, I had an appointment at the gym and I wanted to get to bed early. I had only ventured into one about ten years ago, but had decided it wasn't for me. It was Jade who had persuaded me to join. It had been added to 'The Cavendish', for guests and was also open to the public, a state-of-the-art design with a heated swimming pool, sauna and steam room. Jade had a special discount for her clients at the salon and she'd told me to meet her there at ten o'clock tomorrow morning.

I had tried hard to talk my way out of it, especially as it was at the place where Louise had seen Simon and Sarah together, but she told me that now I was looking fabulous it would be such a shame not to get myself in shape and to start taking care of myself.

She was right! I had lost so much weight and it would be nice to stroll into a gym not feeling bloated and self-conscious. She had suggested a coffee after my induction and that had been the decider. I was also intrigued to see inside the hotel where my soon-to-be ex-husband and his lover had spent their little rendezvous.

As I snuggled down into my bed, I noticed my mobile, which was on silent, was flashing on my bedside table. I answered it. It was Jade.

"Hi hon," she sang. "You all ready for tomorrow morning?"

"Yes," I said, as I smiled. "Tucked up in bed as we speak."

"Good girl. Now," she began, "you're booked in with Greg Smythe." She emphasized his name, almost as if I should know who he was.

"Oh okay," I replied. The name meant nothing to me.

"So, head straight to reception and they'll direct you. "Oh Jen," she said, dreamily. "Wait until you see it! The gym I mean! It's amazing. On the top floor with views right over the town."

"Wow, sounds great."

"Look, I know you're not really in to all of this, but you've got to take care of yourself Jen. You look fantastic, so imagine how you'll look and feel six months down the line, in the safe hands of Greg Smythe. Well, just imagine!!"

"Yes, you're right," I agreed, yawning.

"The girls' at the salon are green with envy that I've got you a session with Greg."

"Really? Why?"

"Apparently he's gorgeous with an amazing body. They got stuck with Brody and Josh and they're not pleased," she giggled. "Anyway, I digress. The reason I called you so late honey, is to tell you that when you've finished get changed and meet me in the 'La-la lounge'. I'm having a meeting there but I want to catch up with you."

"Okay, sure."

"Oh, and I forgot to say, forget coffee, it's going to be champagne!"

With that she hung up. Jade always managed to make me feel happy. I knew very little about her, except that she worked extremely hard and loved her business, but beyond that, nothing. Whenever I saw her, she was smiling and made me feel so good about myself. I smiled as I remembered the day we had first met and thank God we had.

When I woke the next morning, I knew my appointment with Greg Smythe was just for a chat and a weigh in etc. followed by a tour of the gym and equipment. So with that in mind and the fact that I was meeting Jade for drinks after, I chose to wear a grey cashmere dress I'd recently bought which fit like a glove. I teamed it with a pair of knee-high length black boots and a designer black handbag with grey detailing, which all matched perfectly. One last glance in the mirror and I left the house with a new feeling in my stomach. Not one of dread or the sickening feeling I'd had for the past months, but an excited, giddy feeling as if something exciting was about to happen.

The hotel was luxurious. It oozed opulence. I imagined Simon and Sarah checking in on the night they stayed, but I pushed it to the back of my mind and listened to the receptionist's directions to 'The Bodysculpt' gym. It was on the tenth floor. I took the lift and as the doors opened as I reached my destination, I walked out into a buzzing lobby with toned young girls and buff young men passing through, towels thrown over their shoulders and drinking water from brightly coloured flasks.

"Hi there," called out a skinny, pretty woman from behind a desk. "I'm Holly. Do you have an appointment?"

"Yes," I answered, relieved that someone had acknowledged me as I felt completely out of my depth and overdressed, surrounded by people in sports gear. "I have an appointment with Greg Smythe at ten."

"Okay," she said, checking the computer in front of her. "A-ha. You must be Jennifer Aagar." She looked up at me smiling. "Greg will be with you in a moment. Please, take a seat."

She pointed to two leather sofas and I sat down feeling nervous all of a sudden. I didn't feel like 'me' any more. The 'me' I'd known all my life had disappeared and I just didn't know how to act. There were several magazines on a coffee table, but I didn't need to read anything, the comings and goings were enough to keep me occupied whilst I waited for Grey Smythe.

Behind the receptionist were glass walls with 'Bodysculpt' written at different heights in white frosted glass. Behind the glass, you could see the gym equipment. People were on running machines, rowing machines and working with weights. All working hard, some watching the numerous television screens on the walls, others in what I can only presume was 'the zone'. I was so engrossed that I didn't see Greg approach me. Suddenly, I became aware of someone standing over me and looked up to see what I can only describe as a vision! He had dark black hair, cut very short. He had brown eyes with the longest lashes I'd ever seen on a man. He was olive skinned with beautiful defined features. His body was to die for, with muscles bulging beneath tight-fitting Lycra. I felt my heart stop and then race until I swear everyone around me could have heard it.

"Hi. Jen?" He held out a hand and smiled, revealing the most perfect white teeth and dimples in his cheeks. He reminded me of a glossy magazine advert for toothpastes.

Fearing I wouldn't be able to speak, I swallowed before saying, "Yes, that's me."

I stood up and smoothed down my clingy, cashmere dress.

"Great. I'm Greg and I'll be showing you around today. You ready to follow me?" He grinned.

WAS I EVER? Like a small lapdog, panting with its tongue hanging out, I followed. He took me into the gym first. He talked me through the equipment first, explained how we'd work out a programme to suit my needs. My needs! Needs I hadn't had for years rose up inside of me. I was hot with rosy cheeks and wished he would kiss me.

Next he took me to the pool area, which we viewed through more glass and I had to stop my urge to lunge at him. I could feel my perfectly styled hair beginning to frizz with the humidity. He just kept on and on, talking and smiling and walking…me trotting behind with the view of his clearly defined buttocks, wanting to rip off the black Lycra shorts that fit so snugly. I longed for him to turn around so I could get a good view of his front.

"So," he said, clapping his hands. "What do you think? Did you like what you saw?"

"Great." That was all I could manage to say, innuendos running riot in my mind and threatening to jump out as they sat on the tip of my tongue.

"Okay then. Let's get you booked in." He took me by the arm and led me into an office. "We just need to go through some paperwork. It won't take long."

"Great." The only word in the English vocabulary I seemed to know.

And that's what we did. He took my details and made appointments for me twice a week, with him, for personal training. He told me he was going to 'whip me into great shape' and an image of Greg Smythe, naked, holding a long leather whip entered my head. He was simply the most perfect man I'd ever been this close to. I couldn't help wondering how he wasn't on a catwalk in Paris, London or Milan? I was totally and utterly mesmerized.

We said our goodbyes and he walked me to the lift, pressing the down button for me. He smiled and walked over to the receptionist, who pointed him in the direction of his 'ten-thirty', an Abigail Crompton. I detested Abigail Crompton on sight. As the doors pinged open, I took one last look at him and he turned to meet my eyes, holding the gym door open for Abigail. He winked at me and my stomach literally somersaulted. I quickly got into the lift and sighed a sigh of relief as the doors closed.

Once back in the hotel foyer, I headed to the 'La-la Lounge'. I entered almost in a daze, the thought of Greg at the forefront of my mind. I actually wanted to run back, using the stairs and declare my undying love for him. And then it struck me, right there in the 'La-la Lounge' that this was probably the impact Sarah West had made on Simon. With that thought, I was brought straight back down to earth, with a bump!

Out of the corner of my eye, I saw Jade waving at me to join her, a glass of champagne in her other hand. I smiled and walked over to her – thank heavens for Jade!!

Chapter 16

Life was carrying on, in a fashion. I was able to function better on a day-to-day basis. I found for example, that I was no longer planning meals. I would shop three or four times a week now compared to before when things were more 'normal'. I was beginning to see just how regimented my life had been.

The weekends were based around Simon and James. Looking back now, I realised I didn't really have a life, certainly not an exciting one. Simon had been right that day I had smashed his phone on his head, the day he had told me 'to get a life'.

I suppose that's what I'd done – got a life. It was quite lonely, but it was certainly different. I hadn't seen or heard from Anna in such a long time and I was mad at her now. What kind of a friend was she? Not even a phone call to see how I was. In my usual way, I had put her to the back of my mind and couldn't face the conversation we needed to have, and each time she popped back into my mind, I just pushed her further back. Apart from the children and Aunt Rose, my only communication was with Jade. She was so busy though, that I only saw her on a Wednesday evening when she had a gym session at the same time as me. We would shower and change and have a glass of wine or two in the bar afterwards. I loved our get-togethers, she was so vibrant, you couldn't help but feel good when in her company.

My gym sessions were going extremely well. The handsome Greg Smythe, was very pleased with the results so far. I had lost over four kilos and had followed his plan to a tee. It had been four weeks since I'd joined and I went three times a week. Originally he'd suggest twice, but with so much time on my hands, I decided to take advantage of it. I went Monday mornings, Wednesday evenings and Saturday afternoons. I can't say I enjoyed exercising, but I loved the results and the time spent with him. All my clothes that had been hidden away at the back of my wardrobe, fit me so well and I felt wonderful.

I also felt wonderful whenever I saw Greg. He was so encouraging and motivated me to keep training. I'd booked in for a month's personal training and this afternoon was my last session with him guiding me, touching my stomach as he urged me to do more sit-ups. As I drove to the hotel parking, I couldn't help but feel a little sad that it was ending, but it was too expensive to continue and now I knew my way around all the equipment, it wasn't necessary. Simon had given me an allowance to cover costs, but he had objected to paying for my personal trainer.

I walked out of the ladies changing rooms and into reception and there he was waiting for me.

"Hey Jen," he called out, "you ready for our last session together?"

"Not really," I replied, glumly. "I'll miss them."

"Well, we'd better work extra hard today then," he said, smiling, and holding the gym door open for me. "Come on." And he followed in behind me.

He certainly kept his word and worked me very hard. I finished the session a perspiring, red-faced wreck, puffing and panting, gulping down water, droplets falling from the side of my mouth.

Not a pretty sight, so I was more than surprised when he looked at me and said, "Ok Jen, I've really enjoyed our sessions and I'm going to miss you, so I'd like to take you out for a drink, maybe dinner. What about this evening? If you're free of course…I mean, maybe you already have plans with it being a Saturday." He was so confident in his approach.

I almost spat out my water in his face and gulped rather loudly as I struggled to take in what he'd just said. I looked around the gym to see who else could be in as much shock as I was, but we were alone.

"Erm…I…I…" I couldn't get my words out.

"Hey look Jen, no probs if you don't want to," he began.

"I want to," I blurted out, far too quickly.

"Great." He smiled, stroking my back and probably regretting doing so immediately as I was damp, to say the least. "I know a great place off the high street. It's called 'Capriccio'. Do you like Italian?"

"I love Italian."

"Great," he said again. "Is eight good for you?"

"Great," I replied.

"Okay then. I'll make the reservation and meet you there."

"Okay. See you later then, Greg." I picked up my towel and we left the gym together. I headed for the lift and turned to see him greeting his next client.

I felt as if I was walking on air. I mean, a guy like Greg, wanting to take me out for dinner. Things were definitely looking up.

****

I almost ran into the house and actually keyed in the wrong code on the alarm system. After many years of the same code, day in day out, year after year, I felt a little foolish explaining to the alarm company when they called, that I'd simply forgotten the code. I'm sure the engineer who called thought I was in the early stages of dementia.

Flustered, I threw off my gym clothes and jumped into the shower. I stayed there a long time, letting the warm water wash over my body. I felt elated, almost to the point were I could actually burst with the excitement of it all.

Greg Smythe and I were going to have dinner together. I was sure he didn't ask all of his clients out. Suddenly, self-doubt ensued me. Why had he asked me out? I was starting to convince myself it was all a joke somehow and that he wouldn't be there at 'Capriccios' waiting for me at all. Within moments, I had gone from a feeling of complete euphoria, to one of utter despair.

As if to shake me out of this ridiculous turn of events, the water ran cold and I shook my head as if to empty it of such futile thoughts. I altered the flow of water and the cold turned back to warm. I shampooed and conditioned my hair quickly and dried myself off. I looked in the bathroom mirror and smiled at my reflection.

I had come a long way since the day Simon had told me I was too fat to buy sexy underwear for, and I said out loud, to myself, "he likes you. It's all going to be just fine!"

With a huge sigh, I set about getting ready for my 'date'. I stood wrapped in a bath towel, gazing at my clothes hanging in the walk-in wardrobe. What did one wear? What impression did I want to give to Greg Smythe? I had no answers, truth be told.

I just couldn't wait to sit opposite him and gaze into his heavenly brown eyes. I felt like a teenager again. I felt alive and I wasn't going to let my negative thoughts spoil it. I grabbed a black dress with a low v-neck and my black patent leather slingbacks. I picked out a delicate gold necklace with a small diamond pendant and matching bracelet, simple but not brash. A set Simon had bought me years back for an anniversary. A slight pang of guilt flashed through me, but I thought now that our marriage was over, it wasn't important.

As I fastened the bracelet onto my left wrist, my wedding and engagement rings caught my eye. I held my hand out, looking at them for some time. I was going on a sort of date, was it now time to take them off? With a deep breath, I wriggled them off my fingers and placed them in the ring compartment in my jewellery box.

My fingers felt bare. I rushed into Louise's room and found a costume ring that I slid on to my middle. I gazed out of her bedroom window over the garden and my eyes filled with tears. I blinked them away. It hadn't been my choice to end our marriage and Simon didn't deserve my tears, especially not tonight.

By six o'clock I was ready. I looked at myself in the dressing room full-length mirror and liked what I saw. I looked elegant and best thing of all, I looked slim. I smiled so widely that my cheeks ached. I decided that being ready so early was ridiculous, so I got undressed again and poured myself a little glass of wine for courage, just a small one as I was driving.

The time dragged. But soon enough, I was in my car and heading into town. Taking a strawberry red throw to keep warm and adding a splash of colour to my outfit, I felt ready and excited for the night ahead. I parked just outside the restaurant and once inside, was led to my table.

There he was. Greg Smythe, already seated and waiting for me. He smiled and stood up to greet me. He was wearing a designer T-shirt and jeans, and suddenly I felt way too overdressed.

"Wow!" he said and leaned in to kiss my cheek. "You look amazing. And he exaggerated the 'a' in amazing.

"Thank you, Greg," I replied, sitting down. "I owe a lot of how I look to you."

"Awe, come on." He grinned. "It was all your own hard work. I just encouraged you. Now, what would you like to drink?"

We both ordered a glass of white wine, which he sipped very slowly. I imagined he wasn't a heavy drinker, with his occupation relying heavily on how he looked. He ordered a ravioli dish and I fancied scampi with pasta, which came in a rich cream sauce. I looked for some kind of disappointment in his face, but there was none.

"So, Jen, how on earth are you free at such short notice on a Saturday evening?" He paused and then continued, "looking like THAT!"

"Hmm," I sighed, gulping down my wine. "It's a very long story."

"Hey, we've got all night." His stare was so intense that it actually sent shivers down my spine. He made me feel so attractive, so sensual, just by looking into my eyes.

I began to tell him all about Simon and Sarah, not once feeling uncomfortable or awkward in any way. He was a good listener, that was for sure. During dinner he ordered me another glass of wine and a bottle of water for the table. It felt so good to be able to talk so freely about the recent events and how my life had been completely turned upside down. Finally, I told him the divorce was proceeding and that there was no way back.

"Well," he said, sitting back and pouring us both a glass of water, "if you ask me, your husband's a fool."

"No," I said, gesturing with my hands. "He just fell out of love with me and in love with someone else...someone a lot younger!"

"Don't put yourself down, Jen." He leaned across the table and took my hand. "You are a beautiful woman. Don't forget that." He pulled away and called over the waiter. "Jen, another wine?"

"Oh, no, no..." I started to say.

"Come on. One more. I'll drive you home, no probs." He winked at me and turned to the waiter. "Another white wine for the lady, please."

"What about you?" I asked, realizing all we'd done was talk about me and feeling the effects of the wine beginning to warm my body. "Anyone special in your life?"

"No, nobody special at the moment. To be honest, I've worked so hard this past year, I don't get time."

"Are you trying to keep busy for any particular reason?" I found it hard to believe someone like him wasn't in a relationship.

"Yeah, I guess. Last year I had a bad break-up and so I threw myself into the training. I found it was the best way to get through it."

"I'm sorry, Greg. I didn't mean to pry."

"Hey, that's okay. Just know, she's out of the picture. Actually," he paused, looking up at me, "you're the first person I've been out with since. I just felt a connection."

My heart almost melted, my body tingled. "Me too."

"Well, there you go then," he said, winking at me, cheekily.

My stomach was doing somersaults for most of the evening, but when he said there was a connection between us, I felt as though my insides were about to fall out. Who would ever have thought that a guy like Greg could find someone like me remotely interesting? With each passing moment, my confidence grew and it was all down to him.

We both declined to look at the dessert menu as an urgency passed between us that we didn't need to talk about it, it was just there. Greg insisted on paying the bill. The waiter brought us over a small glass of Amaretto on the house, which Greg encouraged me to drink, though I noticed he took only one sip from his glass. He told me he'd drive me back to my house in my car and take a taxi later to his. My heart raced.

"Hey! BMW, nice car Mrs Aagar," he commented as he opened the door for me.

We drove the ten minutes back to mine in silence, but not an awkward silence, anticipation hung in the air and he kept his hand on my knee the whole way. I longed for him to move it further up my leg and I struggled to keep my breathing in check.

By the time we pulled into the driveway, we couldn't wait any longer and he pushed his lips hard against mine. I knew I was about to get to know Greg Smythe a whole lot better!

Chapter 17

We ventured out of my car and to the front door, fumbling about to find the house keys in my bag, he reached in and pulled them out. He unlocked the door and I rushed in to turn off the alarm. My hands shaking as I carefully pressed the four digits, not wanting a repeat of earlier. Suddenly, I was aware of Greg kissing the back of my neck and I turned to face him.

In the darkness his eyes glistened as he stared deeply into mine. As we kissed I leaned slightly back and kicked off my shoes, standing on tiptoes to reach him. He started to pull down my dress at the shoulders and kissed me there, soft, gentle kisses. I thought my legs were going to give way beneath me, I couldn't breathe as my body was overtaken by the passion. Pulling away, I reached for the hem of my dress and pulled it over my head, dropping it on the floor. The necklace I'd ever so carefully chosen earlier that evening snapped and fell onto the floor and I thought how ironic. He stood back and looked at my body.

As I stood there in my black lacy underwear, I was relieved I'd thought it through. I hadn't known that our evening would end like this, but as I'd got dressed earlier this evening, I had chosen the sexy black set with this very event in mind. Aunt Rose's words started to ring in my ears about the importance of such things, and I fought hard to get her out of my head. This was not the time.

The way he looked me up and down, I felt like the most beautiful woman in the world. He reached out and pulled me towards him, unhooking my bra and letting it drop also to the floor. I gasped as he cupped my breasts in his hands.

"You feel amazing," he whispered in my ear, sending shivers down my back. "Absolutely fucking amazing." And he reached down and began to kiss them.

I grabbed at the belt around his jeans and started to frantically unbuckle it, undoing the button and pulling down the zip. I could feel him hard and I was desperate to feel him inside me. He stepped out of his jeans and pulled off his T-shirt, revealing a defined hairless chest.

"I love your mind..." he said, gasping and moaning, and I wanted to tell him he wouldn't find it where his hands were wandering, but felt it would be totally inappropriate and then the alcohol rushed over me and I went with the moment.

He slid his hand inside my lacy French knickers and I felt things I hadn't felt in so long, if ever. "Come on," I said, taking his hand and leading him towards the stairs. "Let's go to bed."

We fell onto the bed, kissing and caressing each other's bodies. It felt as though ten pairs of hands were over me and I had never felt such bliss in my life. He climbed on top of me and with both hands, swept my hair off my face and kissed my face tenderly before finding my lips again and kissing them desperately. I opened myself up to him, unable to wait a second longer. I felt the full force of him inside me and our bodies moved together in perfect harmony, hot and wet, until he reached climax and he flopped on top of me, his whole body weight heaving and breathless.

We lay like that for a few minutes and he rolled over onto his side, stretching and sighing in deep satisfaction. "Thank you," I whispered, tears filling my eyes.

"Thank you?" he repeated, laughing and propping his head up in his hand and looking at me.

"Yes, thank you. For making me feel alive again." And as I turned to face him, I kissed his mouth gently.

This gentle kiss went on for a few minutes, getting harder and more passionate, and before I knew it, he had flipped me over onto my stomach and entered me again. I yelled out in pure ecstasy and turned to look back at him. He was the most beautiful man I had ever encountered and I secretly prayed that this second time, wouldn't be our last.

Eventually, both exhausted, we snuggled under the covers and he put his arm around me. I placed my head on his shoulder and breathed his scent in. I wished we could stay like this forever and I knew in that moment that my marriage to Simon had probably been over for a very long time. What I had just felt, the experience of utter passion, was what he had found in Sarah West. In that instant, I understood completely, why he had left me.

We slept for over an hour. I woke to him sitting on the edge of the bed, looking at me. As I opened my eyes, he smiled. "Hey," he said softly, "I'm going to go now." He stroked my hair. "I had an amazing time with you, Mrs Aagar."

"Do you have to go?" I asked, suppressing the urge to beg him to never leave.

"I'm working at seven in the morning."

"Oh, okay," I said, feeling disappointed. I reached for his hand. "Tonight was perfect."

"Absolutely. In fact," he said, getting up and grabbing his underpants from the floor. "Let me get my phone and I'll get your number." He went downstairs and I heard him putting on his jeans and coming back to the bedroom. Looking like someone out of a catalogue, he passed me my handbag. "Right, call this number on your phone and then we'll have each other's contacts."

I keyed in his number and his phone flashed, obviously on silent, and I thought it was sweet that he didn't want to be disturbed whilst he was with me. I got up and reached for my robe at the end of the bed. He kissed me and promised he'd call later. I saw him to the door and he told me to go inside. I had offered to take him back into town, but he reminded me how much I'd had to drink. He assured me he'd be okay, and I watched him walk down the driveway, waving as he turned back to look at me. He blew me a kiss and disappeared behind the garden wall.

I closed the front door and set the alarm. I couldn't wait to climb back into bed. It was still warm from where we'd been and I could smell him on the pillows and in my hair. I lay back and closed my eyes, re-living every single touch, every kiss, over and over again.

I slept so well. I didn't wake until eleven the next morning. I couldn't believe it. I saw my mobile flashing, informing me I'd had a missed call or a message. It was from Greg.

'Home safely. Sleep well Mrs A...until next time...Gx"

I scrolled down, he'd sent it at 2 a.m. I felt giddy with excitement, like a teenager all over again. I sent him a reply.

'Slept extremely well. I CAN NOT wait until next time!! X'

For the rest of the day I busied myself. After showering, getting dressed and having a coffee I thought about stripping the bedclothes and washing them, but just smelling his scent on the pillow put pay to that. I couldn't settle to anything. I couldn't get Greg or last night out of my head. I decided to occupy myself by calling the kids.

Each phone call lasted no more than five minutes. They were all okay. Okay and busy. They were so pleased to hear me sounding cheerful. There was only one thing, one person who could take my mind off it all − Aunt Rose. I picked up the phone and called her. After a few rings she answered.

"Aunt Rose, it's Jennifer."

"Darling, hello. Oh how lovely to hear from you." She was genuinely happy.

"How do you fancy dinner with me this evening?" I asked, hopeful she'd be free.

"I'd love it. I was just sitting here, wondering what to make. Oh, that's so lovely dear."

"Great then, I'm going to come and get you. Seven okay? My treat."

I made reservations at 'Peacocks', a beautiful quaint little place on the outskirts of town. Getting ready, the euphoria I'd felt all day was slowly turning into longing. A longing for Greg to contact me, a text would have done. But I'd heard nothing all day. I had to fight the constant urge to message him. The longing was turning my stomach into a pit of anxiety.

As I got ready to go out, my eyes wandered over to the bed and I sighed, long and hard. I put on a mulberry coloured woollen dress, yet another one I'd found way back in the wardrobe. I draped a long gold necklace over it and stood back to look at myself. Grabbing my coat and handbag, I set off to get Aunt Rose.

When I arrived, she was ready and waiting, dressed in a brown trouser suit with a beautiful shocking pink throw wrapped around her shoulders. She looked the vision of a perfect English Rose. She got into the car and I closed the door behind and off we went. She was delighted at my choice of restaurant. As we drove up to the old cottage style building, it looked so inviting with the lights leading us to the parking. Inside, there were several people already eating and it was warm and cosy. A real fire crackled in the bar area where you could sit and wait for your table over a glass of something nice. Our table was ready and the waiter led us to one in the corner with a window overlooking the countryside, though now in the dark, we could only see our own reflections. We ordered a glass of champagne and looked at the menu.

"I think I want meat," Aunt Rose announced. "Comfort food. I want comfort food."

"Hmm, I know what you mean." And I perused the wonderful dishes available. "What about the beef stroganoff?"

"Ooh, perfect choice, darling," she gasped, snapping shut the menu. 'And you?"

I decided on duck in a Porto sauce. I felt that I could do with some meat too. The thought of Greg's toned, hard body popped into my head and I shivered.

"Oh darling, are you cold?" Aunt Rose enquired.

"No, no," I hastily replied and she looked at me, her blue eyes squinting, almost suspicious.

"Now then," she said, smiling as the waiter brought our champagne. "What news?"

"Nothing special," I replied quickly, picking up my glass as she did the same. "Cheers."

"Cheers my dear and thank you for this." She took a sip. "Children okay?"

"Yes, really okay. I called them earlier and they were fine, very busy with one thing and another…you know how it is at their age."

"And you, my darling Jennifer, how are you?" she asked, sympathetically.

"Good, Aunt Rose. I feel good."

"Well, you certainly look it. You look more fabulous each time I see you. Pity the bastard didn't leave you years ago!" I spluttered on my drink at her words. "Oh I'm sorry dear, that was little insensitive, but you know me, no harm intended."

"I know," I said, wiping the corners of my mouth with the napkin.

"It's just that you look so alive, darling. More alive than I've ever seen you."

All through our meal we chatted away about this and that. Aunt Rose had spoken to my parents recently and they had said that they would try to get home for Christmas. We both raised our eyebrows as we knew this was unlikely. They were like nomads and would probably wander to some other far out place to see how the locals celebrated Christmas there. I was really alright about it, though. They'd suppressed their nomadic tendencies long enough for me to reach university and after all, Aunt Rose had always and would always, be there. Even though she'd told them about what had happened with Simon, they hadn't called me.

I knew it was too much for them to deal with over the phone, as they hated dealing with emotions as much as they hated staying in one place too long. They had, however, sent their love.

Dinner was a triumph. The food was excellent and the service warm and friendly. Aunt Rose finished it off with Irish coffee and me with a cup of tea. She thanked me again for such a lovely time and we got back it the car and I drove her back to her place.

"I'll see you in,' I said, turning off the engine and unbuckling my seat belt.

"Oh good. I have something for you."

I couldn't imagine what it was and I followed her in. She set about turning on some lamps as it struck me, I hadn't thought once about Greg since the beginning of the night. She beckoned me into the dinning room.

"Close your eyes," she instructed, taking me by the arm. "Okay...open!"

There on the table were lots of wrapped little gifts, and standing proudly next to them was an easel and on it's frame, a blank canvas. I couldn't believe it. I hadn't painted in so long, it was the last thing I had expected. I was also secretly relieved, because with Aunt Rose, it could have been anything!

"I don't know what to say." I smiled, turning to kiss her.

"Say nothing, just start painting!"

Chapter 18

As soon as I arrived home, I put the easel into the study. On unwrapping the gifts I'd discovered Aunt Rose had bought me a selection of paints, charcoals and sketch pads, along with several other canvases. I carried them in from the car, put them on Simon's desk and closed the door. I stood for a moment in the hallway. I hadn't drawn or painted anything in years. I think the last drawing I'd done was of Louise when she was a baby.

I understood exactly why she had felt the need to do this. She was desperate for me to find something just for me. What I couldn't understand was my reaction to them. I just didn't want to think about them and somehow, placing them in the study I could forget about them. I was about to make myself a cup of tea, when my mobile rang from inside my bag.

It was Greg. My heart missed a beat. "Hello?" I answered, coldly. Be cool. Be cool.

"Hey, Mrs A. What are you up to?" The 'Mrs A' thing was starting to irritate me.

"Oh, not much. I've just walked in, actually." I was just about to tell him about my dinner when the doorbell rang. I couldn't think who it could be at this time of night and I peeped into the kitchen to check the time on the clock hanging on the wall. "Er, just hold on a minute Greg, there's someone at my front door." I opened the front door to find him standing there, huge grin on his face.

"Oh okay," he winked. "I'd better let you go, see who it is." And he hung up.

"Greg!" I exclaimed, in total shock at finding him there and thank God I looked presentable.

"Good evening. I couldn't get you out of my head. Today's been a complete waste of time. Just," he stepped inside and kissed me on the tip of my nose. "Couldn't," and again, kissing my nose. "Concentrate." He pushed the door closed and leaned against it, pulled me into him.

We didn't speak again until we were both lying on the tiled floor, naked. I was completely blown away and we were both exhausted. A few minutes later, I could feel the cold floor beneath me and I sat up, reaching for my dress and covering myself up.

"Hello," I said, smiling and bending down to kiss him.

"Hello." He smiled back. "I feel much better now, Mrs A."

"Don't call me that, I much prefer Jen."

"Okay, I feel much better now, Jen!" And he grabbed me and pulled me back down to him, holding me close.

I felt so secure and so content in his arms. It was magical. He asked if he could shower and went upstairs, returning to the landing and throwing me down my robe.

"Don't want you catching a cold." I caught it before it landed on the floor.

I went into the kitchen and poured myself a glass of wine. I curled up on the sofa in the family room and sat back, listening to Greg moving about upstairs and liking how it felt. I sipped my wine, visualizing how it would be waking up next to him in the morning. He came into the kitchen, jeans already on and he was pulling his sweater over his head. Carrying his socks and trainers, he joined me on the sofa. I realised when he began to put on his socks that he wasn't going to be staying after all. Disappointment rushed over me.

"You don't mind if I get off now, do you, babe? It's an early start again in the morning."

"No, of course not." I lied. "It was nice to see you." I hoped he couldn't hear in my voice that I did mind, very much.

"Great!" And with that he stood up, leant over and kissed me. A long lingering kiss, that sent my stomach into a series of flips. "You stay there, darlin'. Enjoy the rest of your wine and I'll call you tomorrow."

Then he was gone. I glanced back at the clock. Eleven thirty, he'd stayed less than an hour. I emptied my glass and went into the hallway, locking the front door and picking up my pile of clothes I'd left on the floor. I opened the study door and turned on the reading lamp and closed the blind. I ran my fingers over the canvas. Opening the sketchbook, the smell of fresh new paper immediately hit me. Suddenly, I felt inspired. I picked out a charcoal and sat down at Simon's desk. I began to sketch an image…I began to sketch Greg.

I climbed into bed around three in the morning. I was completely exhausted having finished drawing Greg. I was ready for sleep. My head hit the pillow and I slept immediately, a deep, peaceful sleep, no dreams or nightmares, just pure sleep.

When I woke around ten o'clock the next morning, I felt more alive than I had in such a long time. I lay there for a few moments, recalling the events of last night and remembering Greg's hands and lips all over me. I smiled and yet at the same time felt an unbearable ache inside. I wanted him again and I checked my phone. Nothing. I decided that it was okay for me to send him a message.

'Last night was amazing…can't wait for next time. Xx'

I put my phone back on the bedside table. It was then I remembered the sketch I'd done and I jumped out of bed and ran downstairs into the study. Forgetting to turn off the alarm I quickly ran to key in the numbers to turn it off. I opened the blind in the study and light flooded in. The drawing of Greg made me smile. He looked beautiful, I'd drawn him naked, lying down on his side, head in his hand. It was a magical feeling and it took me back to life drawing classes I'd taken at college. The thought of painting filled me with new optimism.

My heart filled up even more with hope when my mobile phone bleeped and Greg had replied to my text message, telling me our 'next time' was going to be sooner than I thought.

The next few weeks carried on much the same. I had continued to visit the gym, three to four times a week, taking full advantage of the swimming pool, meeting Jade on occasions and having drinks in the bar, or eating lunch in the restaurant. I snatched glances of Greg, exchanged sly smiles when nobody was looking. We never spoke, except for 'hello' and 'goodbye', but then he'd text me saying how great, sexy or stunning I was, and I was living in a dreamlike state, hardly able to believe that someone like him could possibly find someone like me attractive. Our little rendezvous continued, taking place four or five times a week. He would arrive in the evenings and a couple of times he'd popped around at lunchtime. Those moments were the happiest I'd been in years. There were no more dinners or dates in public, but I was just content with the time I had with him. I carried on sketching images of Greg, never showing him what I'd drawn. They were for me, to look back in future years, to remind me of this time.

James had stayed with me at home for a few days towards the end of October, and though it was wonderful to see my lovely son, I missed Greg unbelievably. I missed his face, his smile, his touch — everything about him. I was struggling to eat and only a message from him would reignite my appetite. I was becoming totally obsessed with him. As James was leaving, he commented on how well I looked and said that his Dad leaving was probably the best thing that had happened to me.

That night, Greg arrived at eleven in the evening. I had been ready to go to bed when the doorbell rang. Seeing him on the doorstep, I grabbed him and squeezed him tightly. He kissed my forehead and put his hands inside my robe, making me squeal a little as the cold touched my body, then sigh with delight.

Later, as we lay together in my bed and held hands I turned to him.

"I missed you so much." I kissed his chest. "I couldn't stand another night without you."

"Me too, babe, me too."

"Stay tonight," I proposed.

"I can't, darlin'," he whispered, stroking my hair.

"Why not?" I asked, turning over to face him.

"Usual reason. Work."

"I'll wake you up in time, don't worry about that," I insisted, kissing his neck and trying hard not to feel or sound too foolish. "I'll make you a high energy breakfast…"

He laughed out loud. "Sorry babe, no can do." And he gently pushed me aside and sat up on the edge of the bed. "In fact, it's getting late now. I'd better make a move."

"Why?" I was bewildered now. "Please stay, Greg."

"Hey," he turned to look at me and stood up, grabbing his clothes.

"What? Come back to bed…"

"Don't go getting all needy on me, Jen. This is going great, but don't pressure me! Don't beg it's not very attractive."

His words stung me and the foolishness I'd pushed down earlier rose up inside my throat and I couldn't speak. Tears stung my eyes and I quickly wiped them away before he saw them. I gathered together my dignity as best I could and smiled.

"Okay," I managed to say, "I understand."

Though I really didn't understand. He was alone and I was alone, what reason was there why we couldn't have one night together? I wanted to cry and I bit my lip as I watched him dress. He told me to stay in bed and that he'd see himself out. And I called out to him to 'call me', immediately regretting it.

Before my mind could start to analyse what had just happened, I decided to go downstairs and make myself a milky drink to help me sleep. As I tied the belt around my robe, I prayed I could avoid the wine cooler. I'd been avoiding it for weeks now, though I think there were two or three bottles still in there.

As I reached the bottom of the stairs, the doorbell rang and my heart raced. He'd changed his mind and had come back. I rushed to the door to open it.

"You changed your mind then…" I began to say, and stopped as I saw it wasn't Greg standing there, but a heavily pregnant young woman.

She was around twenty-five years of age with long brown hair, a pretty face with a little button nose. Her eyes were wide and like large deep pools, as tears brimmed over. I couldn't understand why she was at my door. I wrapped my robe closer around my body and looked over her shoulder, though I don't know who or what I was looking for. I opened my mouth to speak, but before I could say anything, she pushed her way past me and into the hallway.

"I just wanted to look at you, see what you were like," she said between clenched teeth. "And you're nothing special!"

"Excuse me," I said, completely flabbergasted and running my fingers through my messy hair. "Who are you?"

"Who am I?" she mocked. "Who am I?"

"Look, I don't know what's going on here, why you've bombarded your way into my home, but I don't think you should get so worked up in your condition."

"My condition?" she repeated, again in a mocking voice. "Would you like to know who I am?" WHO put me in 'this condition'?"

By now I was so confused, I didn't know what was going on. My mind was in a blur. One minute I was about to make myself a hot drink, the next a stranger was stood in my hall, ranting at me. It did run through my mind that this could be another of Simon's flings, but surely not.

"I'm sorry," I said, calmly. "I just don't understand what's going on here. I'm going to have to ask you to leave now."

"I'm Greg's fiancé," she announced, and I felt my knees buckle.

"What?" I gasped, clutching my chest.

"Oh, shocked are we? Didn't he mention about me and the baby?"

"No…" I began.

"No! I didn't think he would, that's why I thought I'd come around and introduce myself. I saw him leave just now." She was yelling at me and tears poured down her face. I remembered the day I'd tried to confront Sarah at the office and I understood why she was so angry. The difference being, I managed to mess it all up before I could confront her. "Was it good? Where did you do it?" She was uncontrollable now. She walked through the hallway and stood at the bottom of the stairs, looking up. "In your bed? Or on the kitchen table perhaps, he likes that!"

"I'm sorry," I said, feeling rather pathetic. My mouth was dry. "I had no idea. I would never have…"

"Never would have what?" she screamed. "Shagged him if you knew about me!" She stopped shouting for a moment and put her hand on her baby bump. Maybe she felt the baby kicking her, but it stopped her momentarily. She sat down on the bottom stair. "Look at you," she sobbed, eyeing me up and down. "What the hell does he see in you? You must be at least forty-five or something for God's sake."

I walked towards her, feeling totally helpless. "I'm so sorry," I said again.

"You're not sorry, you're a disgusting housewife who'll take a shag wherever she can."

"No," I moaned, tears falling down my face. "I'm not like that, please you have to believe me," I said, desperately.

"Well, you are now." She stood up and came face-to-face with me. "You stay away from him. He's mine! He'll get tired of you soon anyway. Don't think you're the first sad, old hag who's sad miserable life he's tried to brighten up.

I thought for one moment that she was going to hit me and I felt myself tense up, but she didn't. She looked at me as if I was scum and then walked towards the door and left. Left me standing there, sobbing and feeling so worthless.

I quickly shut the door and put on the chain, shaking. I found myself once again sliding down the wall. I sat there, on the floor for a long time. Her words rang in my head, over and over again. How could I have been so stupid to think that someone like Greg would have been interested in someone like me? How could he have done this to her? He was engaged, due to be a Father and he had lied.

Something caught my eye, sparkling on the floor under the hall table. I crawled over to it. It was the necklace Simon had bought me…it had laid there since the first night when he'd undressed me in the hall.

Rage filled me and I rushed into the study, taking the sketchpad and began to rip out each drawing I'd done of him, tearing them one by one into hundreds of tiny little pieces. I'd somehow thought the smaller the pieces the smaller the ache in my gut, but it didn't work. I took my phone and started to call him, but I realised this was futile. Instead, I deleted his contact details and all of the messages he'd ever sent me. Needless to say, I didn't return to the gym again.

Chapter 19

By mid-November I was settling nicely into a depression. The cold, dark nights were not helping my mood and I was ready for bed, snuggled on the sofa by six o'clock most evenings. I kept things cheerful and upbeat when I spoke to the children, the last thing I wanted was for them to worry. Aunt Rose was calling more regularly and I think I'd managed to make her believe I was okay.

The divorce was moving forward and although still icy cold, the relationship between Simon and I was a little easier. I felt that now I understood what he'd experienced with Sarah, I would be a hypocrite to play the victim. I had come to see now that our marriage was all but an empty shell. Days filled with nothingness, emptiness and two people who had simply grown apart.

I wasn't eating enough and I was drinking too much. I'd kept Jade at arm's length. She had tried to coax me back to the gym, and in the end I had to tell her what had happened with Greg. She wasn't at all shocked and she didn't judge me. She kept me updated on him from time to time and she'd done some delving into his 'situation'. Apparently, I was one of many. Great! His girlfriend, Tea, was constantly stalking him at work and she had always taken him back after each fling he'd had with a client or another member of staff. They were due to be married in April next year.

Jade insisted that I keep up with my regular cut and colour, and she enrolled me into Pilates classes at the local village hall. She was the best friend that I'd ever had. Unlike Anna, who still hadn't once picked up the phone to see how I was. I felt sorry for myself, but more than anything, I felt alone — totally alone.

As if she had somehow read my mind, Anna called me the next day. I had been sorting through my clothes and bagging up items for the charity shop when the phone rang.

"How are you doing?" she had asked in a rather condescending way, after announcing she had news for me.

"Oh, not too bad, thank you." I knew I was off with her, I couldn't help it, but she seemed oblivious.

"Good, good. Now, my news!" She paused, waiting for a response from me, but I stayed silent on the other end, rolling my eyes, counting to ten before I said something I knew I would regret. "I've set you up on a date."

"WHAT?"

"Yes, you heard me right...a date. He's lovely. His name is Sebastian Houghton."

"Anna, I don't care what his name is! Un-arrange it as soon as possible!"

"Oh don't be so silly, Jennifer Aagar," (I hated it when people used my full name, it reminded me of a teacher back in primary school). "He is perfect for you, just perfect. I met him last night at a charity do, you know, the one Polly Mason runs for cancer awareness? It was a fabulous turnout and everyone asked where you were. I told them about Simon and what had happened. They were all so very sorry for you. Really, you wouldn't believe how many people were talking about it..."

The problem was, I could!! I could imagine very well JUST how sorry they were and how it would have kept most of them going all evening with gossip on my ever so sad situation. I wanted to scream at her for discussing my private business with other people, especially with people whose losses were probably far more traumatic than mine, but there simply wasn't the chance, she didn't take a breath. I couldn't understand how I had never seen it before now, how she loved the sound of her own voice. HOW had I been friendly with this woman for so long?

"I promised everyone that I'd pick up the phone today to see how you are...I said to them, you hadn't been in touch and well I was far too busy helping with last night's function to contact you. I said to them, if she wanted to talk she would have called me." AT LAST, a breath. "Now then, enough of that. One of the people speaking last night caught my eye. Did I mention he would be perfect for you? Anyway, I got chatting to him and he's a widower, so I mentioned I had a friend in need of some companionship and voila!" She was triumphant.

Taking a very deep breath, I chose my words carefully. "Thank you for that, Anna. But I really am not ready to go on a blind date."

"Oh nonsense! I think it would do you good to get out. None of us have seen you around in a long time. You've got to stop wallowing in self-pity and get yourself out there. We all thought that you'd go great together, all of us!"

Why could I not stand up to her? She made me feel so small, so insignificant. This wasn't what a true friend did. How did she know if I was wallowing or not? She had no idea what I did day-to-day. Obviously she'd taken a good guess, but she couldn't know for sure. And who the hell were the 'we' and 'us' who all thought they knew what was best for me? They totally summed up the definition of busybodies with nothing better to do until teatime when their husbands returned to their perfect homes. I was angry, but unable to vocalize my feelings.

"So, get yourself ready, he's picking you up at seven-thirty this evening."

"Anna! This is really out of order. I can't possibly…"

"Yes you can. You'll thank me for this one day. Call me tomorrow and let me know how you got on. Bye bye."

I slumped onto my bed, shaking my head in disbelief, my hands shaking with fury. I was livid, totally livid! Who did she think she was to do this to me? I found it hard to breathe and had to walk around the bedroom, pacing up and down, round and round, muttering under my breath.

The truth was, I was too much of a coward to call her back and tell her where to shove her meddling…right up her fat arse. I decided that as from this moment, she would NEVER again affect me in this way. I couldn't let this poor Sebastian, whatever his name was, down. He had probably been speaking last night about losing someone close to him and as he was a widower, it would surely have been his wife. It was a hopeless situation. I would have to go, I had no choice.

****

I was ready at seven o'clock. I had dressed in a duck-egg blue polo-neck sweater and brown trousers with brown ankle boots. It was cold and raining outside and I wanted to be warm as well as comfortable, as well as showing no cleavage or ankle. I'm sure the poor man wouldn't be remotely interested in my breasts or legs, but I just felt out of my depth and didn't want to give him the wrong impression. After my experience with Greg Smythe – the bastard – I wasn't in the mood for men, even if they were in mourning.

Bang on seven, the doorbell rang. I hadn't heard the car come up the drive as I was in the kitchen swigging back a glass of white wine and the double doors were closed. Damn! He'd probably smell alcohol on my breath and think I was a raving alcoholic. I quickly put the glass in the dishwasher and went to open the door.

For the first time since I'd known I was going out with him, I started to wonder what Sebastian Houghton would look like? If he was tall, dark and handsome and it was love at first sight then I would have to swallow my pride and call Anna, thanking her for what she had done. Now, thinking he might be half decent, I became a little nervous as I opened the door. Inside my head, the words 'please be nice, please be nice' repeating rigorously in the hope this would turn whoever he was into a prince charming.

It didn't work. A prince charming he was NOT. Sebastian Houghton was short with a balding head and a pot-belly. He stood there with a bunch of red roses, smiling at me and sweating profusely. "Hello," he said, his voice squeaking a little and he cleared his throat. "Hello. You must be Jennifer. I'm Sebastian."

Hoping with all my heart that the horror and disappointment all rolled into one wasn't conveyed on my face. "Sebastian, hello." I held out my hand for him to shake as

I didn't want to 1) kiss his perspiring cheeks or 2) him smell the wine on my breath. He looked at me and I stood there. "Do come in, sorry, where are my manners? It's just I've switched all the lights off ready to go…I mean I didn't know what time the reservation was, Anna didn't say and well I thought it best for us to just go…" Great, I was rambling and he was probably thinking how boring the night was going to be. "Sorry, do you want a drink or something?"

He stepped forward but not inside and presented the flowers. "Why don't you put these in the sink and I'll go and start the car?" He smiled such a warm smile that my nerves faded. He seemed very sweet and very kind.

"Thank you, thank you so much. They're lovely. I'll be right out."

He had made reservations at 'Peacocks' my favourite place too and where I'd taken Aunt Rose recently. Sebastian was extremely pleased when I told him this. It was an old thatched cottage renovated about twelve years ago by Henry and Lydia Peacock – hence the name. The atmosphere was a warm and cosy as always and we were shown to our seats and given menus.

"So Jennifer, what would you recommend?"

"Ooh, I don't know…let me see…" I perused the menu. "Yes, they still have the cod or the duck is very good. Are you a meat eater?"

Patting his paunch, he looked at me over his gold-framed reading glasses. "What do you think?" We both laughed and I felt myself relaxing. "I love meat and I think I shall go for the duck. Now Jennifer," he began taking off his glasses, "I want you to choose whatever you fancy. I am of the old school and I shall insist on paying for this evening, so go ahead, choose something special."

"Thank you Sebastian, you're very kind and I have a feeling there is no point in arguing with you over it." I smiled at him as he was shaking his head. "I will have the duck too."

"Perfect," he said, and called over the waitress. "I think we're ready to order."

During dinner our conversation flowed easily. He was utterly charming and had a very gentle soul. He was the Chairman of a local shoe manufacturer, where he had worked for twenty years. He really cared about the company and the people working there. His wife, Ellie, had passed away five years ago and he hadn't been on a date until this evening.

"Not that I see it as a date, you understand." He quickly chipped in and I felt a little awkward, not knowing quite how to respond. "Look," he said, putting down his knife and fork. "We have to speak about the elephant in the room."

"What do you mean?" I asked, taking a sip of champagne.

"Oh come on now my dear, you know exactly what I'm talking about." He had a look of embarrassment on his face.

"Really, Sebastian, I honestly don't." And I didn't.

"This. Us. Your friend, Anna."

"Oh," I finally said. "Was she ghastly?"

"Well, that's one way of describing her, but I'm on about her setting me up with you."

"I'm truly sorry. It's just not something I would normally go along with, but you've met her, you've seen first hand just how bossy she is!"

"More to the point, why did she set you up with ME?"

"Oh don't say that Sebastian, please. Don't undersell yourself. I am having a wonderful time. Believe me."

"Well, me too and you're very kind to say so. It's just the way she described you. I hope I'm not speaking out of turn here, but I honestly believe I was in with a chance." I frowned, not quite knowing where this conversation was going. "She told me that I was perfect for you. Told me that you were all alone and grieving over your husband. She told me all about what went on, which frankly I think was a little intrusive."

"You don't say. I am horrified at the way she's behaved. I cannot understand why she's being like this. We've been friends for years and she has been so odd since Simon left, well...you know he left me for a younger woman," why did people always say that? 'Younger woman'. As if it needed to be made perfectly clear from the outset.

"Yes, she did mention it. I think it's perfectly clear why she's behaving oddly. Why she's setting you up on dates with balding, overweight gentlemen who are clearly not your type. I think that your friend, Anna, is a little jealous of you, my dear. Maybe she's a little nervous that her own husband may find you attractive now you're, shall we say, available."

"No, no, not at all. They're very happy."

"Well, as a man standing on the outside, I think she's trying to fix you up as soon as possible. She almost pounced on me last night." I sat there in shock. "Look, you are a beautiful, amazing woman, I can see that from just sitting with you tonight and talking to you. I hope we can be friends, Jennifer, good friends, but I hope you understand that I know that is ALL we can ever be."

From that moment on, I knew I had found in Sebastian Houghton, a wonderful, caring friend and that I had lost an old, uncaring one, forever. Needless to say, I didn't call Anna the next day to 'fill her in' and nor did she call me.

Chapter 20

It was late one Monday afternoon at the beginning of December, when I received a call from the local district nurse, Carol. "Mrs Aagar, I don't want you to be alarmed, but I'm calling about your Aunt. She's had a little accident."

"Oh no! Is she okay? What happened?"

"Nothing too serious, she had a little fall this morning and unfortunately she's sprained her ankle. I've just popped in to see her and she's very reluctant, but I feel she should have someone here to look after her."

"Of course," I said, without hesitating. "I'll be there as soon as possible. She can stay with me."

I hurriedly got into my car and sped off to collect her. When I arrived she was sitting in the living room, leg up on a footstool.

"Oh my dear," she began as I sat down on the sofa, "I'm so sorry to inconvenience you like this."

"Hey," I said, stroking her arm. "You're not an inconvenience at all. My goodness, all the things you've done for me over the years."

"Can we stay here, darling? Only I just prefer to sleep in my own bed. It would only be for two nights though, because I've phoned Daisy Simmons and she is going to keep me company until I'm back on my feet again."

"No, Aunt Rose. Please let me take care of you," I insisted.

"And you can, for the next two days. You have your own life."

"Huh, some life," I interrupted.

"You will be fine, Jennifer. You'll get through it. You're strong and beautiful. Yes, right now things seem unsettled and uncertain, but look at you, you will come out of all this a much happier person. Although, I have to say you're looking rather thinner than the last time I saw you. Are you taking care of yourself?"

I burst into tears and sobbed. She took my hand and squeezed it tightly, a look of concern on her face.

"There, there my dear. It's okay. Let it all out," she said, gently.

"Oh I'm sorry, I'm here supposedly looking after you and look at me. I'm an idiot. I've BEEN a complete idiot!"

"Why don't you nip home and pack a bag for your stay and then you can tell me all about it over dinner."

"Dinner," I gasped. "I haven't even thought about dinner."

"No need. The beauty of being a member of the WI is that there's always someone on duty to help out. Tonight it's Mrs Chapman and she's bringing some sort of stew over." She raised her eyebrows in disapproval. "She never shuts up about it. Apparently it's very nice, so we shall find out for ourselves this evening. And the good thing is, if it's no good, I've got a few bottles of red we can wash it down with."

I did as I was told and returned an hour later. Mrs Chapman was just leaving as I arrived. The food smelt delicious and after taking my bag upstairs, I helped Aunt Rose to the table in the dining room, and plated up our meal.

"Well," she said, after taking a mouthful of the stew with all its vegetables and tasty gravy. "I have to say, this isn't bad after all, but we don't need to tell her that."

"You're awful, Aunt Rose!" I scolded, smiling and pouring us both a large glass of wine.

"So, come on. Tell me all," she said, making it all sound ever so thrilling.

"Ugh," I sighed, taking a large gulp from my glass. "I met someone."

"Oh, how exciting."

"No, not exciting. Well, yes, in the beginning it was, very exciting. But the end was disastrous."

"Oh darling, the end's always disastrous. Got messy did it?" She reached over and touched my hand.

"Yes."

"Lots of sex?"

"Yes, lots," I replied, feeling quite ashamed. "But that's all it was really, sex."

"Well darling," she said in a gentle, comforting voice. "You know what they say don't you?"

"No." I sniffed. "What do they say?"

"Sex, my dear, is like a Sunday roast. If you thought about the mess it made afterwards you wouldn't bother!"

We laughed and I cried some more. She talked to me, soothing me by reminding me of how I'd been a faithful, dutiful wife for most of my adult life and that if 'this Greg Smith or Smythe, or whatever his name was' had been honest with me from the start, I would never have gone there. I had to put him behind me now and move on from this sad chapter in my life.

I filled her in on my blind date with Sebastian, set up by Anna. She scowled and informed me she had never liked Anna, always had found her 'a bit too much up her own arse' and that I was well rid.

Aunt Rose always talked such sense. She never shied away from the truth and always, always made me feel so much better about myself or whichever dark, looming problem was on my horizon.

I cleared away the dishes and we spent the rest of the evening in the lounge cosy and warm in front of the open fire. We reminisced on events in our lives and she told me more tales of her exciting life. At one moment I felt she wanted to tell me something, but thought better of it. It was only when I snuggled down into bed in one of the guest rooms that I wondered what she was going to say. As a child I'd seen many men, always very handsome and dashing, but they'd come and gone. Not one had lasted for very long. She had however, always seemed content with her life. I wondered what skeletons Aunt Rose had hidden in her closet.

The fragrance of the cotton covers and pillows brought memories of summer holidays spent here with Aunt Rose, flooding back. I had always felt safe and loved here. Happy and carefree and nothing had changed. She had always given me the stability my own Mother never could. I felt I could let my emotions out, and I cried long and hard until eventually I slept soundly underneath the pink and white Laura Ashley bedding.

The next day I did what I could for Aunt Rose, but there were so many kind neighbours and lifelong friends nipping in and out, doing this and that, I felt a little redundant. That evening I cooked a roast dinner and we laughed at the mess in the kitchen. We ended up once again in front of the fire, chatting into the early hours. She was such a strong and fascinating woman that listening to her tales made the time just fly by. There were no tears as I climbed the stairs and got into bed, I slept as soon as my head hit the pillow.

We said our goodbyes late in the afternoon once Daisy had settled in. I felt a little sad driving home and wished I'd stayed longer. Why hadn't I insisted harder that I was going to stay and take care of her? As I drove up to the house, it was almost dark, the house looked cold and unwelcoming. I turned off the engine and sat there, just looking up at my beautiful home.

I had no idea what I was going to do. I couldn't imagine where my life was going to take me from here. I had agreed with Simon that we would sell the house and split the money, now the reality of this struck me hard.

I had agreed to it one rainy day in Tony's office and on a high from my passion-fuelled evenings with Greg. I had agreed to everything, feeling as if nothing could phase me…now, sitting here in my car, all alone, I felt as if my world was turning upside down. My body felt completely numb and with a heavy heart, I went inside.

Chapter 21

It was two days before Christmas and I was busy decorating the house. Normally, in fact every year since I'd lived in here, the tree would have been up and decorated over a week ago. I loved Christmas! This year, it was such an effort. Just going for the tree was an almighty struggle, both physically and emotionally. Simon had always gone for the tree and I was so embarrassed about it all that I went to a different place and they delivered the blasted thing to my front door.

Aunt Rose had agreed to come for Christmas dinner and I was expecting the children anytime now. I had prepared their rooms and stocked up the fridge, freezer and cupboards ready for them. I had literally just turned on the tree lights when they arrived. The headlights from Louise's car shone through the window of the living room and I closed the curtains before they came in, waving at them then realizing it wasn't in fact Louise's car. No sign of her red and white Mini that she treasured, but a large four wheel drive Audi and getting out of the driver's seat was a man. Not Scott, someone else. A tall dark haired older man in, I hazard a guess, his late forties.

I rushed to open the front door to be greeted by my lovely son, James. I reached out to hug him and he flashed me a look. "Brace yourself," he whispered in my ear.

"Mum!" Isobelle called out. "Hug!!" she demanded, pushing James out of the way. "Did you know?" she asked, whispering also and then hurrying into the hall.

Confused, I turned back to look at them, mouthing the words 'who is he?' but they just stood there looking back at me, eyes wide.

"Hey, Mum." It was Louise, walking in. "This is Michael. He's spending Christmas with us. Hope that's okay," she said, matter-of-factly.

"Erm…yes…of course," and I bobbed my head around her to catch a glimpse of the mysterious Michael.

"Please to meet you," he said, following in behind her. He kissed me on my cheek, a quick peck (no hug then).

"Oh, and you Michael, pleasure to meet you. Come on in," I said, stepping aside to let him pass.

"James," Michael said, rubbing his hands together as if cold. "You want to give me a hand with the luggage and gifts?"

"Yeah, sure," James said, going back outside to assist him.

I looked at the girls standing there and I shook my head at Louise.

"Well," I said, between clenched teeth and keeping my voice low. "Care to explain what's going on."

"Later, Mum." She just dismissed me.

"Well, I'd like to know now!" I insisted, checking to make sure that Michael was still busy outside.

"Please Mum, not now." She walked past me and went back outside.

"Do you know what's going on, Izzie?"

She beckoned me into the kitchen, shaking her head and saying, "Not a clue! She's told me absolutely nothing, Mum. I even spoke to her yesterday to arrange times for today and she didn't even mention him."

'Where's Scott?' The two of us were keeping an eye on the front door as James struggled through with an arm full of gifts, shouting to me as to where he should put them. "Under the tree, darling," I called out to him, turning my attention back to Izzie.

"Mum, what is she thinking?" Izzie looked at me with a look of horror on her face. "He's Dad's age for God's sake!"

We stopped talking as Lou and Michael came back inside with cases and more presents. I offered everyone a drink, a choice of coffee, tea or wine. We all took wine. They went upstairs with their bags and I sat at the kitchen table with my wine, my second glass, willing Izzie and James to come back down first.

I was disappointed as it was Michael who came down first. This was going to be awkward.

"Well, Jen," he said, rubbing his hands together again. "You have a lovely home, really lovely." He smiled, showing off a perfect white smile.

"Thank you, Michael," I said, offering him another glass of wine. "So," I started to say and was unable to think of another single thing to say to him. I poured his wine and sat back down.

"Now," he said, suddenly. "I see you haven't got dinner on yet."

I looked at him horrified. Glancing at the clock I pointed out that it was only four o'clock.

"No, you misunderstand me, Jen. I said to Lou-lou..." (LOU-LOU?), "I hope Mum hasn't got dinner on yet because I want to treat you all to a sumptuous dinner somewhere fabulous.

"Oh, that's very nice of you." I was taken aback. "Thank you, Michael."

"Pleasure Jen, my pleasure." He grinned an enormous grin and shook his head, sighing. "I can't believe Si left you like that. It's had a profound effect on Lou-lou. He sounds like an absolute fool to me to be honest. Look what he had, you for a start. How he could contemplate looking at another woman with you here waiting at home and, if you don't mind me saying, a beautiful home, well he's simply a fool."

I sat there, flabbergasted. He knew everything by the sounds of it. All of it! Lou-bloody-lou had obviously been very open with him, whoever he was. I emptied my glass and he immediately filled up again. I started to zone out, not really hearing what he was continuing to say. He had a way of almost just stopping short of insulting you, only to make it sound like the most charming compliment you'd ever heard. Heaven only knows what Aunt Rose would make of him and I smiled to myself as I imagined the conversation over Christmas dinner. One thing was for sure, she would certainly get to the bottom of what had gone on and most importantly who he was!

Eventually, the others joined us and we all sat at the table, sipping our wine and listening to Michael talk about himself. He was a city trader and didn't mind telling us how much money he'd made. He had grown up in Italy and his Father was British, his Mother Italian. That explained the dark, good looks then. He explained how he'd come to England aged eighteen and gone to university, blah, blah, blah!

I had to stop myself from nodding off. The three glasses of wine and his voice droning on and on was proving to be a fatal combination. I studied Michael and just couldn't work him out. Louise was listening intently to his every word and he amused her too, she kept giggling like a schoolgirl when he said something remotely amusing.

As he continued to chatter on, I couldn't work out what their relationship was either. He was extremely handsome, tall and very masculine, but there was a strange femininity about him at the same time. I wondered if he was in actual fact gay, and that he and Lou-lou were just friends.

I looked up at the clock. It was six thirty. For two and a half hours we had sat there just listening. At one stage, James had got up and made coffee and they were gratefully received.

"Right," I said, clapping my hands as I stood up, shocking everyone. "If you're taking us out for that dinner, Michael, we had all better start getting ready. Any ideas where you'd like to go?"

Louise — or as she was now known, Lou-lou — glared at me for interrupting Michael.

"That is for you to decide my dear Jen," he said, infuriatingly rubbing his bloody hands together. I looked around the room for help. "Anywhere Jen, choose anywhere you like. I want to take you somewhere where you feel special again."

"Grants!" James almost shouted out.

"Okay, Grants it is," Michael agreed, having no idea about Grants.

"No!" snapped Louise. "No way," and she glared at James for suggesting it. "It's far too expensive."

"Lou-lou," Michael said, stroking her face. "If your dear Mother wants to go to Grants, then Grants we shall go. Agreed Jen?"

"Well," I said, trying hard to avoid James's grinning face for fear I may break out into fits of laughter. "It would make me feel very, very special, darling." She narrowed her eyes at me, furious.

"Perfect. That's sorted then. Now, give me their number and I'll make reservations. Shall we say eight?" We all nodded except Lou-lou. "Jen, put something on that makes you feel amazing. We're going to get you feeling like your old self in no time." He looked as if he'd just made a rousing political speech and I hoped that he was wrong. There was no way on earth I wanted to feel like my 'old self' ever again.

****

We walked into 'Grants' Restaurant amidst the hustle and bustle of a busy setting. I watched Michael as he charmed the head waiter. Normally, you would have to reserve a table weeks in advance, but somehow here we all were, the five of us dressed up to the nines and being led to our table. Michael was in deed a smooth operator, a charmer and I still hadn't made up my mind as to whether I liked him or not, nor had a single moment alone with Louise to ask her what was going on. Where was Scott, her boyfriend of over three years? We were all totally bemused.

Once we'd sat down the waiter handed us our menus and informed us of the 'specials' of the evening. Michael, for the umpteenth time since leaving the house, reminded us all that we 'could choose whatever we wanted'. Cost, apparently, was of no object. The sole purpose of this evening was to cheer me up, to make me feel – and I swear I was tiring of this word-'special'.

James took immense pleasure in ordering the most expensive starter, the lobster, followed by a main of fillet steak with all the trimmings. Isobelle, as fair as ever, simply chose her favourite fish dish, no starter. I decided I should perhaps humour him, so I also chose the lobster to start, followed by a lamb dish. One thing was for sure, he did seem genuinely thrilled at spoiling us.

I could see James was thinking he was a complete and utter moron. Izzie was extremely polite, and Louise, well she seemed oblivious to everything that was going on around her. He was very tactile, touching her hands and face, stroking her hair, which was a complete mystery to me, as she had never seemed like the tactile type. Michael couldn't take his eyes off her and he certainly seemed fond of our Lou-lou!

Who could blame him? She looked absolutely stunning. Dressed in a knee-length slinky black dress, cut into a low V at the back, with a high neck, accessorized with a long gold chain with diamonds set intermittently. I wondered if he had bought it for her, as it looked very expensive and wasn't her usual style. She certainly seemed more grown-up than when I'd last seen her.

It was becoming very clear that they were more than just friends.

Michael had ordered a bottle of Dom Pérignon and he raised his glass, announcing how thrilled he was to be spending Christmas with Lou-lou's family, ending his speech with a 'cheers.'

We all raised our glasses to him and they clinked one after the other. "This is very kind of you, Michael, but not at all necessary," I said, sipping the expensive and oh so delicious champagne.

"Pleasure, Jen. An absolute pleasure."

Turning my attention to my three children, I asked them, "Have you any plans to see your Father over the holidays?"

"I haven't!" snapped Louise and Michael gently stroked her arm.

"Yeah," James said, slightly squirming in his chair. "Izzie and me said we'd pop in at some point."

"Good," I said, smiling. "That's nice."

"Nice? What's nice about it?" Louise suddenly blurted out.

"Oh not now, Lou," Izzie said, rolling her eyes.

"I just don't understand you two!" Louise continued, "look what he's done to Mum."

"Mum's fine," James said before I could comment. "Have you actually bothered to look at Mum since you've arrived?

148

She looks fantastic. She is okay, Lou. You've got to move on from this now."

"Lou," I said as gently as I could, seeing her eyes brimming with tears that were about to fall down her perfectly made up cheeks. "I am okay, honestly. I think you have a lot to sort out with your Dad, but please, my darling, don't hold a grudge because of me. I'm dealing with it all better than I ever imagined I could, so come on, let's try and work this out...together."

"Can I just say something?" Michael said, but not waiting for an answer. "Lou-lou is struggling with what Si's done." We shot glances at each other. "He has been extremely selfish and Lou-lou, well, let's just say it's left a mark on her. I think..."

"We don't care what you think quite frankly, Mike, mate!" James interrupted. "None of us have even met you until today and we'd appreciate it, if you kept out of our family's business."

"Don't speak to Michael like that! And he hates to be called Mike!" Louise shouted out angrily. The other diners started to look over at us and whisper.

"That's enough! All of you, that's enough," I said, firmly, embarrassed at the scene we were causing.

"Your Mother's right," Michael agreed, not at all ruffled by any of it. "Let's try and enjoy our dinner and this wonderful champagne. Lou-lou," he said, turning to face her and taking her hand. "Calm down, darling, and remember we're all here for you."

Immediately the anger from her face lifted and she smiled and nodded. He patted her hand, almost as a sign of approval and calm was once again restored.

Whoever the bloody hell this man was to her, wherever it was she'd met him, he could reach her emotions far quicker than any of us ever could. In a strange way, I started to like Michael and his irritating, obnoxious little habits.

Chapter 22

Having arranged to bring Aunt Rose over to stay with us Christmas Eve, so as she could be with us on Christmas morning, I put on my shoes ready to go, when James appeared in the hallway. He insisted on going to collect her.

"It's no trouble, James," I said, grabbing my coat.

"No, Mum…let me go, please," he said, a look of desperation on his face.

It amused me and I gave in, waving him goodbye as he took my car keys and left. He wanted to get away from Michael, that was clear. He was starting to grate on James, and I giggled to myself as I imagined him filling Aunt Rose in on the latest gossip from the Aagar household.

I decided to carry on wrapping presents up in my bedroom. As I did so, I sat on the floor cross-legged and I began to think about past Christmases. What a difference a year can make. It was incredible to think that Simon would no longer be part of our lives in that way, at least not in my life.

Outside it was raining and the wind blew strongly against the windows. I felt as if a cloud had come to rest on top of my head as well as on the roof outside.

Looking at my bed I felt a pang of yearning for Greg – or at least a yearning for what Greg represented – passionate nights (I say nights, more like just hours) spent in underneath my covers. It was simply the physical closeness I missed, not really him, just the contact and warmth of another body close to mine.

I sighed as I attached a gift card to the last beautifully wrapped present. Well, I told myself, looking for some kind of positive, I didn't need to shave my legs quite so often.

James returned with a radiant Aunt Rose who was dressed in a smart grey suit and soft pink polo neck sweater. She kissed us all and James followed in with an armful of gifts. Michael appeared in the doorway.

"Oh," she said, rather dramatically just for effect. "And who is this?"

"Like James hasn't filled you in, Aunt Rose!" Louise said in a joking, yet rather sarcastic tone.

"So, THIS is Aunt Rose," Michael said, pushing forward to get closer. "I'm Michael Kingston. Lovely to meet you." You had to admire his bravery.

"Likewise," she said, leaning in as he bent down to kiss her cheek. "Well now, is it too early for a sherry?"

"Is it ever too early for sherry?" Michael said, linking her arm as we all laughed and followed them into the living room.

****

Spending Christmas Eve with Aunt Rose and the children, not forgetting Michael Kingston, was magical. It was fun and filled with laughter. I had expected her to detest Michael on sight, but she didn't. She too, seemed drawn to his stories of his life in Italy and they exchanged tales of evenings spent in Rome and Milan. I even got the impression that James was warming to him, especially as he offered to take him to the next Grand Prix in Italy.

"My goodness!" Gasped Aunt Rose.

"What is it?" I asked, praying it wasn't a heart attack or something.

"Look at the time!' She laughed.

I glanced at the clock on the mantelpiece, whilst Michael checked his watch and the children looked at their mobile phones. It was ten minutes past midnight.

"We missed Christmas!" exclaimed Izzie.

"No," said Michael, cheerfully. "Christmas has only just begun, Izzie my darling." And rubbing his hands together asked, "Who's first?" And he picked up a large present from underneath the tree.

"We don't normally open our gifts until morning." I pointed out, feeling he was taking over a little too much. He looked at me and put the present down.

"Do you know what?" Aunt Rose said. "I think this year, in this year of change," and she winked at me, "I think we should open our presents now. After all, it's not like any of us here believe in Santa Claus any more."

We all smiled and I couldn't think of a single reason to disagree with her, and immediately Mr Charm himself knelt down and searched through the abundance of gifts.

"Aha," he cried, passing a beautifully wrapped small box to Aunt Rose. "This, my darling Aunt Rose, is for you from Lou-lou and me." He placed it gently in her hands and wrapped his hands over it. "We hope you like."

I was beginning to think Father Christmas DID exist after all, here in my living room in the form of Michael. He made everything seem almost perfect and I could see exactly how he'd won my little Lou-lou over. If Scott had been here now, he'd have been upstairs with James playing on the Playstation or Xbox or whatever it was they spent their time on, whilst Louise, Isobelle and I would be preparing for Christmas Day. Simon would be watching something on the television and that would have been our Christmas Eve. Normally, Aunt Rose would be on a cruise ship for the entire holiday returning only in the New Year, but after her problem with her ankle she had delayed it and I'd insisted she stay with us.

"Well," she said, admiring whatever it was inside the little black box she'd just unwrapped. "This is absolutely beautiful.

"Michael knew you'd like it," Louise said, rushing over and planting a kiss on her cheek.

"Well, he was right, I do," she replied, almost at a loss for words and turned the box to reveal to us all what was inside. It was a sapphire broach, encrusted with what certainly looked like diamonds, set in platinum and in the shape of a flower. It really was magnificent and something Aunt Rose would certainly have chosen for herself.

As Michael reached under the tree, we all sat on the edge of our seats, hoping we would all be as fortunate as Aunt Rose.

One by one, he handed us each a beautifully wrapped gift and each of us waited in line for our turn. For Isobelle, they had bought a pair of vintage silver drop-earrings with vivid sapphires set in the centre. They were stunning and she held them up to her ears, they brought out the blue in her eyes. Isobelle was speechless.

James took his gift rather warily. It was wrapped in a black matt finish paper with a silver metallic tag placed on top. It was the size of an A4 envelope and no thicker. Once unwrapped, it was simply a white envelope. He looked at us all. He opened it with encouragement from Louise and gasped.

"Oh God!" he gasped, hardly able to contain his excitement. "Thanks man!" he said to Michael and actually got up and hugged him. It was an experience day to drive all types of sports cars, from the classics to the most up to date.

"Hey!" complained Louise. "It's off me too, you know." And he turned to hug his sister too. "Now," she said, a mischievous look in her eyes. "Mum's turn."

Michael found my gift and walked over to me. Judging from the size of the beautifully wrapped box, it was sure to be a piece of jewellery also. I accepted the gift smiling at him and glancing over at Louise who looked so happy with a glint of excitement in her sparkling brown eyes. I slowly began to unwrap it, taking care not to tear the paper. This had always driven Simon and the children mad, but it was the way I liked to do it. A black velvet box lay under the paper and I snapped it open. A platinum necklace with a heart shaped diamond pendant caught the light and it took my breath away. I sat gazing at it, open-mouthed.

"This is all too much, really!" I whispered.

"Jen," Michael began, his voice soft and soothing. "Lou-lou and me want to share our happiness at finding each other with you all. I know it's a little over the top, but the pleasure I saw on her face choosing all these gifts, well, let's just say, that gave me pleasure."

"Well, we've nothing for you!" Aunt Rose blurted out in her usual Aunt Rose way, and once again laughter filled the

Aagar household, the loudest laugh coming from Michael himself.

I looked over at Louise and I could see she was truly happy, but I knew at some point, I would have to talk to her alone and find out how my eldest daughter could have a new partner and yet none of us knew anything about him.

We finished handing out our gifts and exchanging our thank yous and Louise reached under the tree and handed a present to Michael.

"I hope you like it." She reached over to him and kissed him gently on the lips.

"I love it my darling because it's from you." All the females in the room sighed as he opened it up to reveal a 'Rolex' box, which held an antique gold watch. He put his hands around her neck and drew her head to his chest, kissing the top of it. "Now, where did I put yours?" He stood up, patting his trouser pockets, a look of confusion on his face.

"Oh don't worry…" Louise started to say.

"No, no. I know I put it somewhere." We all turned to see if there were any gifts left under the tree, but there were none. "Ah yes, there it is." He took a small box that was hanging from the tree. There seemed to be no end to the magic this man could bring. He held his hand out to Louise and she took it, standing up. He knelt down on one knee and I gasped. "Lou-lou, I wanted to ask you this question the first day I met you, but I knew I had to wait. Well my darling," he continued, slowly opening the box to reveal a stunning diamond solitaire engagement ring. "I can't wait another day. Will you marry me?"

Tears filling her eyes, Louise yelled out, "Yes, yes I'll marry you." He slipped the ring onto her finger and of course, it was a perfect fit.

Aunt Rose looked at me and smiled. It would appear Michael had even won her over. "Champagne," she announced. "We need champagne."

Chapter 23

We had all giggled our way up to our beds around two in the morning. I lay in bed before dozing off with such a feeling of contentment, that I couldn't stop smiling. To see one of your children find someone who made them that happy was all you could ever hope for. I woke up in the very same position in which I'd fallen asleep, on my back snuggled under the duvet, the best sleep I'd had in a long time and even better news, no dribble.

As I lay there drifting in and out of sleep, I heard the doorbell ringing. At first I wasn't sure if I was dreaming, but then it rang again and I realised there actually was someone at the door. Checking the alarm clock, it was ten o'clock. Christmas morning, who could it be? I flung off the covers and grabbed my robe from the end of the bed. I heard James on the landing calling out he'd get it and running down the stairs.

"James," I shouted, "the alarm, don't forget to turn off the alarm."

I heard the beeps as he keyed in the code and the rattle of the chain as he unlocked the front door. I was surprised that any of us had remembered to put the alarm on and I wondered who had, as it certainly wasn't me. Standing at the top of the stairs, I waited to see who it could be. I didn't have to wait too long, as a familiar voice greeted James with 'happy Christmas'.

It was Simon. My heart actually sank a little as I saw him appear in the hallway, he looked up at me and I felt myself shudder.

"Happy Christmas, Jen." He said, carrying an armful of presents.

"Happy Christmas," I replied, praying that Sarah wasn't with him and a wave of relief washed over me as James closed the door.

"I'll put the kettle on," he muttered, yawning and scratching his head. "Mum? Tea or coffee?"

"Coffee for me, please," I replied, coming down the stairs.

"What the…" Simon gasped as he entered the living room, seeing no gifts under the tree, but piles stacked up, unwrapped.

"Oh yeah," I said, following him in and opening the curtains. "We opened our gifts last night. We felt like a change." I have to admit, I was getting a little pleasure from the hurt expression on his face.

"But we never open presents until Christmas morning." He actually looked as if he might cry.

I had to bite my tongue at this point. I wanted to say 'well, Simon, some of us had an affair this year and so the rules went out of the sodding window!' But I didn't. I just looked at him and said, "I know, but Michael really wanted to and well…it's a long story. Why don't you put your gifts under the tree and I'll wake everyone up. We didn't even know you were coming, Simon. To be fair."

"Who's Michael?" he asked, bewildered. He followed me through the double doors into the family room and kitchen. "Who's Michael?" he asked again.

I pulled out a kitchen chair for him to sit down and started to help James with teas and coffees.

"Well? Is he your new boyfriend?" he insisted, and James and I looked at each other and let out a cry of laughter in unison. Searching for an answer, he looked extremely unkempt and miserable. He clearly hadn't shaved for a few days and his hair was long into his neck and badly needed cutting.

I smiled to myself as I remembered it was always me who regularly booked his appointment at the barbers in town. "No, Simon, no." I touched his shoulder softly, a feeling of sympathy running through me. Sitting down next to him, I continued. "He's not my boyfriend, he's Louise's."

"Boyfriend!" exclaimed James, sarcastically. "I hardly think boyfriend describes him."

"Okay, partner then. Actually, he's her fiancé since last night. They got engaged," I said, matter-of-factly, forgetting the pinnacle of our Christmas Eve.

"Engaged?"

"Look, it's all very unexpected for us too. She turned up the day before yesterday with him and we were just as shocked as you are."

"What happened to Scott then and why didn't anyone call me?"

"Dad," James said, placing two coffees down on the table in front of us. "Why haven't you called us?"

Simon didn't answer. James went to wake the others and I filled him in with what had gone on over the past couple of days. "So, there you have it," I said, sipping my coffee.

"Right then," he muttered, looking forlorn. "Well my gifts won't live up to expectations then."

"Are you okay?" I asked, almost wanting to kick myself for being quite so nice.

"I'm okay? Why, do I not look okay?"

"Well to tell you the truth, Simon, no." I so wanted to reach out and touch his hand, but I squashed these feelings deep down inside of me and took a gulp of coffee, hoping the urge would go.

Before we could say any more, Isobelle ran into the kitchen, throwing her arms around him. "Happy Christmas, Daddy." She kissed him and grinned a big, wide happy grin.

"Happy Christmas, Izzie. I've missed you," he whispered in her ear, squeezing her ever so tightly. She shot me a glance and smiled at me. She too could sense his pain and I wondered if all was not well with the lovebirds.

Louise followed in, half asleep, but propped up by the ever jolly Michael. James helped Aunt Rose into the kitchen and sat her down next to Simon. She didn't look too pleased to see him, but she said nothing.

After our coffees and Simon congratulating Louise and Michael, and Michael apologizing for not asking Simon for Lou-lou's hand in marriage, we all moved into the living room so that the children and Simon could exchange their gifts. I waited for Michael to pull something amazing from under the tree or from behind his ear, but nothing came. I felt almost sorry for Simon, especially as everyone was raving about the gifts we'd opened last night. Looking at the presents he'd bought for them, aftershave and perfume, I wondered if maybe she, Sarah West had gone with him to buy them? And where, I wondered, was she?

After more coffees and croissants, Simon showed no signs of moving. He'd settled down in his favourite armchair. This hadn't gone unnoticed by Aunt Rose.

"So," she began, as I busied myself at the kitchen sink. "Is he staying for dinner or what?"

"I've no idea. Do you think I should offer?" I whispered, not wanting anyone to hear us.

"Well, it's more than he deserves!" She looked a little horrified at my suggestion.

"I know, I know. But have you seen the state he's in? He looks dreadful. Maybe something's happened."

"Don't you go all soft of him, my girl. Do not forget what he's put you through!" she said, her eyes fixed on me, sternly. "Anyway, he's not your problem any more, something happening or not!"

"Aunt Rose, it's Christmas Day. It might be nice for the kids," I suggested. "I'm okay with it, but if you're not…"

"Oh don't worry about me. It's your house…" then she added. "For now!"

I stood in the doorway of the living room. Simon was nodding off. Talk about déjà vu. "Simon," I called out. "Will you be staying for dinner with us? Or do you have other plans?"

"People to see?" Shouted Aunt Rose from the kitchen.

"Would it be alright for me to stay?" he asked, looking a little humbled.

"Everyone okay if your Dad stays?" I asked, and they all just nodded, Michael beaming from ear to ear. "Right, that's settled then."

Simon looked at me, smiling and mouthed 'thank you'. I hadn't expected to be spending Christmas Day with the man who I would soon be divorced with, but somehow it felt like the right thing to do.

Chapter 24

The day had passed quickly. It was one of those beautiful, crisp, sunny days. Everyone had got involved with preparing dinner and we sat down to eat around eight in the evening. It turned out that Michael was an amazing cook. He was so happy to be part of our day and it was quite heartwarming. He made us all feel special and that was quite a unique gift.

Simon had been quiet, but in good spirits. He had kept checking his mobile phone throughout dinner and it had irritated me a little until I reminded myself that I didn't want him back and so I had to let him go, completely.

After dinner, Michael and Louise had insisted on clearing away, it seemed he shared her passion for organization and cleanliness and this amused me. Aunt Rose retired to her bedroom after a long day of laughter, eating and drinking. She was quite merry and James helped her back up the stairs as she wished us all a goodnight.

Simon and Isobelle went into the living room to watch TV, Simon lighting the fire, whilst I stayed at the table, sipping champagne and watching the chemistry between my eldest daughter and her fiancé. I made the most of each little moment for I knew, in no time at all, they would all be gone and I would be once again, alone.

Everywhere was looking clean and tidy, spick and span as I imagined Michael would say, and he stretched, throwing the tea towel onto the worktop. Simon had disappeared a while ago into his study, but he suddenly appeared in the kitchen doorway, a confused look on his face.

"Have you started drawing again?"

"Oh, just a little," I said, dismissively.

"Er, more than a little, I'd say," he said. "There's piles in there."

"Mum…" Louise began, "is it true? Are you?"

I shook my head. "Not really."

"It's great if you are. Can we see?" she asked, excitement in her voice.

"No!" I said, glaring at Simon.

"You draw, Jen?" Michael piped up.

"Well, I try. I used to years ago, mainly before the children came along, but Aunt Rose kitted me out with all sorts to help revive my passion, apparently."

Rubbing his hands together, Michael pleaded for me to show them what I'd done. Simon left the room and returned moments later with several pieces of my work, thankfully I'd destroyed all my interpretations of Greg Smythe. He placed them on the table, fanning them out so each one could be seen. Simon almost looked proud.

"Wow!" Michael gasped. "These are fantastic! And this one," he said, picking up a drawing of our garden. "This one is simply beautiful. I love the way you've captured the essence of its lifelong memories." I smiled, as that is exactly what I'd intended for it to be. He admired it a little longer, before announcing, "well, maybe I shouldn't say this in front of Simon, in light of your upcoming divorce settlement, but I know someone who would probably snap these up. If you did more, I could arrange a showing for you."

"What?" I was in shock.

"Yes! These are too good to lay in some stuffy study with no one to appreciate them, Jen my darling."

He then went on to tell us about his connections with art dealers and how he'd been involved in many art galleries. This man just never stopped giving. Isobelle and James came into the kitchen, wondering what all the fuss was about. I was thrilled that everyone was so supportive, but most of all, thrilled that they loved my work.

Everyone decided to call it an end to our perfect day, but I noticed the outside light was on in the garden and Simon was out there, pacing. Pacing meant he was thinking, not just your average run of the mill thoughts, but deep, dark thoughts. I grabbed a throw from the sofa and wrapped it around my shoulders and joined him.

"Drink?" I called out to him, handing him a glass of champagne.

"And you?" he asked as I showed him my glass.

"Everything okay?" I asked, imagining he must have spoken to Sarah whilst he'd been locked away in the study.

"What do you mean?"

"Do you not want to talk?" I was using my most sympathetic voice I could.

"Do you think I need to talk?"

"Oh for God's sake!" I cried out, losing my patience. "Can you please not answer every question with another bloody question!!"

"Sorry," he replied, rather pathetically. "I just feel so…so lost, Jen."

"But why? I drank my champagne rather too quickly and almost wished I hadn't asked. He was after all, no longer my problem. "I thought that you and Sarah…" (I almost choked on her name). "Well, I thought you two were really happy." I put far too much emphasis on the word 'really'.

"It's not easy Jen," he began, as he stared sullenly into his glass.

"Well, relationships rarely are, Simon."

"Everything's turned upside down. I miss this house, I miss the kids…" he paused and we both looked at each other. I really hoped he wasn't going to say he missed me. It was as if time slowed right down, the pause seemed to go on for an eternity. I didn't want him back and this moment confirmed it. "I…I miss us!"

I couldn't say anything. 'US'. He missed us. We both knew there hadn't been an 'us' for a long time. He probably missed the routine and safety that I'd provided for so long. I had to find the right words, right now, to fix this.

"Simon, look it's normal you're struggling with the newness of your relationship with Sarah…but you do love her, don't you?"

"Yes, yes I do love her," (okay, don't rub it in). "But…but she…she isn't you, Jen!"

I can't deny I didn't feel a small amount of satisfaction that this young, slim, pretty woman still didn't really have what it took to make him forget me, but I knew I couldn't let him see this. "No, she isn't me, Simon. And that's why you were with her in the first place, because you don't love me anymore."

"Can I just come home, Jen, please?"

"What?" I stood there completely frozen;, on the outside from the cold and on the inside from his words. He wasn't even thinking of how I was feeling, what he'd put me through. He was a selfish man and I had to simply convince him that returning to Sarah would be the best for him and he would be satisfied with that.

"And how do you think Sarah would feel if she knew you were saying these things? Asking me if you could come back home?"

"I doubt she'd care. She's staying at her parents' place."

"Oh, I see." This explained why he'd turned up bright and early on my doorstep and been happy to stay for dinner with us. "Did you have a fight?"

"She totally overreacted to something," (oh God he was now on a roll − I felt like I was on Dr Phil or one of those shows, where in a minute the host would congratulate him on allowing his emotions to show). "I asked her if she could iron this for me," and he pulled at his shirt. "She erupted, Jen. It was just like when Louise has one of her tantrums. She told me to iron my OWN shirt." He was shaking his head in disbelief and looking at me for some assurance.

It took all my strength not to laugh in his face.

"And that's why you want to come back, because she wouldn't iron your shirt? Tell me, Simon, what did you think at the time? Jen would iron it."

"Yes!" he exclaimed, thrilled that I'd understood, ironic that he hadn't heard the sarcasm in my voice. She was very welcome to him!

"I think you need a good nights sleep and tomorrow you can call her and see if the two of you can work something out." I took his glass and beckoned for him to follow me into the house. "You can stay here."

"Jen," he called out to me. "I'm so sorry. For everything I've done to you."

"I know," I whispered, turning back to look at him.

"You look amazing, by the way."

"I know," I said, and we both laughed. "Thank you, Simon."

"If only I'd seen you with these eyes before, Jen, I swear I'd never have done it. I should have looked at you more often, seen you. I'm sorry, so sorry."

I walked over to him. I didn't tell him it wasn't his eyes that hadn't seen me, but that I'd had a complete makeover since he'd gone. I held him in my arms as he cried. I cried. We cried together. We cried because it was sad and the damage couldn't be repaired. The truth was, even though I couldn't take Simon back, I wished he'd never left me, wished he'd never strayed into the bed of another woman. But he had and our lives were changed forever.

Chapter 25

The next morning we all sat talking rather loudly at the kitchen table having breakfast. Simon had got up early and was in the study talking on the phone to Sarah in the hope of overcoming their differences, and we all hoped that if we talked loud enough, we could drown out their sickly sweet conversation.

He emerged about an hour later and it was clear to all he couldn't get away fast enough. We all tried to push out of our minds the thought of their make up sex, but it hovered somewhere at the back of our imaginations.

The day after that, James and Isobelle took Aunt Rose home. She had had the most wonderful time and she kept telling us. She had embraced Michael and all his funny little ways with such ease it was a delight. In a few days time she was off on her cruise and she had a lot to organize — mainly packing.

In the middle of the week and two days before New Year's Eve, Michael, Louise, Isobelle and James packed up ready to leave. I felt sick inside and was dreading the closing of the front door and the emptiness that it would signify. As they were leaving, Izzie mentioned the annual New Year's party at Anna and Tim's house.

She had been over there regularly this visit, and James had confided in me that she and Anna's youngest, John, were getting very close. She mentioned that he had asked if I would be going, but I said I wouldn't after the events of the 'end of summer' party. James thought I should go and not sit home alone on the last evening of the year. I decided to push this situation to the very back of my mind — I had two long, lonely days to think about it.

As I waved them goodbye, Michael reminded me to continue with my artwork and that he'd be in touch soon to discuss options. He seemed almost sad to be going. I stood on the driveway until the car had turned on to the road and disappeared. I was dreading going back inside on my own. Head down, I slowly walked on the gravel and back into the house. I closed the door slowly and locked it.

I headed straight for the wine cooler and picked myself a bottle of Moet left over from Christmas. Checking the clock on the kitchen wall, five o'clock, I nodded and decided it was okay. The phone started to ring. It was Aunt Rose.

"Hello my darling, headed for the bubbly yet?"

"As we speak," I replied, popping the cork. Well, what was the use in pretending otherwise?

"I've poured myself a sherry. It's these dark evenings, darling. I'm all packed and my taxi is due here any minute, but I just wanted to tell you that I love you and I'm so proud of you and your beautiful children."

I was almost moved to tears and I swallowed hard. "Aunt Rose, that's a lovely thing to say. You know how much we all love you, don't you?"

"I do indeed. Now, your parents called earlier. They tried to get us on Christmas Day, but couldn't connect. They send their best wishes and all their love. They said that next year…"

"They'll be home for Christmas." We both said it in unison and we laughed hard.

"I'll never understand that sister of mine and it's too late to try now, my dear. Your Father and her are well matched, that's about all I can say."

"Thank goodness for you."

"Will you be okay whilst I'm away, darling?"

"Yes of course, I promise. I'm going to continue drawing and painting and there'll be lots to show you when you get back. You have a wonderful, wonderful trip. I can't wait to hear all about it when you get back."

"Bye bye, my darling," she said, her voice breaking, just a little. "I shall be thinking of you and take care of yourself."

****

New Year's Eve arrived. I climbed out of bed with a heavy heart and went downstairs to make a strong cup of coffee. Last

165

night I had drowned my sorrows in a bottle of Pinot Grigio and I now I was suffering. The house was far too quiet since the children had left, everything felt wrong. I ached for the sound of their laughter and the sight of us all sitting together at the kitchen table eating. Now the only noise I heard with some regularity was the creaking pipes as the heating started to come on.

Sipping my coffee, I reflected on the past twelve months. It was still hard to believe what had gone on. I knew I needed to make a decision about this evening and whether or not I was going to Anna and Tim's house. It was only half past eight and the day ahead seemed long. Tapping my fingers on the table, my irritability grew. I had to come to a conclusion before my head literally blew off. I jumped as the home phone rang. It was such an effort just to make my way into the hallway to answer it.

"Hello?" I asked, no idea of who it could possibly be on the other end.

"Jen!" A happy familiar voice rang out. It was Jade.

"Jade," I said, smiling and thankful it was her. "How are you? Did you have a good Christmas?"

"Great, absolutely great, thank you. Now listen, I'm calling you to invite you down to the salon. Are you free in, let's say, an hour?"

"Erm…" I tried desperately to find an excuse, but she saw through me immediately.

"Jen," she began in a soft, gentle voice, "don't find some silly excuse not to come. Anyway, I'm not taking no for an answer! You've won our special client of the year award and so get yourself down here ASAP."

Lies, all lies, but how could I refuse such a generous offer?

I arrived at Jade's salon feeling drained and deflated. I left three hours later feeling completely rejuvenated and looking refreshed. I'm sure being around Jade and her incredibly upbeat workforce helped, apart form the pampering of course. They all wore genuine smiles and worked their magic with happy conversation.

As I walked back to my car, I passed a boutique where I had often stopped and looked in the window, admiring the clothes displayed until I would catch a glimpse of my reflection in the window and walk away feeling too dowdy to enter the shop.

Today however, I decided I was going inside, I made my mind up that I was going to buy something to match my mood and what's more, I was going to wear it to Anna's party tonight.

I opened the door and a little bell announced my arrival. I was greeted at once by an overeager member of staff, who eyed me up and down with a look of anticipation on her face. Within minutes she had selected five items off the rails and ushered me into a changing room. She hung the dresses on a little hook inside and swished the curtain shut, announcing she would be waiting right outside.

Ridiculously, I was filled with fear. I dreaded the curtain being pulled back to reveal me, half naked and struggling to fit inside a dress too small. That was until I stripped down to my underwear and was reminded of the new 'me'. Slim and toned, my skin glowing from my facial, professionally made up and not a hair out of place – I had nothing to fear.

I set about trying on the dresses. Each one fit perfectly and I threw back the curtain with gusto, thriving on the pleasing reaction from Kirsten, as I discovered was her name. I settled, with the full agreement of Kirsten, on a black cat suit with a halter-neck and a daringly low back. The trousers flared out slightly at the bottom and there were tiny sparkling stone detail around the neck.

It was beautiful – I felt beautiful. Suddenly, the thought of the party filled me with complete and utter exhilaration and not the dread I'd felt all along. I couldn't wait and I left 'Sassy's Boutique' feeling happier than ever.

Chapter 26

I tried all afternoon to reach Anna. I wanted to drive over and leave my car there and get a taxi back, or perhaps even stay over as was usual in the past. Trouble was, I didn't know if she would want that, or indeed if I was welcome. I couldn't get her on her landline or her mobile. In the end, I decided I would drive that way; I could leave when I wanted or stay if I was invited.

One last look in the mirror and I grabbed my black throw, scattered in Swarkovski diamonds and headed out of the door. I had never felt so wonderful for such a long time, and felt a slight pang of regret that it took the traumatic end of my marriage to look and feel this good. I pushed the negative thoughts out of my mind and got into my car.

I parked up on the road outside the house because the driveway was already full and felt my stomach churn as I walked up to the front door. Normally I'd have been here since late afternoon, helping as well as taking my orders from Anna, now it was eight o'clock. I pushed the door open as it was slightly ajar and made my way through the hall into the kitchen where most of the guests had gathered.

I saw Anna in the centre of a group of our oldest and dearest friends, and I helped myself to a glass of champagne from the breakfast bar and walked over to her.

"Hello everyone," I said, in my happiest voice.

"Jen!" Anna gasped, "I didn't think you were coming." Her face had dropped and those who noticed me started to fidget and look uncomfortable. Some even looked at the floor rather than meet my gaze.

"I tried calling you all day but you weren't picking up." I managed to say, starting to feel as awkward as everyone around me. This was NOT going as I had imagined it would. "Isobelle had mentioned that John insisted I come. Is it a problem, me being here?"

Nobody spoke. Anna said nothing, just stood there, flushing from her neck upwards. It was like a scene from a movie where the silence becomes almost unbearable. My heart started to beat fast and my face was as flushed as Anna's.

"Anna," I began, trying desperately to make eye contact with her or anyone. "Is there something wrong?"

Before she could answer me, people began to disperse, and as I looked through the doorway that led into the living room, it was as if the crowd parted in a small well-rehearsed moment to reveal Simon standing there with Sarah. But it was only as Miranda Birkett, who had been standing next to Sarah, moved aside, that the reason everyone had not wanted to look me in the eye, became apparent.

For there, in all her blooming glory stood a very pregnant Sarah West.

Time seemed to stand still and I felt as if all of the guests could hear my heart beating. I wanted to faint, it actually felt as that would be a fitting end to the whole thing, but all I could think of was how everyone would remember the New Year's Eve party where poor Jennifer Aagar discovered her husband's mistress was with child.

I drank my champagne down in one go and put the empty glass down on the sideboard next to me. "I think I'd better be going," I said to Anna, "I don't want to make your night any more uncomfortable."

I walked steadily out of the kitchen and back into the hallway, squeezing through huddles of people who had just arrived, feeling as if they were all whispering VERY LOUDLY. As I got outside I took a deep breath, desperately needing air in my lungs. I heard footsteps running behind me as I reached the end of the driveway. I dreaded turning around in case it was Simon or God forbid, Sarah, but it was Anna.

"Jen," she called out when I didn't stop, I just wanted to get into my car and escape the horror of the evening. "Wait."

Tears were now running down my perfectly made up face, spoiling the beautiful work the beautician had done earlier. "What?" I sniffed, opening the car door.

"I…I didn't think for one minute you'd come," she said, puffing, after her little run from the house to the pavement.

"Why not? Why would you think I wouldn't come?" I asked, walking back towards her, an anger rising up inside of me and probably showing on my face.

"Well, you knew we would have invited Simon, I just presumed you'd stay away."

"Presumed or hoped?" I snarled, wanting to slap her face.

"Jen, come on don't be like that! This whole thing has been very difficult for Tim and I…"

"Ha! Difficult for you AND Tim," I snapped. "What about me? Don't you think it's been difficult for me? You were supposed to be my friend, Anna."

"I AM your friend!" she shouted back.

"Well, it doesn't feel like it, Anna. It's New Year's Eve for God's sake. You've ignored all of my calls all day long and PRESUMED I'd stay at home. Alone! YOU should have called me!"

"I've been very busy." She was smug now, almost looking down her nose at me.

"Oh my God!" I couldn't believe how cold she was being.

"I tried to help you," she said matter-of-factly. I frowned as she continued to try and explain in which ways she'd 'helped' me. "I set you up with a perfectly nice man. Was he good enough for you? No!" She shook her head in disgust.

"You set me up alright! Sebastian and I were never going to come to anything, he knew it and you must have known it too. He is lovely and kind and a good friend now as it happens, but you MUST have known he wasn't what I was looking for." I paused for a second. "Anna, what's going on here?" I asked, wiping the tears that had fallen down my face.

"I don't know what you mean." And I knew she knew exactly what I meant.

She had distanced herself from me since Simon had left me, and at first I thought I'd been oversensitive, but now standing here face-to-face, it was as if she didn't care at all.

"What have I done to make you so cold towards me? My husband left me for another woman and you shut me out. Why, Anna? We've been friends for all these years..."

"LOOK at you!" she blurted out. "Who do you think you are? Dressed like...like THAT!" She looked me up and down, green with envy, pure and simple jealousy.

Suddenly it all made perfect sense. Standing there in her navy blue A-line skirt with a two-piece beige top and matching cardigan, edged in mother of pearl sequins and a pair of navy blue court shoes and American tan tights, everything became crystal clear. I knew exactly why she'd shut me out. My husband may have left me, but I'd come out the other end and this had shocked her. Sebastian had been right all along.

She had always been the dominant one in our friendship, she had probably expected me to fall and crumble, I hadn't and she was mad. Not only had I picked myself up, I looked fabulous and she couldn't take it. So she had shut me out and accepted Sarah with open arms, or so it seemed.

"You'd better get back to your party, Anna. Your guests will be wondering where you are."

"Don't be bitter, Jennifer," she said, now completely composed. "It really isn't attractive."

There was nothing I could say to her, no words to express how let down I felt. I got into my car and drove away as she headed back indoors, head held high and shoulders back. Nothing was going to spoil her New Year's Eve Party.

Chapter 27

I sat on the sofa in the family room, huddled up in one of the throws. All dressed up and nowhere to go. Never one to drink spirits, I'd come home and poured myself a very large whiskey. I was in complete shock. The picture of Simon and Sarah standing together amongst our friends in Anna's house haunted me. Sarah's baby bump, how far gone was she, I wondered? The faces of everyone there, Anna's words, all of it, just kept replaying in my head.

Once again, the feeling of dread I'd first experienced way back on that September day taking James to university, rose inside of me. I had accepted that my marriage to Simon was over, accepted that he'd fallen out of love with me and in love with someone else, but a baby had never entered into my head. Another sip of whiskey, another gulp to get it down and into my system – anything to dull this pain. I felt cold and I pulled the throw tighter around me, shivering. I wanted to cry, but no tears came.

I was still sat there at midnight when the New Year arrived. A new year, but nothing had changed and I was still in shock. Sarah would still be carrying Simon's baby. I was still alone.

My mind started to race as I imagined what she would have, a boy or a girl? Would this child have the same character traits of my children? Would Simon love this child more than ours?

Suddenly at twelve thirty, I heard a key in the front door. I turned towards the double doors that led into the hallway and waited to see who was going to come through. Footsteps sounded on the floor, keys were thrown onto the hall table.

I was relieved to see James and Isobelle. They stood there looking at me for a moment. Sadness and fear was etched on their faces. They had obviously arrived at Anna and Tim's after I had left and not known what to expect when they saw me.

"Mum," Izzie cried out, rushing towards me, arms open wide and ready to hug me. "Are you okay? We've just come from the party. We'd been into town and got back just before midnight and we…" She paused mid-sentence. James came and sat on the other side of me and there I was, huddled up with two of my beautiful children. "We saw Dad and Sarah," she said, quietly, a glazed look in here eyes.

James put his arms around my shoulders and finally, my tears came. My whole body shuddered with the force of them. I sobbed out loud, the first time I'd let them see me cry. I'd tried so hard all these months and yet, here in the early hours of what was supposed to be a new start, they saw I was hurting.

"I'm so sorry, Mum. So sorry," James whispered, kissing my head.

"I can't believe Anna invited them!" Izzie seethed. "John had no idea or we'd never have insisted you go, Mum. I feel terrible."

"You weren't to know," I sniffed, wiping my eyes with a tissue James had passed to me. "I don't understand why I'm so upset. I know your dad and me are over, I just didn't consider he'd have a family." I started to cry again and Izzie took the glass of whiskey away from me and went to make a cup of tea. James held me tightly in his arms as I allowed the tears to flow and I couldn't stop them if I'd tried.

The next morning I could hear Izzie and James pottering about downstairs and talking in hushed voices. The home phone rang and Izzie answered it. I heard her mention Louise's name and I decided to let them tell her everything before going downstairs.

I must have drifted off again, because the next minute James was standing over me, a cup of tea in his hand. He smiled at me and I sat up.

"Morning. I thought you might like a cup of tea in bed."

"Thank you," I replied, propping myself up with pillows. "Happy New Year," I sang out as he opened the bedroom curtains. He looked back at me and I giggled, much to his relief. "Was that Lou on the phone?"

"Yeah," he sat on the edge of the bed. "We'd tried to call her before we came to see you last night, but she wasn't picking up. Apparently she was at some amazing party with Michael. Who else?" he finished off, sarcastically.

"Is she okay?"

"Furious as you can imagine. She's going to call Dad now. Izzie told her best not to, but then why shouldn't she? We're all as shocked as you are you know, Mum."

"I know, darling," I whispered, touching his hand. "I'm so sorry you had to see me like that."

"God, don't worry about that. We just didn't want you on your own. I mean, we're sorry we didn't get back here for midnight. You were all on your own and..."

"Hey, come on. Next year I won't be." I smiled at him, he looked so worried about me and I felt a pang of guilt that I'd lost it in front of them. "Well, I think I'm going to stay in bed and savour this cup of tea, then I'll get up and call Louise. Will you be staying for dinner? And don't feel you have to if you have other plans."

"I'm staying. We all are. Louise is coming too so you don't need to call her. We're not leaving you alone to deal with this, Mum. Okay?"

"Okay," I replied, thankful that they were there with me.

****

They packed their bags and reluctantly left me three days later. I waved them off with a big smile on my face. It was a genuine smile as they had helped me through the past few days and I felt strong enough to be alone again. Izzie and James, it seemed, were dealing with it all quite well. Louise however, I felt really wasn't. She was so angry with Simon, almost disappointed in him. He had tried calling her a few times, but she didn't want to talk to him.

Apparently after hearing the news from Izzie, she'd called Simon and given him a piece of her mind. She wouldn't discuss the conversation with us, other than to say he hadn't anticipated our reactions to Sarah being pregnant. He told her that he honestly believed that I'd be okay with it. I honestly think he didn't mean to be or realise that he was being cruel or insensitive. Funny how you can be married to someone for all those years and yet never really know them.

The days passed quickly and were uneventful. I took the Christmas tree and decorations down followed with several glasses of wine. The house looked depressing without the warm glow of the fairly lights. I piled everything up on the landing remembering how Simon would always put it all in the loft. I couldn't face going up there, so I pushed them all up against the wall and decided I'd leave it for another day.

By the end of January I pushed the boxes of decorations one by one into the guest room. Out of sight, out of mind.

The calls from Louise, Isobelle and James were becoming more and more frequent. Whereas before they'd call me once a week, usually to return my missed calls, now they were taking it in turns to ring me. They were making sure I was okay, though none of us ever actually mentioned the events of New Year or the baby. One of them would call between six and eight in the evening, and as my drinking habits were slowly getting out of control, I'd make sure not to have more than two before eight o'clock. The last thing they needed was another reason to worry about me.

Then, towards the end of March, Izzie had called to inform me that the baby, a girl was due in June, the tenth. Simon had kept her informed throughout, deciding to include them in his new life. She also found it no problem to talk to me about everything, which I was pleased about. Louise refused to have any contact with him, and James found it difficult to be civil with him. I think James felt he was being unkind to me if he'd accepted it all, despite my reassurances otherwise.

Louise was struggling and I felt helpless. I couldn't talk to her about it and she loathed Sarah. She saw her as the woman who took her darling Father away from her. It made sense because she and Simon had always been so very close. Louise was the apple of his eye and she'd been a 'daddy's girl' from day one. I didn't push it with her, because it caused her too much pain to talk about it. I could only hope that Michael was still being her tower of strength.

I tried so hard to stay bright and breezy throughout Izzie's call. Simon and Sarah had decided to call the baby Sophia. I couldn't get the name out of my head...Sophia Aagar, over and over again. I finished off the bottle I'd opened earlier that evening and climbed the stairs to bed, hoping sleep would stop the whole thing for just a few hours at least.

The next day I pulled myself together enough to attempt a food shop. I filled the shopping trolley with healthy, appetizing foods as well as several bottles of my favourite wine. That evening I decided to call the children myself in the hope of showing them that I was coping and coming to terms with everything. Our conversations were brief, but I kept it all very jovial, calling Louise last when I knew she'd be at home and feeling more relaxed.

She sounded anything but relaxed! Nor was she in the mood to talk. I finally got it out of her that Scott had posted something on Facebook about her after a drunken evening and it had niggled her. She wouldn't disclose to me what he'd written and despite me trying to convince her not to worry too much, she had cut me off.

As I tried to settle down for the evening once again in front of the television with just a glass of wine for company, Louise's words kept popping into my head. I went into the study and turned on the computer. I remembered that they had once set me up with a Facebook account, and I logged on and sat staring at my profile page. Married to Simon Aagar, who by the way, was not on Facebook he thought it ridiculous and couldn't understand why I had let them create me an account. I had no way of knowing how to change my status from married to whatever it was I was, and I certainly didn't have the inclination right now.

Searching through my friends, I clicked on Louise's profile. There I found Scott. He didn't have any privacy settings and so I was able to see his wall, then I realised Scott and I were friends too. Whatever he'd written had obviously been deleted, as I couldn't find anything that would disturb Louise.

It was then that I had the idea to search for Sarah West. There were a lot of Sarah West's. Eventually there she was, smiling and posing on a swing – on a bloody swing. For Heaven's sake. My heart was beating so fast, I felt as if I was in the middle of some high level police investigation, determined to search out the truth.

I clicked on her name. My mouth was dry so as it allowed me entry, I left it and went into the kitchen, pouring myself a glass of wine. As I sat there in front of the screen, I knew I shouldn't be doing it, putting myself through it, but I couldn't resist. I clicked on her photos.

There it was...out there for the world to see. Was I some kind of masochist, causing myself this pain or just too curious for my own good? And anyway, why didn't she have any privacy settings? STUPID COW!! The first thing James had done was sort out my privacy settings. Maybe she wanted the whole wide world to see her postings and photographs.

Suddenly, there right in front of my eyes, her profile picture changed. Gone was the carefree, smiling face of a young and single woman. In its place was a photograph of her and Simon. Sarah stood there, pregnant and blooming. A smile so wide it reminded me of a Cheshire cat. Her shoulders back, head held high, smug. That's how she looked, smug! Simon next to her, the proud Father. She had her hand on her baby bump and his was placed on top of hers. I couldn't breathe. Worst of all it had been taken at the New Year's party at Anna's.

Pushing the knife further into my own heart, I clicked on the picture. She had titled it just a few seconds ago: 'The expectant parents.'

Within moments, friends were leaving comments about how happy they looked, how suited they were, congratulations and so on it went...I ran to the downstairs toilet and was sick. I felt as if my heart had been wrenched from my body.

Reality had hit home and it had hit me hard.

Chapter 28

Over the next few weeks, I continued my new obsession with Facebook. Or should I say, with Sarah West's Facebook page. I would wake up, make myself a coffee and plonk myself in front of the computer, heading straight for her profile.

I'd discovered that their affair had started long before I had thought. By looking through the various albums I'd seen pictures of them together as far back as December, the year before last. There were office party pictures, leaving parties, award evenings, and even holidays. I say holidays, it was more like city breaks.

I was horrified. At first they appeared just in the same shot, at the work related events, but by May, the year before at George Peterson's retirement dinner, they were sat beside each other and she had her stupid hands around his stupid neck. Then by August they were appearing in albums titled: 'Paris', then April last year:

'Rome' and 'Barcelona'.

I had my diary open on the desk and each time I'd check my entries finding the corresponding dates to her photographs. The business trips Simon had been on — all lies. He had in actual fact been with her, not at some boring seminar that he'd moaned on about upon his return. I hadn't had a clue, not even an inkling. Had I been stupidly blind or just a boring, trusting wife?

But what would our marriage have been if it had been without trust? (I remembered once Anna telling me she didn't trust Tim as far as she could throw him and he didn't trust her...I told her that this was no way to live, but she had said I was naïve).

I thought about privately messaging Sarah or calling Simon to talk over the years of deceit, but she would probably then change her privacy settings and I needed to see these things, know what was going on, even though I knew it was not healthy. No matter how hurtful it was to see them together, knowing all the time I was at home being the dutiful wife, I couldn't stop looking. I wasn't ready for her to take control of this situation too.

I found myself fixated on every part of her...her face, her body, what she was wearing...everything. The only saving grace through all of it was that she wasn't what I'd imagined a mistress to look like...I wasn't sure what she was supposed to look like, but not like Sarah. I had to laugh as I remembered back to the day at Simon's offices when I'd mistaken Sara for Sarah. Yes, my Sara was certainly more the mistress material than his.

One morning in May after spending far too long investigating the life and social events of Sarah West, I looked up from the computer and out of the window. It was a beautiful day and I was wasting it looking at Sarah's life whilst my own was wasting away.

That was it, I decided to get dressed and go out. I called Jade to see if she was free for lunch. Thankfully she was and we arranged to meet at twelve o'clock at a little Italian in town that had only recently opened.

Jade was already seated and waiting for me when I arrived, she waved at me as I walked through the door and already my day was brightened. She had ordered me a glass of Prosecco. We ordered a scampi dish in a delicious creamy sauce with pasta, and I sat and listened to her harmless gossip from the salon. As always she had me in fits of laughter and made me feel so positive.

As we were halfway through our lunch, a familiar face came towards me. It was Susan Parry. "Jennifer!" she called out to me as she approached our table. "How are you feeling?" She cocked her head to one side in a sympathetic gesture, managing to get a good look at Jade at the same time.

"Hello, Susan," I said, swallowing a mouthful of pasta. "I'm fine, thank you. And you?"

"Oh, I'm great, really great. It's you I'm worried about, all of us are." She continued talking to me, but eyes on Jade.

Susan Parry was a woman I'd known most of my adult life. She had children the same age as me and had socialized in the same circles throughout my married life. I couldn't recall seeing her at the New Year's party, but I'm sure she'd have been there at some point during the evening. I wondered if she'd witnessed my arrival and quick departure.

"No need to worry about me, Susan. I'm absolutely fine." I smiled and took a large gulp of my drink, only to find it was gone. Jade discreetly caught the eye of the waiter and asked for two white wines, smiling an assuring smile at me.

"It's just that, well….after what happened…you know…" She paused and it was blatantly obvious that she was enjoying every minute of my awkwardness. "At New Year." She said the words slowly and so quietly, almost mouthing them.

"What happened at New Year?" Jade asked loudly, a look of confusion on her face. I hadn't told her. After her kindness at giving me a beauty treatment and haircut especially for the evening, I hadn't had it in me.

"Oh, it was awful!" Susan blurted out, thrilled at the chance to repeat it to a stranger. "Didn't she tell you?"

"Jen?" Jade looked at me, willing me to explain.

"It was nothing really…" I started to say.

"Nothing?" Susan repeated. "It was awful. She turned up at Tim and Anna's party — do you know them?"

Jade shook her head and the waiter appeared with our drinks just as Susan grabbed a chair from the next table and sat down at ours.

"Ooh, bring me one of those too, please," she said to the waiter. "My party hasn't arrived yet."

Jade and I looked at each other, unable to stop the situation developing before our eyes. I picked up my glass and nearly emptied it of its contents. Jade shook her head slowly at me as if telling me to take it slowly.

"I'm Susan by the way. And you are?"

"Jade."

"Pleased to meet you, Jade. How long have you known Jennifer then?"

We felt completely ambushed. I wanted to tell her to leave, but somehow I felt myself shrinking back into my chair, allowing her to continue with the gossip about my life, which she couldn't wait to tell.

Not even waiting for Jade to answer her question, Susan continued with excitement in her eyes. "Well, there we all were at the party and who walks in but our Jennifer here. None of us expected her to come, you know after what had gone on and Simon being there with HER!"

"I am actually here, Susan," I said, tiring of her gossip.

"I know you are, darling," she carried on, now in full flow and smiling at the waiter as he brought her wine over. "Anyway, Jen spots them, Simon and Sarah. Complete with bump!" She stopped and waited for a reaction. Jade frowned. "Pregnant. The mistress is pregnant! It was one of those moments you never forget, the look on your face, Jen. I will NEVER forget it. You poor thing." She reached out and touched my arm.

"Oh that?" Jade sang out, laughing. Susan and I looked at her, startled. "Oh God, for a moment I wondered what the hell you were going to say." Susan looked confused and a little disappointed. "Jen and me think it's hysterical. I mean let's face it, Susan...for example, how old are you?"

Totally flabbergasted, mouth open Susan tried to speak, but no words came out. I sat back, confidently watching the show. Jade always knew the right way out of a sticky situation.

"Erm, let me guess," Jade continued, looking directly at Susan and completely unnerving her. "Fifty-six? No?"

"No!" Susan snapped. "I'll be fifty next year!"

"Really? Oh sorry. Gosh, I'm usually so good at guessing peoples age. Well, actually that's not one hundred percent true, is it Jen? I thought you were at least six years younger than your actual age when we met, didn't I? I must be losing my touch. Anyway, Susan, we think it's simply hilarious that at his age, Simon is having another child. We pity him, don't we Jen?" I nodded in agreement, sipping my wine and now feeling totally chilled out. "Are you married, Susan?" Jade asked her, leaning forward awaiting Susan's response.

"Yes, it will be twenty-five years in September, actually," she replied, no idea where this conversation was now going.

"Ooh," Jade tutted. "Are you worried, Susan?"

"About what?"

"Your husband," Jade said, matter-of-factly. "What's his name? Your husband?"

"Pete," she replied, becoming more and more anxious.

"Well, aren't you, on some level, worried that Pete might do what Simon's done? I mean look at Jen! If Simon could do it to Jen, what chance do you and the others have?"

"My Pete would NEVER cheat on me!" she exclaimed. The colour had completely drained from her face, she looked at me and I just shrugged my shoulders and smiled.

"Do you trust him, Susan?" Jade asked, bluntly.

"Er, well…yes."

"Really?" Jade insisted. "All I'm saying is you never know. Imagine if next year it's you turning up at Anna & Tom's to find your Pete there with his mistress, with child."

"It's Tim, not Tom. Anna's husband." She was now in a totally perplexed state.

"Oh and he's another one! She'll have to watch him."

"Tim? Really?" Susan took a huge gulp of her wine, her huge diamond solitaire ring clinking on the glass.

"Trust me. I'm a hairdresser."

"It's so nice of you to ask how I am, Susan," I said, finally finding my voice. "But as you can see, I'm doing just fine."

"Yes, yes, I can see that," she said, looking around the restaurant for a way out of our little chat. "Oh, there's my friend just arriving. I'll let you get on with your lunch. Please excuse me. It was nice seeing you again and nice to meet you, Jade." She stood up and put the chair back.

"Lovely to meet you, Susan." Jade smiled, putting her hand out to her and shaking it firmly. "And if you ever feel you'd like to update your hairstyle, here," Jade began fumbling in her handbag. "Take my card. I'm sure my stylist could take years off you."

As Susan walked away we tried hard to suppress our laughter. Once again Jade had rescued me.

"Sorry I didn't tell you," I whispered.

"Are you okay?" she asked, touching my hand. "Really okay?"

"I'm getting there," I said, squeezing her hand.

That evening I went into the study and deleted my Facebook account. I wasn't, it appeared, a masochist after all.

Chapter 29

I was beginning to feel as though I had finally accepted everything: the upcoming divorce, Sarah, the baby and now I had to face the fact that I would have to start looking for somewhere new to live. Simon had, via our lawyer, Tony, said that there was no rush, although he hoped that by next Christmas I would have found a new place and that our house would be sold.

I thought back to Christmas Day and how I'd welcomed him back into our family for the day and how he'd cried in my arms. Now he wanted it all done and dusted by the next one, no doubt focusing on the fact he'd have a baby by then.

It was something I kept pushing to the very back of my mind until bedtime came. Then it would creep in, usually just as I'd turned the light out and snuggled down. If sleep did come, my thoughts would disturb me in my dreams and I'd wake at around four in the morning, lying awake until about six when I'd fall back into such a deep sleep not stirring until much later, feeling groggy and irritable.

My drawings and painting helped me enormously during the day and I was occupied for hours upon hours. I found myself sketching myself when I was pregnant with Louise, using photographs that Simon had taken in our garden. I did a series of paintings in the garden, with each of the children in them, first just Louise, followed by Isobelle and then James. They were really starting to look like a collection that maybe I could show at a gallery.

Eventually, one Friday evening I decided to bite the bullet and start looking for somewhere. The local newspaper carried details of places, so I circled the ones I thought might be worth looking at and searched for them on the websites.

Sat there all alone in the study, looking out onto the front garden, sadness washed over me, but I knew I had to just get on with it now. I'd always have my memories and especially now through my paintings, where the house and garden came to life on a canvas of beautiful colours.

Once I'd narrowed it down to my price range and preferred requirements – three bedrooms, a large diner kitchen, living room, en-suite, small garden – I found myself becoming a little excited about the prospect of setting up my very own home. It no longer brought terror at the thought of being alone. I'd already faced that fear and was conquering it.

One property in particular caught my eye. It was an apartment in an old mansion house that had been divided up into three homes. The one I liked had everything I needed and a beautiful south-facing garden. I could even imagine my furniture in each of the rooms.

Saturday morning, I woke up bright and early after a wonderfully peaceful night's sleep and contacted the agents to make a viewing. The lady on the other end of the phone was extremely helpful and almost as excited as I was over my viewing of No. 2 Manor Place. I arranged to meet her there at ten o'clock that morning. That gave me time to get ready and drive the ten minutes down the road to where it sat on the edge of the village, in beautiful countryside.

I was about to leave the house when the phone rang. It was Izzie.

"Izzie my darling, I'm about to walk out of the door, can I call you back?" I decided not to tell her where I was going until I'd seen the place and got a feel of it.

"No need, Mama dearest. Just to let you know, we're all on our way up to you, leaving in about an hour. That okay?"

"Oh okay," I was a little surprised they were all coming home without previous warning. "Great. Well, I'll be here. See you soon."

"See you later," she called out before hanging up. I couldn't put my finger on it, but there was mischievousness in her voice, I knew Izzie very well and she was excited about something.

All that would have to wait, I had an house viewing to attend.

Driving up the private lane, surrounded by fields and trees, the sun shining, I felt a good vibe about this place. I could see the house at the end of the lane and it looked very grand. As I parked up, Ella Anderson from Peterson's Estate Agents greeted me. Her smiling face and happy disposition put me at ease straight away.

"Hello, Mrs Aagar, lovely to meet you. I'm Ella."

"Hello. Lovely to meet you Ella, and please call me Jennifer."

I followed her to the main door. It was huge and painted black and opened into a spacious communal hall with high ceilings and beautiful marble floors. An enormous crystal chandelier lit the entrance and it felt very opulent.

"Here we are, Jennifer. Number two," Ella said, turning the key in the lock. "The previous owners have actually moved out so it's empty. You'll be able to imagine all of your things in the rooms and get a good feel for the amazing space."

She had convinced me already and I couldn't wait to get inside what could potentially be my new home. Ella was right about the space. From the moment I entered, light streamed in from the garden through glass doors leading into each room, and large windows gave beautiful views from the living areas out onto the garden. Cream soft carpets covered the floors and gave a cushioned feel underfoot.

The kitchen was beautifully fitted out with white high gloss units and grey slate floors that complimented them, there was room for a table, and French doors led out onto a private patio area. There were four bedrooms, two were en-suite and I could visualise myself waking up in the master bedroom.

"I love it!" I said to Ella as she opened the doors and stepped out into the garden.

"Isn't it beautiful? I can just see you living here."

"Me too," I agreed, following her outside, the sun shining as if she had arranged it all just this way. "Do you have anyone else interested in it?" I asked, standing back to look at the apartment properly.

"Yes, there were two couples who came to see it yesterday, no offers as yet, but I think this place is meant for you! I really do."

I spent another half an hour walking around. My heart felt completely full up and I couldn't wait for the children to see it. I arranged with Ella to make another viewing for later in the day. We parted company, her knowing she had a sale, me knowing that I'd found a place where I could really be happy.

****

They all arrived at two o'clock. I'd gone home and made a lasagne with a crisp salad for lunch. I couldn't believe that I was going to leave our beautiful home, our family home, and I was actually feeling okay about it. More than okay, I was delighted. As I started to dish out the food, James popped his head into the kitchen and told me to wait a minute. I looked around to see the three of them standing there, faces beaming. I was right, there was something going on, they were up to something. I put the dish back into the oven and asked them what the big secret was.

They beckoned me outside and I followed them, gasping as I saw a beautiful new four wheel drive BMW gleaming and parked in front of the house. "Lou, you've got a new car!" I said, walking over to investigate further.

"No, actually it's Michael's. I borrowed it," Louise informed me, opening the boot and everyone gathering around, looking at me.

"What is going on?" I asked, growing impatient.

Izzie took me by the arm and pulled me to the open boot. I couldn't quite take in what I was seeing. There inside a cage were two fluffy, white golden retriever puppies, tails wagging and yawning after their journey.

"Oh, they're gorgeous, Lou," I said, opening the door of the cage and stroking them. "Are they yours?"

"No!" James said, picking out one of the puppies and putting it in my arms. "They're yours!"

"What? I gasped in utter shock. "What do you mean, they're mine?"

"Well," Louise began, scooping up the other puppy and closing the boot. "We know how lonely you get being here, in this big house, all alone, so we decided to get these two for you. Call it an early birthday present."

"No, I can't take them," I insisted, giving the cute bundle back to James.

"Why not, Mum?" Izzie asked, looking extremely disappointed. "They'll be such good company for you."

"And a nightmare to take car of! Anyway, I'm moving form here, there won't be room for two dogs where I'm going."

"You don't know that," Louise butted in, "we'll help you find somewhere that's dog friendly."

"But I've already found somewhere," I said, walking back inside. "And it's got cream carpets and a tiny garden and there wouldn't be anywhere for them to sleep. That was going to be my surprise over dinner…I'd arranged for us all to go and see it."

They all scuttled in behind me, puppies included. I could hear them whispering between each other, James leading and was the first to try and persuade me into a complete change of lifestyle. Like I hadn't had enough change so far!

"Look Mum, look at him…" he laughed, pushing 'him' into my face. "He loves you."

"What were you all thinking?" I asked, bemused, pushing puppy away. "I'm not a dog person, never have been." I actually wanted to cry at the thought of these two visitors becoming permanent residents.

"They'll be great for you, Mum. Just what you need," Louise said in her firm, 'don't be so silly' voice. "You can walk them, get out of the house, you'll meet new people. Just what you need!"

"Please don't. Don't tell me what I need!" Silence fell. James grabbed the other puppy from Louise and went out into the garden. Not really knowing what to do, Izzie stood there for a few moments before following James.

"Mum," Louise said softly, "I'm sorry. We just thought that..." she paused, trying to find the right words. "We've just been so worried about you, we thought the puppies would make you happy again. We remembered when we lived at home, you were always so, so happy. We don't know what to do, Mum, we feel so helpless." I looked at my eldest daughter, usually so strong in character, standing there unable to make things better for me and on the verge of tears. "It's James's fault! He's an idiot!" she suddenly announced before I could say anything.

She slumped down at the kitchen table, defeated. I turned to her and took a deep breath. "He's not an idiot, Lou. None of you are." I looked out onto the garden and watched James and Izzie playing with what were after all, delightful pups. "Come on, let's go and pick names for my new house guests, shall we?"

"Oh, that's OK, we've already picked their names for you. Max and Millie."

The three of them stayed the whole weekend, I cancelled my second viewing with Ella. She sounded more disappointed than I felt. I let the dream of Apartment No. 2 with its plush cream carpets and under-floor heating fade away from my mind and tried to bond with Max and Millie. My two new house guests were, apparently, here to stay.

Chapter 30

The weeks passed by, and Louise, Isobelle and James replaced their phone calls with weekend visits, taking it in turns. First to come was Isobelle, who had always wanted a dog, then James the following weekend.

They would turn up on their allocated weekend, fuss the puppies to within an inch of their lives, walk them, feed them and even groomed them and every Saturday afternoon at three o'clock, they were dragged along to puppy training class. I went to their first lesson with Izzie. I too was literally dragged along. I was not bonding with Max and Millie like the children had hoped. My house was a mess of dog hairs and muddy footprints.

It had rained nearly ever day since they had arrived. They woke me each morning at five without fail. I was tired and I was irritated.

The beginner's puppy classes were disastrous. Our puppies were the worst behaved there, they didn't listen, sit or basically follow any instructions. After the instructor had snapped at me, making me feel like I was a five-year-old child again, I swore I would never go back. So, I left it up to the children to take my car, puppies in tow and attend puppy school without me.

Throughout the week I would climb back into bed after letting them out, and sleep on and off until around ten o'clock. I hated getting up late. I felt groggy and moody. I would attempt to walk them around the lake in the park. I say attempt because Max and Millie would take it in turns to lie down, refusing to go anywhere.

I hated them. I'd never hated anything or anyone in all my life. Well, that wasn't strictly true, there was of course Sarah West. If this woman hadn't entered my life, or rather, Simon's life, I would not be in this situation. I would be making dinner right now, Simon would walk through the door and we'd eat together...I could feel the rage and hatred building up inside me. Then I realised something. Simon would be sitting opposite me and we would be eating dinner together, but in silence and blocking out anything I was saying.

Sighing, I looked over at the two puppies sleeping in their beds in the hallway. They were snuggled together, their full little bellies heaving up and down, their paws twitching as they dreamt of new adventures, no doubt plotting how they could terrorize me the next day.

No matter how much I wanted to hate Sarah West, blame her for everything that had gone wrong in my life, I couldn't. Something inside me softened. After all the months of sitting here alone, now I wasn't alone. I went over to Max and Millie and bent down, I wanted to stroke them, but Max opened one eye and I quickly retreated. They were at last asleep after creating havoc all day, so I let them be and headed upstairs for an early night.

When I woke the next morning, I couldn't believe that I, and puppies, had slept through until nine o'clock. They had slept through the night for the first time. Not a murmur from them. I actually felt a little unnerved and quickly went downstairs to find them still sleeping. It was nothing short of a miracle.

I crept past them and made myself coffee and toast. I sat at the kitchen table chewing and swallowing slowly and quietly so as not to disturb them. Still, they slept soundly. They wouldn't make very good guard dogs I decided and it amused me. Maybe they had picked up on my mood, knowing they could be out on their ears if they didn't buck up.

As I took a last mouthful of my coffee, they woke up and were bouncier and livelier than ever, but somehow, I didn't mind.

****

For the first time since Max and Millie had arrived, I set off on our daily walk to the park with a spring in my step and a smile on my face. It was sunny and warm and I'd just needed a cardigan over my T-shirt today, jeans and trainers instead of the wellington boots and the waterproof coat I'd been forced to wear due to the rain.

Once at the park entrance, I breathed in the fresh air and felt a feeling of happiness that I hadn't felt in such a long time. It didn't involve the children, or Simon or any man for that matter; I was happy with me and it felt good.

With my new approach to the walk, I was daydreaming and not paying attention to where the pups were leading me — the dog trainer would not be impressed — and I found myself on a narrow, twisting lane. Feeling brave, I decided to let the dogs off the lead as it seemed quiet and wasn't a main road.

At first, all went well, they stayed close to me and came back when I called them, rewarding them with treats. As we got further down the lane, Max, gaining confidence, started to run further ahead, I called him, but he didn't come back. Millie, on the other hand and the more timid of the two, stayed by my side, glancing at me to see if a treat was coming her way for good behaviour. I quickly put her on the lead so that she didn't get any ideas.

Running, I began to shout out his name. Panic was setting in as he was now out of sight. Eventually, the road came to an end. I came across the most beautiful cottage I had ever seen.

It was painted white with an olive green front door. Perfect borders edged the gravel driveway, pots of flowers sat on the windowsills and it made me eager to draw it. It was picture perfect. I caught my breath and listened for any sound from Max.

On the opposite side was another white cottage. It was run-down with its paint peeling off, revealing red bricks underneath. The windows were broken and the garden was considerably overgrown and it was obvious that nobody had occupied it for some time. A rusty old gate was partly opened and Millie and I pushed through it into the garden.

Even though it was totally abandoned, it had a wonderfully peaceful feel to it. Around the side there was a wall and an opened arch gate leading into the back. There we found a very happy Max, who, with a wagging tail, was sniffing his way through the weeds.

Suddenly with the sun shining down on the south-facing garden, almost lighting up the cottage, I caught my breath. I knew this was where I wanted to be. It was all meant to be. The chic apartment I'd viewed all those weeks ago, as wonderful as it was, was never meant to be my new home, this was!

Visiting the magical cottage I felt was meant to be mine, became a daily ritual. I just stood there looking at it, imagining how it could look whilst the puppies ran into the garden, seeming as content as I was.

I'd hoped to bump into the owner of the other cottage, but it never seemed as if anyone was home. I had knocked on their door once, hoping to catch a glimpse of my new neighbours-to-be and ask them if they knew how to contact the owner of my cottage.

On our way back home, I made a detour into the woods at the end of the lane. It was a nice warm afternoon and there were plenty of other dog walkers around and a lot of joggers, who Max enjoyed chasing, forcing me to put him back on the lead.

On a high from seeing the cottage again and seeing as we were deep inside the woods, I let the dogs off, allowing them to explore. I took pleasure from all the people who admired Max and Millie as they passed them. They were, I had to admit, the cutest puppies!

My good mood was short lived as Max disappeared down a steep muddy incline. Millie stopped in her tracks, sensing there'd be trouble and ran back to me. I stood at the top of the path looking down at Max, who was running through a heap of soggy leaves that hadn't dried out from the rain, nose to the ground, oblivious to my calls.

Suddenly, something caught my eye in the distance and I'm sure Max had spotted it too as he was running towards it. I squinted, trying to make out what on earth the beautiful, vibrant blue object could be. It struck me, it was some kind of exotic bird, lying there injured and Max was hurtling towards it.

Putting Millie quickly on her lead, I raced down the hill towards the pitiful bird, screaming at Max to 'stay'! People were gathering, looking down at the spectacle before their eyes, wondering I'm sure, what all the commotion was about.

As I ran, I tripped over a fallen branch and lost my footing. I ended up flat on my face, my sunglasses that I'd had fashionably on my head, fell down and were now crooked and covering my face. I could hear people gasping, others laughing and I was mortified, completely embarrassed. I heard someone running behind me and turned to see a man running down the hill with ease and towards me. Flustered, I got to my feet just as he reached me and took my arm to help me.

"Are you okay?" he asked, a concerned look on his face.

"Yes," I replied, breathless and feeling extremely foolish, I popped my sunglasses over my eyes to hide my shame. I was covered in mud from head to toe. "Its my dog, Max. He's only a puppy and he's spotted a bird over there." I pointed in the direction of the tiny blue bird about to be devoured. "I think he may harm it."

"Okay, don't worry, I'll sort it out." He smiled at me, patted my shoulder and rushed off towards Max.

I turned to face the crowd of people watching from the top of the hill gesturing to them that I was okay and brushing off leaves and twigs from my arms and legs, even my hair. Grabbing a shaken Millie, I gingerly made my way over to the handsome stranger who had come to mine and the birds rescue.

"It's okay," he assured me, nudging Max away and cupping the tiny creature in his hands.

"Is it still alive?" I asked, hoping Max hadn't maimed it for life.

"Already dead I'm afraid," he informed me, making a little clearing in the ground.

"Oh no, poor little…thing…" I wanted to shed a tear until I realised it wasn't a bird at all.

He'd tried his best to save my blushes, but it was too late, I'd seen it. Not an exotic bird as I had imagined, it wasn't a tiny, injured creature lying there, waiting to be rescued from the jaws of Max…it was in fact a sock! A SOCK!!

"Oh God!" I gasped under my breath. "It's a sock. A bloody sock." I once again faced the crowd and shook my head, signalling to them that the bird was indeed dead as the tall, dark, handsome stranger buried the sock.

Gradually they dispersed, leaving a mortified me all alone with him.

"I'm so sorry," I whispered as I bent down beside him.

'What's there to be sorry about?" He smiled, getting up to his feet and holding out his hand to help me up. "I've not had had that much excitement in a long time, believe me."

"But it was just a sock!" I exclaimed, shaking my head in shame and glaring at Max, who was now jumping all over him.

"Exactly! Just shows you how boring my life is!" He smiled at me again, his perfect white teeth almost sparkling, as did his brown eyes. "I'm Alex. Alex Stone."

"Jennifer Aagar," I said, offering him my hand. "Thank you for coming to my rescue, Alex Stone. I'm mortified."

"Really, there's no need, Jennifer."

"Call me Jen." I smiled not loosening my grip on his hand, dazed and transfixed by just how good looking he was.

"Ooh dear," he let go of my hand and turned it over to examine a wound. "You appear to have cut yourself."

"Oh…" I looked and saw blood oozing from my wrist and suddenly became aware of the pain. "I must have done it when I fell over."

"Hmm," he suppressed his laughter as he surely replayed my spectacular fall in his head. "Look, I live just two minutes away from here, come on, I'll clean that up for you."

"Oh no, really, no need…" I began, but it really was hurting now. "Well, if you're sure it's no trouble."

We gathered up the dogs and he helped me back up the hill and back into the warm sunshine. He was so attractive, olive skin, tall and slender. He was in running gear and wearing a cap so I couldn't see his hair. I imagined it to be dark, peppered with a little grey perhaps. As he walked in front of me, leading the way up a small path into the other side of the woods, I couldn't help but look at his muscular thighs and firm buttocks.

I felt my cheeks flush as I imagined him naked and found myself longing to reach out and touch him. Well, his bottom. Max followed our new friend as if he were his new master, whilst Millie, faithful as ever, stayed by my side.

"Gosh," I said after a few minutes of walking, "I've completely lost my bearings."

"Nearly there," and he pointed towards a wall with a gate that led on to the back of a garden. "It's just there."

As we neared the gate, I could see a white house and I realised it was the back entrance to the perfect cottage. Could this go any better? Max was certainly going to get a treat once we got home. Finding me a place to live and now Alex.

I let out a laugh. "What?" he asked, "what's funny?" He fumbled in the pocket of his sweatshirt for the key to unlock the gate.

"Oh nothing really, it's just…" I paused, taking in the beauty of the garden.

"What?" he asked, smiling at me and staring intently.

"I was just here earlier. Well, at the front, looking at the cottage opposite."

"Oh, Mrs Fearnley's old place. How did you manage to come across it?"

"Max," I said, bluntly and we both laughed. "Is it for sale, do you know?"

"Not sure what the family plan on doing." He went on to tell me all about it as I followed him up to the back door that led into a stunning kitchen with stone floors and wooden work surfaces. It was open-plan and double-fronted so I could see the old cottage. He sat me down at the breakfast bar. "The old dear died about six years ago. We'd bought this place a few years earlier and totally renovated it."

'We'. Damn it! He said WE!!

"The place was already falling apart then, but after she died, well, they just let it go to pot. I gave up asking them what their intentions were, but I have a number if you want to contact them," he said, cleaning my wound with such concentration, I found it quite endearing. "There we are, all done!" And he finished off by sticking a large plaster over the cut. "Can I get you a tea? Coffee?"

"I'd love to, Alex, but I should be getting back." Max barked as if in agreement. "We've been out for ages now and I've so much to do." I lied.

He let me out through the front door and I was just about to regret my decision and say I'd stay, when I saw a photograph in the hallway of Alex and the most stunning brunette woman on their wedding day. I felt a pang of disappointment and knew I'd made the right choice. He ran to the front gate and opened it for me. "It was really lovely meeting you, Jennifer," he took off his cap to reveal a head of dark hair, with just as I'd thought, a hint of grey. "If you decide you want the family's number, just let me know. Any time."

"Thanks, I will." I walked away, turning to have one last look at him. "Thanks for everything, Alex."

As I headed home I felt as if I'd been given the most beautiful gift ever, only to have it snatched away from me.

"Oh well," I sighed, patting Max and Millie. "What you've never had, you'll never miss!"

I would just have to forget about him but not the cottage.

Chapter 31

Unbelievably, forget him I did. I hadn't stumbled across Alex again in the park and I avoided the woods as best I could. I started to sort out the house. There was so much to do. I'd spoken to Simon and he'd agreed to give me a year to find a new place. We agreed that we would put the house on the market next January, that way, giving me time to find somewhere and get a feel for the market.

I hadn't told him about the cottage. I figured if it had been empty for six years, it wasn't going to be sold any time soon. Plus, I didn't fancy turning up on Alex's doorstep to have his perfect wife open the door to their perfect home. So I busied myself with sorting out and kept an eye on the local newspaper for anything new that came up for sale.

Sorting out and painting kept me occupied. I'd cleared out the summerhouse, which Simon had claimed for his own as his shed and turned it into an art studio. The weather was warming up and I was inspired to paint by the breathtaking beauty of the garden. How I would miss it. However, I wasn't going to allow myself to wallow any more.

In September it would be a year since Simon and I had split up and I was doing okay. I was dreading the baby coming, and it wasn't long off now, but I had to move on.

My paintings were piling up and Michael had been pushing me for a date when I would be ready to display them. Mr Miracle as I liked to call him, had found a vacant shop on the high street in town and got the owner to agree to do a pop-up gallery. All I had to do was tell him when and he would sort it all out.

It was the end of May, one week until my birthday. I had just finished painting my vision of how the cottage would look. I propped it up against the painting I'd done of Alex's place. They looked like a pair and I felt they should be sold as such.

And suddenly, I felt ready. I felt it was the time to show my work.

I called Michael and he set the date and it coincided with my birthday, next Saturday, 3 June at seven o'clock in the evening. His secretary emailed me over different designs for the invitations for me to choose from and that was that.

He organized everything, even down to the staff to serve champagne, to the guests through the evening. I was nervous and excited all at once. But best of all, I didn't have to worry about not having my annual birthday bash and all the memories that would have unleashed.

I picked up the phone to call Aunt Rose, Michael's biggest fan, and tell her the good news. After all, she was the one who had encouraged me to take up painting again so it was only right she be the first to know.

She wasted no time in organizing me. She picked me up the next morning bright and early, and took me to a designer she knew from way back. Once we arrived there at the little shop in the city, where magic was weaved, I was fitted out in a classic, stylish cocktail dress in midnight blue. It had an asymmetric neckline, capped sleeves with a bow detail to one side. It had a fitted waist and fitted like a glove. The designer picked out a thin, silver metallic belt to go with it.

Aunt Rose had paid for it before I had left the dressing room and I had no idea of the cost. I would have argued more but she got such pleasure from treating me, I had learned to just thank her.

To this day, she was still trying to make up for the huge hole my parents had always left in my life.

I got home and hung my designer dress in my dressing room. I kept looking at it, unable to believe that I could fit into something so perfect. I felt so alive, so happy and the most wonderful feeling of all, I didn't feel alone.

The phone rang, bringing me back to the here and now. It was Sebastian.

"Jennifer, darling. How are you?"

"Sebastian! I'm good, and you?"

"Wonderful, wonderful. Be even better if I could take you out for dinner this evening. Are you free?"

"I am. And if I wasn't, I would have cancelled it just for you." I giggled, flirting outrageously, knowing I could and that he would never take me seriously. "I've lots to tell you."

"Fabulous. I'll collect you around eight and I've already made reservations at 'Silva's'. Is that okay for you?"

He knew it was my new favourite restaurant and I that I would be thrilled. "That's perfect, Sebastian. Thank you." And I hung up, looking forward to a lovely evening with my wonderful friend.

Later that night as Sebastian ordered a bottle of champagne, I started to tell him all about the exhibition. He couldn't have been more supportive or pleased for me. He was such a genuine person and I counted my blessings that he had come into my life. I also felt comfortable enough to tell him all about Alex Stone. I was describing how we'd met, all about the sock and how he'd cleaned up my wound whilst we sat in his kitchen.

"Sounds like destiny to me, my darling," Sebastian said as he topped up my glass with champagne. "It's as if you were meant to meet him. And thank goodness to whoever the someone was who misplaced a sock." He frowned. "How does one lose one sock? I often wonder that, you know when sometimes you see the odd shoe lying about at the side of the road…I've never lost a sock or a shoe."

I giggled and agreed with him. "Only one little problem though…he has a wife."

"Well, that's very unfortunate." He looked at me, but I was transfixed at the sight over his shoulder. "Jennifer," he continued, "he has a wife you say?"

"Yes! A wife," I blurted out. "And he's just walked in," I said, ducking down trying to take cover.

"Ooh, is that his wife?"

"No!" I whispered, leaning in further so that Alex hopefully wouldn't see me.

"Oh, this is a little awkward. Are you sure it's not his wife?"

"Yes," I continued, "it is definitely NOT his wife. I saw her picture at the house, on their wedding day!"

He topped up my glass again. "Drink this, but slowly."

"Ugh, I thought it was too good to be true. I was willing to accept we could never be because of his beautiful wife, but I knew he was too good to be true. What is it with men of a certain age?" Sebastian coughed, looking at me. "Present company excluded, obviously."

Thankfully, the waiter arrived to clear away our starters and I stopped ranting. I looked over to where Alex was sitting, his handsome and perfect profile. I just felt so disappointed with him. His lovely, perfect wife, sitting at home in their lovely, perfect home whilst he brought out some bimbo to one of the best restaurants in town. Him and his wife had looked so happy in the photograph and it can't have been that long ago. Narrowing my eyes, I studied the 'other' woman.

She was my idea of perfect. Unfortunately. She had silky, long blonde hair, falling over her perfectly structured shoulders, curling up slightly at the ends. Her skin was lightly bronzed as if she'd just returned from some exotic beach holiday. She wore a sleeveless white, lacy shift dress, legs crossed under the table, feet sitting pretty in a pair of strappy high-heeled beige shoes, a matching handbag placed on the floor next to her chair.

On her wrists, she wore several bangles that sparked as they caught the light from the candles sitting on the table. A perfectly manicured hand held the glass of champagne from which she sipped from intermittently as she listened intently to whatever cock and bull story the charming Alex was feeding her. She kept throwing her bead back and giggling, stroking her throat as if to bring it to her attention.

UGH!!! I swallowed what was left in my glass and signalled for Sebastian to refill. Poor Sebastian, I could see he was horrified at the way I was staring over at the handsome couple.

"If looks could kill," he whispered, filling my glass as instructed. "Are you okay? I've never seen you like this, Jennifer darling. You look as if you could kill someone."

"Oh I'm sorry, Sebastian," I said, trying to bring my face out of the contorted expression it was wearing. "I'm just a little…" I search for the word I was looking for. A word suitable to describe exactly the way I was feeling.

"Jealous?" he suggested, smiling, and then a sympathetic look came over him.

"No," I replied, smiling back. "Disappointed. I don't know why. I don't even know the man very well, but I do know he's married. I suppose, deep down, I'd hoped for more."

"I'll say you did! I think you've fallen for him and you were hoping he'd fall for you? Hey, we all fall for the people we can't have at some point in our lives." He winked at me and I knew he was referring to me, in a joking manner.

I managed a half smile and we fell quiet once again as the waiter appeared with our main meal. "You must think me ridiculous," I said, attempting to eat my dinner.

"No, of course not," he said, tucking in and nodding in approval as he chewed a piece of his fillet steak.

"But he's married. Married AND fooling around. What a catch!"

"Now Jennifer, you don't know for sure that something's going on with this woman, and you never know, he might be separated or divorced from his wife."

"I do though, I just know that's not his friend, or his sister or…or his niece!" I said, playing with words, as it was clear she was a lot younger than him.

"Or maybe his daughter," Sebastian offered, smiling and raising one eyebrow.

I let out a rather loud laugh and we clinked our glasses, gaining the attention of the other diners, including Alex, who on seeing me had a look of 'where do I know her from?' expression on his face. He thought for a moment and then excusing himself to the mystery blonde, headed over to our table.

"No, no, nooooo," I murmured, putting my head down quickly and praying he was going to the gents.

"Jennifer?" (damn it). He bent down, trying to get a look at my face as I refused to look up at him. "It is you, isn't it? From the woods the other day?" He looked at Sebastian and smiled.

"Oh…" I spluttered, looking up as if I had just that second noticed him. This was excruciatingly embarrassing. I peered over at the blonde who was now squinting at me (and I have to say, as she twisted her face, she did look as though she was constipated). This gave me a little confidence. "Yes, yes it's me."

"Alex Stone," he said reminding me, like I could ever forget. "You remember, I helped bury the dead bird, the one your dog killed."

"He didn't kill it!" I said, smiling at him (Hmm, he was witty as well as handsome).

"Oh no. That's right, because it wasn't a bird after all, it was just a sock." He looked pleased with himself at making me giggle and he turned to Sebastian. "Did your wife tell you about how she likes to rescue abandoned socks from the woods?"

"I'm not his wife!" I shouted out rather loudly and way too quickly.

"Yes, she did tell me," Sebastian added, ignoring me and shaking hands with Alex. "And, like the lady said, she's not my wife. We're just good friends, aren't we darling?" He looked at me and I mouthed a 'sorry'.

"This is my very good friend, Sebastian Houghton."

"Pleasure to meet you Sebastian," Alex said, looking directly into my eyes. The intensity of his stare made my stomach somersault and my heart beat that little bit faster. Suddenly the fact that he was an adulterer with a pretty wife at home seemed to escape me.

"Likewise, Sebastian, and lovely to bump into you again, Jennifer. I hope to bump into you again some time."

As he walked away, I felt a surge of sadness run through me. I wanted to leap on his back, put my arms around his neck and kiss him…what a ridiculous image that conjured up.

Suddenly, Sebastian called out to him. Alex turned around. "Maybe we'll see you at the exhibition."

Alex walked back over to us – much to the annoyance of the blonde – and I kicked Sebastian under the table.

"What exhibition?"

"Jennifer is displaying her art work next Saturday in town, also her birthday by the way, it should be marvellous. You should come!"

"Maybe I will come, thank you, Sebastian." He nodded and walked back to the blonde.

"Great!" I seethed.

"What?" Sebastian asked, surprised at my reaction.

"What if he brings HER?"

"Then we'll know he's un-avail-able." He winked, relishing in his own genius plan and delighted at his matchmaking skills. He started to twitter on about fate…how if Anna hadn't set us up on our date, then we wouldn't have come here tonight and he wouldn't have invited Alex to the exhibition. "Like I said, fate!"

After all the excitement, I couldn't face dessert, so Sebastian paid the bill, insisting it was his treat, and we left. We waved goodbye to Alex and his little friend, and Sebastian drove me home.

As I lay in bed, sleep nowhere to be found, I couldn't get Alex bloody Stone out of my bloody head. I had fallen for him, completely. And it scared me, scared me to death.

Chapter 32

My week passed quickly. There was a lot of organizing to do for the exhibition. Actually, it was more overseeing than doing, as Michael had everything in hand. He had hired people to do most of what was required.

I felt alive, more alive than I'd felt in years. The only problem with feeling 'oh, so alive' was that I also felt 'oh so emotional'.

On the day of the opening, which happened to coincide with my birthday and what would have been our wedding anniversary, I decided that I was going to call some agents in town to make enquiries about the cottage, to find out if anyone knew anything about it. Despite the fact that the man of my dreams had turned out to be more of a nightmare, it didn't put me off still aiming for the cottage of my dreams. I just somehow knew that it was where I was meant to be.

After my third attempt without success, I called 'Hamley and Ford'. I finally hit the jackpot. They did indeed know the family of the previous owner and could contact them on my behalf, letting them know of my interest in the property. As luck would have it, only a few days earlier a family member had contacted them with a view to marketing the cottage in the near future. Fate, I decided, was really on my side.

I daydreamed that Alex Stone would fall in love with me and that his wife had left him and he was so happy that I was buying the cottage. The phone, as always, rang and pulled me back into reality.

"Happy birthday, Mum." It was James.

"Aaah, thank you, James," I said, as he announced he was putting Izzie on the phone.

"Happy birthday…are you getting excited yet?" she asked, her own excitement hard to hide.

"Very!" I declared, and I was. I was also very nervous.

"It'll be fabulous, I just know it will. We can't wait!" Izzie went on, telling me that Louise was driving and they were actually on their way. Louise shouted out 'happy birthday' to me, and I shouted a 'thank you' back at her. "We're going to collect Aunt Rose and then we'll be with you. We're so proud of you, Mum."

Nobody mentioned the fact it was also the day Simon and I had got married all those years ago and why would anyone think about it anyway? There was no point in remembering something that was no longer of any consequence.

I got ready, but instead of my usual trip to Jade's salon, she and Maxime came over to the house. I had the champagne on ice and sat back whilst they pampered me. How different my life was to this time last year when I was busy preparing for people to arrive to our party. I'd not even applied lipstick for my birthday party last year, let alone found time for a haircut.

Without warning, events and memories flooded back in. This happened from time to time, when I least expected it, when I thought I was doing okay, suddenly a painful thought would slip in just to throw me off guard.

"Hey, birthday girl," Jade said, nudging me. "Get back to the here and now and how fabulous your life is turning out to be."

"How do you do that?" I asked, astonished. She instinctively knew whenever I was drifting; from that very first day at the coffee shop she had been there. Not constantly in my face or pestering me on the phone, just there in the background. It was as if she had an inbuilt sensor that went off every now and again when I took a dive.

"Just part of the service," she replied, smiling and continue to blow-dry my hair. I studied her through my dressing table mirror. She was very pretty and slim. I had asked her bits about her own personal life, but other than she was happily married to someone called Pete, who worked in banking, I really didn't know anything else. She kept her cards close to her chest, or maybe there was nothing to tell.

By the time she had finished my hair and Maxime had completed my make-up, everyone arrived, bearing gifts of flowers and good luck cards. I felt so lucky.

"Doesn't she look amazing?" Maxime asked, as we all gathered around the kitchen table with our glasses of champagne. Everyone agreed that I looked fabulous and Aunt Rose made a toast in my honour.

"Thank you so much, all of you," I began, feeling slightly emotional, but trying hard not to show it. "Thanks for the lovely flowers, Jade and Maxime for once again working their magic. Aunt Rose," I said, turning to face her. "You are my rock and without you I wouldn't be here today displaying my paintings. So, thank you."

"Here, here," James agreed, as they all raised their glasses. He opened the French windows onto the garden and Max and Millie bounded in, causing havoc.

"Come on, it's time," Jade announced as we all emptied our glasses.

I kissed them all goodbye except for Jade. Michael had organized a car to pick me up and she was coming with me. I was arriving after all the guests had had a chance to view my work and then I would make my entrance.

Slipping into my designer dress I felt a million dollars and looked pretty good. As we drove into town in the black, sleek Jaguar, I looked at Jade.

"I can't ever thank you enough," I whispered, tears filling my eyes.

"Hey missy, watch that eye make-up. Maxime will be furious if you smudge." And she passed me a tissue.

"I mean it, Jade. If I hadn't met you that day…"

"You wouldn't have had hot coffee poured all over you."

"Now that's true," I agreed and we both laughed out loud.

The driver pulled up outside the gallery and opened the door for us to get out. I could see people wondering about and it was quite busy.

'Wow, looks like a great turnout," Jade said to me and acknowledging the driver.

"I can't believe it," I said, bewildered at the thought of all these people here to see my work.

Michael greeted us at the top of the steps, beaming and rubbing his hands together.

"Jennifer, can I just say how beautiful you look. Just like one of your paintings, a vision." He kissed us both on our cheeks and smiling at Jade, told her she too was looking stunning.

"Michael, you've done an amazing job," I said, stepping aside as a group of people arrived.

"It's going very well," he started to say, when a young woman dressing in black and white appeared at the doorway.

"Excuse me, Mr Kingston, it's time," she informed him and turned to go back inside.

"Time for what?" I frowned.

"Come on my dear," he replied, linking us one in each arm. "You'll see, you'll see."

Jade looked at me and grinned. Michael really was, as she had once put it, the campest straight man she had ever met.

Inside the gallery, the atmosphere was electric. People were talking amongst themselves, standing heads cocked, discussing MY paintings. Talking about ME! Two stunning waitresses and one to-die-for waiter also dressed in black and white, mingled between the guests serving them champagne and canapés. Soft relaxing music played in the background and my work was hung at different levels all around the room.

It was perfect. Michael hadn't let me near the place since yesterday afternoon and now I know why. He wanted to surprise me and not let me worry about the empty spaces not filled until now with people. He was a Godsend.

He ushered me over to the far end of the room where there was a large desk complete with lamp and a guest book open for people to write their comments. An elegant brunette with a high ponytail and glasses sat behind it, taking details from sales that had been made.

Michael turned to face the crowd and the music stopped. I looked at him, not sure what was about to happen.

"Ladies and Gentlemen," he announced, "if I could have your attention for just a moment…" he paused, waiting for everyone to give them their full attention. "As you know, this is the first showing of Jennifer Aagar's work and I think you'll all agree with me when I say it won't be her last." People began to clap and I began to blush. "To those of you who will be leaving disappointed at not making a purchase this evening, I would like again to assure you that her new work will be shown at her next exhibition in six months time."

I looked at him in disbelief. I couldn't believe what I was hearing. We hadn't discussed another display and all my work was here. There was nothing left other than the paintings hanging here on the walls.

"As I've said," Michael went on, "I'll be in touch with each and everyone of you who have raised questions about other paintings Ms Aagar will be doing, so without further ado, I would like to introduce you all to Jennifer Aagar."

I smiled and felt my neck on fire, thanking my lucky stars I hadn't gone for a dress with a low neckline. Everyone clapped and I simply stood there, surveying the room and waiting for them to stop. I tried to take it all in and prayed I wouldn't have to make a speech.

Someone, who I vaguely recognized though couldn't place, started to walk through the crowd towards me. She stopped and waved her hands in the air to get my attention.

"Excuse me. Can I just ask one little question?" she called out and Michael nodded for her to continue. "Thank you. Claire Webster, local MP, I just wanted to say how impressed I am with your work Ms Aagar and I wondered if you had any further paintings for sale similar to the ones over there." And she pointed to the two cottage paintings.

"Oh," I said, quietly, clearing my throat. "But they are for sale. You can buy them here tonight."

"No!" she exclaimed. "They're already sold."

"As is everything, my dear Claire, as is everything," Michael interrupted, coming to my rescue. "The cottages are a limited edition, they came as a pair and have been sold as such, but don't despair, I'm going to have a private chat with you in a moment. Now, If I may," and he clicked his fingers as the lights dimmed and 'happy birthday to you' rang out through the speakers. "Please join me in celebrating Jennifer's birthday." A huge cake with candles appeared carried in by the handsome waiter. I wanted to die of embarrassment.

As everyone sang and clapped and camera's flashed, I blew out the candles, unable to make a wish as my head spun and after all, weren't all my wishes coming true right now, right here in this room? Totally overwhelmed, I thanked everyone, especially Michael and my family for all their support.

It was just as I'd finished speaking that I saw them. All of them, together in one place and I swear my heart stopped. Everyone went back to private conversations and I stood there, frozen. It was as if time had literally stood still. Noise ceased and everything went into a blurred kind of slow motion. I felt dizzy as faces became unrecognisable, except for theirs!

Simon, Sarah, Greg and Alex, past, my present and my (wish it could be) future. They were all there, mingling with each other, each unaware of their significance in my life.

I suddenly knew what to expect from the menopause. I flushed from my toes to my face, beads of sweat appearing on my forehead and my mouth was as dry as the desert. I knew I couldn't stand there for another second and I quickly made a getaway, looking for the toilets. I headed in the opposite direction to the four I wanted to avoid and hoped it was the right direction.

Once inside the ladies' toilets, I leaned on a basin and looked at my reflection in the mirror. My face was bright red. I let out a sigh as if I'd run a marathon...I felt like I HAD run a marathon! My heart was beating so fast and so loud it was echoing inside my ears. My hands were shaking and my legs had turned to jelly. Why had my life, since Simon had left at least, turned into some kind of dreadful pantomime?

I was just wondering who on earth had invited these people, when the door opened, and I looked up to see an attractive brunette in her early twenties, walking towards me with some gusto.

"I know who YOU are," she announced, taking me a little by surprise.

"I'm sorry?" I stood up straight and turned to face her. I definitely didn't know her.

"Greg's told me ALL about you!" she exclaimed, her eyes almost popping out of their sockets.

I couldn't think what that meant and even though I tried to speak, I couldn't. No words came, my mouth was dry and I was not feeling too good.

"You're the one who split him and Tea up! She was pregnant and you didn't give a fuck! He told me how you kept chasing him, couldn't leave him alone." She was chewing on some gum, looking at me with disgust, hands on her hips and shaking her head.

"I can assure you," I retaliated, finding my voice. "It wasn't like that at ALL!" It was now my turn to emphasize my words.

"You should be ashamed of yourself, a woman of your age. He didn't wanna come tonight, but I said to him, 'you go and hold your head high'. Just coz you're some big-to-do artist doesn't mean you're better than him you know." She paused for a moment and then it was as if a light bulb had suddenly gone on in her head. "Can I ask you somethin?"

"Oh, ask away..." I said, in utter disbelief.

"Did he erm...you know...pull out?"

"I beg your pardon?"

"Greg...when you were 'avin sex. Did he pull out?" As if this was the run of the mill question, she opened her clutch bag and searched for her lip gloss, all signs of anger at my apparent bad behaviour seemingly gone. She pouted in the mirror and touched up her botoxed lips (okay, so I had also become a bitch since my marriage ended – apparently). "That's what all the girls at the gym say. He doesn't want another kiddie situation, so he pulls out."

"Really?" That was all I could manage to say. I cringed inside at the thought of my fling and passionate evenings with Greg Smythe, the man who 'pull's out'.

She snapped her bag shut, checked herself in the full-length mirror before walking out and leaving me standing there, praying to God no one else was in either of the two toilets. I gingerly pushed the doors open one by one and relief swept over me when I discovered they were both empty.

Taking an extremely deep breath I made my way back to the main room. Simon and Sarah were now talking to Michael. "Oh God," I muttered to myself, walking over to them.

"Jen!" Simon called out as he noticed me walking over to them. "WOW!" he exclaimed. "They're amazing, all of them," he said, gesturing to my work on the walls. "Well done."

"Thank you, Simon," I replied, a little taken aback by his praise and complete enthusiasm.

"Yes," Sarah added, a little timidly. "Congratulations." She managed a smile, but avoided eye contact with me. She was heavily pregnant and it showed.

"Now," Michael blurted out, as if sensing an awkward silence was about to hit us. "If you'll excuse us, I have to introduce Jennifer to the buyer of the cottage paintings, he's been asking after her all evening." He took me by the arm and led me towards the paintings, which were hanging near the entrance, giving me no time to process the feeling I had upon seeing Sarah.

Two little red dots stuck on the wall underneath them, informed me that they were indeed sold. "We've had so much interest in these two," he told me as, much to my relief, I noticed Greg Smythe and his ever so young friend leave.

"They're my favourites, I have to say," I said, slightly sad that they'd be leaving me.

"Well, we sold them first thing to our first customer through the door. Now where is he?" He surveyed the room looking for the mystery buyer, and leaning in said, in a low voice, "he paid full price!"

"Great," I said, struggling to accept this was all really happening.

"Aah, there you are," he called out, "Mr Stone." Alex! It was Alex who had bought the paintings. This night was turning out to be like a scene from a 'Carry on' movie. "Mr Stone, this is Ms Aagar."

"Yes, I know," Alex beamed and shook my hand anyway. "We've already met." I slightly grimaced at him and I searched the room for his wife or his mistress, though I couldn't see either of them. "I love your work, Ms Aagar," he said, a slight sarcasm in his voice.

"Please, call me Jen," I said, in a far more sarcastic voice than I had intended.

"It's funny though…" he started to say, eyeing up the paintings around the room and he laughed.

"What? What's funny?" I asked, becoming a little irritated by him.

"Oh, I don't know, I just thought there would be more paintings of birds, of the exotic type." He shot me a glance, a look of triumph on his face.

I wasn't laughing.

"Birds?" asked a rather bemused Michael.

"Yes, our Jen here has an excellent eye for bird spotting."

"Really?" Michael looked at me. "Well, I'm sure Jennifer will get to work on them as soon as she plans the next stage of her work."

Aunt Rose joined us and it was a welcome relief. She looked so proud and her eyes were lit up with excitement. "Oh darling, it's so lovely to see all your work displayed like this. Oh now then," she said, spotting Alex. "Who is this dashing gentleman?"

"This is Alex Stone. Alex, my Aunt Rose."

"A pleasure to meet you." He smiled, bending down and kissing her gently on the cheek. I didn't get a kiss and something in me just snapped.

"He's married!" I blurted out to the shock of anyone within listening distance. "Married, but having a fling on the side it would appear. Isn't that right, Mr Stone? Though it seems as if he is unaccompanied this evening."

Staying composed, despite my outburst and the fact that most of the room had stopped to listen, he turned to Aunt Rose. "It was a pleasure to meet you Rose," he said softly. He nodded at Michael and then turned to look at me. "I was married, yes, you're right," he began, as I stood there, waiting for the ground to open up and swallow me. "Sadly, my beautiful wife died a few years ago and the lady you saw me with the other evening, well she was a date. So, you're wrong, I'm not having an affair. It was my first date since my wife died. I didn't arrange to see the lovely lady again however, because for some strange reason, and at this very moment, I can't imagine why, I had hoped to take you out."

I said nothing. What was there to say? There was nothing I could say. As he walked out of the door and out of my life, all I could think about was the cottage. There was no way I could buy it now after what had just happened.

It then dawned on me, that in the world of Estate Agents, I would be known as Jennifer Aagar – the woman who pulled out!

Chapter 33

Two weeks after the exhibition and many hours of feeling utter shame, I was finally, slowly starting to feel as if I could face the world again. Aunt Rose had been horrified by my behaviour and I had an awful lot of explaining to do.

Thankfully due to her total and unconditional love for me, she soon felt pity rather than disgust. Michael, in his usual way, had managed to sweep me away from prying eyes and whispering tongues, back to where Louise, Isobelle and James were gathered and hadn't mentioned it since.

Then finally, as if in some cruel, ironic twist of fate, Sarah's waters had broken. Suddenly, all eyes and wagging tongues focused on that and my outrageous episode was forgotten, or at least mopped away with the waters.

So that was that. Baby Sophia was born later that evening and we would forever share the same birthday. Apparently, Sarah had been experiencing niggles and contractions all day.

It was a strange feeling, watching your husband's mistress/new partner, being ferried off to hospital to give birth, but I didn't feel any pangs of sadness or bitterness. It wasn't the child's fault and this baby would be a huge part of my children's lives and was an innocent in all of this.

Life went on. Simon was once again a father. My children had a baby sister and I had found a new career to keep me busy, not forgetting two mischievous puppies to take care of.

Thankfully I hadn't bumped into Alex since that dreaded evening. I had called the agents on the Monday morning to withdraw my interest in the cottage. I hadn't had the heart to look for anything else since. I knew I would have to start looking, and soon, but not yet.

My paintings were coming along nicely. I had started to sketch out a pregnant woman and continued along the theme of a babe in arms etc., inspired of course by little Sophia. Michael had kept in touch and was already talking about another showing of my work towards the end of September. This kept me busy and kept my mind off recent events.

One sunny Saturday morning, I was about to head out to the summerhouse to paint, when the phone rang. It was Louise. She wanted to come and stay with me over the weekend. At first I thought it was another mercy mission, but something in her voice told me it was more about her. Something wasn't right. I didn't ask her any questions over the phone, instead deciding I'd wait until she arrived to see if she wanted to talk or not.

Max and Millie went wild when she arrived, jumping up and licking her face. Though I have to say, this was only allowed with the children. With me, strangers and any other family members, this was forbidden.

I'd prepared a tasty prawn salad in a home-made cocktail sauce, with fresh crusty brown bread for our lunch. We sat down to eat at the kitchen table, not a glass of wine in sight, thinking she'd be relieved at that.

She looked so pretty in a red T-shirt and white jeans, and I studied her for a moment. She seemed to have lost weight since I'd last seen her, about ten days ago when she popped in after visiting the baby. She had taken the arrival of Sophia far better than I'd anticipated, even though she hadn't quite accepted Sarah, so it couldn't be that on her mind.

"How's things?" I asked, brushing her long dark hair away from her face and kissing her forehead lightly.

"Oh, okay." She smiled, but looked a little apprehensive.

"Right then, tuck in."

"Shall I open a bottle of wine?" she asked, getting up from the table and opening the cooler.

"Yeah, sure," I replied, a little surprised and now I knew something wasn't right. I watched her closely as she opened the bottle. Sunlight shone in through the kitchen window and I realised, no engagement ring.

She poured each of us a glass and set the bottle in the middle of the table. We ate in silence for a little while, me searching for the right words to say, wondering if I should mention the ring at all.

"I hope salad's okay, I just thought with the warm weather…"

"Michael and me split up last night," she interrupted, bluntly.

"Oh, I'm sorry to hear that, darling." I put my hand on top of hers. A tear fell down her cheek and she pulled away to wipe it from her face. "What on earth happened?"

"I…I…" she sniffed, shaking her head. "I don't know Mum, I just don't know."

"Do you still love Michael?"

"Yes! I love him so much. He's kind, funny and he takes such good care of me."

"Then what's happened?"

"Scott!" she replied, bluntly, and finishing the wine in her glass in one go, she reached for the bottle. "Bloody Scott. That's what's happened."

"What's happened with Scott?" I asked, finishing my glass and topping myself up too. "I thought you'd cut all ties with him." She shot me a glance. "Izzie told me, but only because I'd enquired. She didn't give me any other details."

"She didn't tell you why we split up?"

"No, darling. Honestly."

"I found him with someone else. It wasn't long after…after Dad. She was a friend of ours. He'd been distant for a while, but you know me. I just ignored it. Then one Saturday I went out shopping. I realised I'd left my purse in another bag, so I went back and caught them in our bed. He moved out the next day."

"I can't believe it! I wish you'd told me, Lou. It just doesn't sound like the Scott we all knew and loved. I'm so sorry…"

"It's okay, Mum. Things, like I said, weren't good for a long time. I'd already got to know Michael and he was a good friend to me through it all, then, well, we just got closer…" the tears came again.

"So, how does Scott come into all of this?"

"I met with him last week and we had dinner. Dinner and drinks." We looked at each other and we both knew what that meant. "I stayed over and I turned my phone off. Michael was out of his mind with worry and I…I knew he would be. What's wrong with me? How could I have done that to him, Mum?" she sobbed.

"Everyone makes mistakes, Lou," I tried to reassure her, my own recent mistakes at the forefront of my mind. "Did you tell Michael that you were with Scott?" She nodded, putting her face in her hands. "Okay. So, did he tell you it was over?" I asked, rubbing her back.

"No! That's what makes it worse. He said it was okay. But it's NOT okay," she wailed.

"Lou, now you listen to me, if Michael's willing to forgive you, maybe you should try and work things out. Unless of course you don't want to and you want to get back with Scott."

"Oh my God, no! I knew sleeping with Scott again was a mistake immediately. I only stayed over because I couldn't move, I was so ashamed."

"How did you leave things with Michael?"

"He suggested I come and stay here with you and clear my head. How can he be so understanding?"

"Because he loves you, my darling. He waited a long time to find you, maybe he just knows what he wants." I smiled at her. Her eyes were wide open, looking at me for answers.

"Do you really think so?" she sniffed.

"Yes, I do. Why don't you call him and ask him to drive up here tomorrow? Put his mind at rest."

Yeah, I think that's what I'll do. Thanks, Mum." She left the table and taking her mobile phone, she went upstairs to call him.

I sighed with relief because even though she was so upset now, I knew Michael would help her through it and that brought me great comfort. I took our salads, covered them and put them in the fridge for later. Neither of us were really in the mood for eating right now.

****

Louise appeared about an hour later, even though her eyes were red and swollen from crying, she seemed brighter.

She told me that Michael had been relieved to hear her voice and that he wanted the plans for their wedding late next year to go ahead. He was travelling up tomorrow to see her. He certainly was a good man.

I heated up some soup that I'd made the day before and we sat and chatted all evening. Around ten o'clock, exhausted and weary, Louise made her way up to bed. I undressed and snuggled into a bathrobe. I was tired, but not enough to sleep and couldn't face a restless night of tossing and turning, so I settled down in the family room in front of the TV.

It was about half an hour or so later that the doorbell rang. I got up from the sofa and it rang again. I went into the living room and looked out of the window to see who was there. There was a dark Audi on the drive parked behind Louise's mini, but I had no idea who it belonged to.

Not wanting whoever it was to ring the bell again and disturb Louise, I cautiously opened the front door.

I couldn't believe who I saw standing there, and I stood in a shocked silence for some moments.

"Can I come in?"

I could hardly say no. I stood back and let Sarah pass with the baby in her arms. She made her way into the kitchen as if it was the most natural thing to do. I followed her, waiting for her to speak.

"I'm sorry to bother you like this," she said, her eyes misty and looking as if she hadn't slept for days, which she probably hadn't considering she'd got a new baby. "I know I shouldn't have come here…but…I…I just didn't know what else to do."

I settled the puppies back into their bed and thanked God that they were terrible guard dogs and not barked once at the doorbell. I closed the kitchen doors, hoping Louise hadn't heard any of this.

"Has something happened to Simon?" I asked, fearing the worst. She shook her head and collapsed down onto the sofa in the family room. "What's happened, Sarah? Why are you here?"

I automatically started filling the kettle with water to make a pot of tea as it seemed like the right thing to do. This was very awkward.

I prayed that by now Louise was sleeping soundly, not Sarah's biggest fan, I didn't want her to come downstairs. Now that would be especially awkward.

I stayed by the kettle waiting for it to boil, which seemed to be taking an eternity and waited for Sarah to say something. I arranged a tray with cups and a jug of milk and set it on the coffee table.

Once I'd made the tea, I took it over and sat on the chair opposite Sarah. Sophia was sleeping soundly in her arms, thank goodness, and looked like an angel. Sarah still hadn't spoken and I honestly didn't know how to handle this situation. She was my husband's mistress for heaven's sake, the mother of his new child. What were the rules for such events? Did I call Simon? I poured the teas and asked her again.

I sat back in the chair and tucked my legs underneath me, trying to look as though I was completely relaxed, but I was anything but.

"Does Simon know you're here, Sarah?"

She shook her head and slowly lifted her head up to meet my eyes.

"He probably hasn't even noticed we've gone," she muttered and I struggled to catch her words.

"Oh, I'm sure that's not true..." I began.

"It is true! He doesn't care. I don't even think he wants us around." She was becoming distressed and Sophia began to stir. "I can't stand it, I just can't. He's so uncaring, so hard on me..."

"Hey, come on, it's okay." I stood up and sat next to her, handing her a tissue. She looked so completely lost and I knew I was going to have to put any of my own feelings about her to one side for the baby's sake. "Do you want me to call him? Just to let him know that you and the baby are safe?"

"No, please don't," she insisted. "He'll come over, any excuse to see you and I couldn't bare it."

"Sssshhhh. Okay, don't worry I won't. Just calm down, you're going to upset the baby," I said as gently as I could, trying not to sound patronizing. "Why did you come here, Sarah?" I didn't react to what she'd said about Simon wanting to see me.

She looked at me and swallowed hard as if she was scared to speak. "Can you hold her?" She held Sophia out to me. "Please, Jen, just for five minutes. Please?"

I took the little bundle from her and held her close. Funny how something you would have imagined would be the hardest thing you'd ever had to do, turns out to be one of the easiest. She had a real look of Louise when she was born: dark hair, olive skin and the longest eyelashes. My heart melted. Not for one second did I link this baby with their affair. I didn't feel for a moment that she was the result of their deceit.

"She's beautiful, Sarah," I whispered, and my eyes burned with tears.

"Does she remind you of Lou?" she asked, her own tears falling rapidly down her pale cheeks. "Simon says Lou looked just like her."

"Yes, she does have a look of her." I saw a slight hurt in her eyes. "But I can see you in her too." I lied.

I was confused as to how compassionate I was being with the woman who had brought so much pain into my life.

"Drink your tea while it's still hot," I suggested.

She sipped her drink, her eyes heavy, and each time she blinked I felt sure she wasn't going to open them again, sleep not far away.

"Sarah, I have to know why you came to me. I don't understand. Wouldn't you rather be with your parents right now?"

"Oh they'd just love this — Mum especially. She'd say 'I told you so'. I can't tell them, they've never warmed to Simon."

I felt myself warming to them immediately. After all, I was being extremely understanding, but I wasn't a bloody saint.

"But you felt you could talk to me?" The woman he betrayed, I wanted to say, but I stopped myself, this was not the time.

"You must think I've got a nerve." She looked at me and I knew she was hoping I'd be kind.

"Guts, Sarah, I'd say you had guts." And a little smile appeared on her lips.

"I just thought…" she paused for a second, trying to find the right words, "I just thought if anyone could understand what he's like, it would be you."

That was true. I can't deny I didn't feel a flash of pleasure that he was showing his true colours. Pleasure, that their heady days of passion and romantic trips away were now a thing of the past. This was the reality of it all.

It suddenly dawned on me that no matter how beautiful, or how precious Sophia was, she would have been the very last thing that Simon would have wanted or desired when he started his affair with Sarah. It all seemed so pointless now, such a shame.

"He doesn't help at all," she blurted out. "He is so insensitive. I'm so tired and all he does is complain about how he's struggling to work during the day because Sophia is crying all night and disturbing him. Not that he gets up to do his share. I don't know what the hell I ever saw in him," (Holidays, older rich man, by chance?) "I thought he was the most amazing, most wonderful man I'd ever met. I mean, he was so thoughtful, so romantic in the beginning." (Oh, they all are in THE beginning, my dear). "Sure, he became a little distant when I told him I was pregnant, I think he thinks I did it on purpose, but I didn't." (Didn't you? Hmm I wonder).

She went on and on and on. She was getting everything and I mean EVERYTHING off her little chest, and I wanted to shake her and scream at her to 'shut up'. It was difficult to hear all about your husband's romantic gestures whilst they were having an affair behind my back, how he'd told her he couldn't live without her…it took all my strength to constrain myself and not slap her across the face.

In the end, I didn't need to do anything. The sight of Louise standing in the doorway was enough to make her silent.

Chapter 34

"What the hell is SHE doing here?" Louise yelled. She stood there in a pair of bright pink pyjamas, her hair all over the place, looking like a small child herself, eyes squinting.

"Lou, it's okay, darling," I said, getting off the sofa.

"Oh my God!" she screeched at the sight of Sophia in my arms. Horror filled her face and she rushed past me and confronted Sarah. "Get out of my parent's home. Now! How dare you come here, how dare you!"

"Lou," I said, softly, trying to calm her down as Sophia began to whimper. "Go back to bed. Honestly, everything's okay."

"No! Don't you say this is okay, Mum, this whole situation is not okay. Just for once, stand up for yourself." She turned back to face a frightened looking Sarah. "What's wrong, Sarah?" she said in a sarcastic tone. "Couldn't wait to measure up for your curtains, imagine your own furniture in our house?"

"It wasn't like that…" Sarah started to say.

"Oh and just what was it like? Wanted to show off the baby to Mum? Kill her, just a little bit more! You little bitch!"

I should have tried harder to stop Louise, but maybe she needed to say these things out loud.

"I just had to…" Sarah tried to explain, but her efforts were futile.

"Had to what, come on, tell me? Had to what?"

"Get out of that flat. Get away from your Father," Sarah said, trembling and running her nervous hands through her lank, greasy hair.

"Oh, oh I see…" Lou was laughing, mocking her. "And the first place you thought to go was here. What the hell is wrong with you? Do you have no compassion? Can you imagine what this must be doing to her?" She turned, pointing at me.

"I know, I'm so sorry. I just needed to talk to someone. I can't cope. I didn't know what else to do. I'm not thinking straight...I am so sorry." Sarah started to sob uncontrollably.

I decided the best thing to do was to put the baby upstairs in the guest room away from the shouting. Louise's voice was getting louder and louder and Sarah was getting more and more upset. It wasn't good for the baby to be around that. I carried her upstairs without them noticing me leave the room and settled her down with pillows all around to prevent her moving.

I stood there for a little while and looked at the little bundle sleeping peacefully, blissfully unaware of the drama filling her parents lives. My heart almost ached at the thought of the circumstances that brought her into the world, into my world. Right in this moment, I knew the human capacity for forgiveness, I didn't understand it, but I recognized it because I felt it.

Hearing Louise ripping into Sarah, I went back downstairs. She was saying such terrible things to Sarah, things that shouldn't have been said, and I prayed that Simon had chosen another understanding woman who would one day be able to forgive the dreadful things she was hearing.

"Louise!" I said sternly upon entering the room. "That's enough now. Please!"

"Are you serious?" Louise asked me, horrified, and I knew that she felt betrayed and that I was protecting Sarah instead of her. "I can't believe this. How the hell can you stand there telling me it's enough? You sat here holding their love child in your arms whilst she was describing in full detail how you're fucking husband shagged her brains out, while you were here at home probably ironing his fucking shirts like the downtrodden woman you are! No wonder he left you!" She started to walk away and as she reached the hallway, she turned to me. "What I'll never understand is why he left you for HER! She's not even pretty. She can't even look after my baby sister, she's pathetic!"

Sarah and I looked at each other, both weary, neither of us knowing what to say. I sat next to her on the sofa and we stayed there for a long time in silence.

Finally she sighed heavily, "I'm sorry for coming here. I don't know what I was thinking...well, I clearly wasn't. I should go and check on the baby," she said, starting to get up, but I put my arm out to stop her.

"She's fine. I put her in the guest room, the door's wide open and we'd hear her if she cries."

"But Louise..." she started to say and I beckoned her to sit down.

"Don't worry about Louise. She adores your daughter, she's just having problems at the moment and unfortunately, you're one of them."

"Simon was right about you. You are amazing," she sniffed.

"He said that?" I had to ask. I passed her another tissue.

"All the time. Well, since he left you anyway. I think all this has been a case of the grass is always greener...I think he'd come back here, back to you, tomorrow if he could." Her eyes were filled with pain.

"Well, firstly, he can't come back here, and secondly, he's made his bed. He has to lie in it."

"Honestly? You don't want him back?"

"Honestly. Sarah, I loved my husband more than anything. I thought we were forever, and that once James had gone to university we'd have time for us, time to enjoy all that we'd worked for together..." my words trailed off at the sadness of it all. "Look," I continued, trying to hold myself together. "I think Simon is struggling with your new circumstances. Don't forget, he's a lot older than you and he's gone out to work everyday when we had our three, I brought the children up, that's just the way it was. He isn't used to changing nappies or ironing his own shirts. You two need to sit down and talk. Simon needs to face up to his responsibilities now."

"God, you must hate me."

"No," I reassured her, "I don't hate you."

"Jennifer," she whispered, her head hanging in shame. "I'm so sorry what we did to you. Can you forgive me?"

"In time. They say time's a healer."

Before I could say another word, she flung her arms around me, holding on tightly and saying over and over how sorry she was.

I let her hold on to me and I managed to put my arms around her. I found myself breathing her in. It was not how I'd imagined Sarah West to smell, all those times when I'd looked at her pictures on Facebook. I'd wondered, ridiculously, what perfume she used, how she smelt when Simon was making love to her.

Of course, this probably wasn't fair play to her, she had just had a baby and there was a faint smell of vomit. She was still carrying some of her baby weight and she felt fleshy under her baggy sweatshirt.

I realised then that this was probably what Simon was thinking. The fragrant smelling, young-bodied woman he'd spent passionate nights with was gone for the moment and a crying, screaming baby had taken her place.

Part of me actually felt sorry for them both, part of me felt they deserved it. And then there was the part of me who finally saw that I had a whole new life in front of me and it was wonderful...puppies and all.

****

I had insisted that Sarah stayed the night. She was in no fit state to drive home. I settled her into the guest room where Sophia was sleeping soundly and I had a feeling that Sarah would sleep well also. I closed the door quietly so as not to disturb them.

Then I peeped in on Louise. She was, surprisingly, also fast asleep. I was relieved that I didn't have to have a discussion about my decision to let them stay over. I was too tired.

It was one-thirty in the morning and I crept back downstairs and called Simon. It was a weary voice that answered.

"Simon," I said in a hushed voice and closed the study door. "It's me, Jen."

"Jen?" It was obvious I had woken him. "What's wrong? Has something happened to the children?"

Well yes it had, but not to the children he was referring to.

"I just thought you should know that Sarah and the baby are staying here tonight?"

"What?" he asked, now he was wide-awake. 'What do you mean, they're staying at yours?"

I started to explain to him what had happened and he was in utter shock, not even aware that they'd left the house as he had gone to bed early.

"God, I'm sorry, Jen," he said. Suddenly, everyone was sorry. "She shouldn't have done that."

"Well, she did and we can't turn back the clock now." If only we could. I didn't want him to think I was a complete pushover or down trodden as Lou had described me earlier. "The worst thing of all is that Lou is here and she didn't react very well to Sarah being here. I think you should come over in the morning and try to sort out this mess."

"I can't in the morning, it's not possible. I have back-to-back meetings all day."

"Then I suggest you cancel them and be here at eight. Like you would have done to meet Sarah all those months ago!" I couldn't help myself.

I hung up. What a selfish bastard. No wonder Sarah had walked out. Incredibly, my alliance was with her now and he would have to deal with the situation he had created. I should have been more furious, but somehow and much to my relief, I couldn't be bothered!

Chapter 35

At seven-thirty the next morning, I was already dressed and downstairs waiting for Simon to arrive. I'd heard Sarah moving about with Sophia in the night, but she'd stayed in the bedroom. I'd snuck in before I went to bed with clean towels so that she could take a shower in the guest bathroom when she woke up. Both her and Sophia had been fast asleep.

I was starting to agree with Simon, I was bloody amazing after all. My only conclusion was that any love I'd had for him had died. If I still loved him, I'm sure I wouldn't be able to deal with my guests.

Around eight o'clock I heard his car on the gravel outside. As it was such a lovely morning, I put the puppies in the garden, I didn't want them fussing around us. I opened the front door and was waiting there as he walked up the path. I signalled for him to be quiet and gently shut the door. He followed me into the kitchen and closed the doors over.

"Coffee?" I asked, and he nodded, throwing his keys onto the kitchen table, a sound I hadn't missed. I glanced over at him disapprovingly.

He looked tired and older. I thought back to the day we took James to university and remembered how handsome he'd looked, how I'd thought we were going to get our lives back, share happy times, make new memories.

I shook my head, wanting these thoughts gone.

"What?' he asked, studying me as I made coffee.

"What?" I said, frowning.

"You were shaking your head."

"Was I?" I carried our coffees into the family room and placed the mugs on the coffee table. "Let's sit in here."

"You definitely shook your head just then," he insisted, sitting next to me and I'd wished I'd sat on the chair instead of the sofa.

"Maybe it's a nervous twitch I've developed since you left and your new family came to stay." I couldn't resist a dig at him.

He sighed and reached for his drink. I felt sure he'd regret sitting so close. Sighing again, he ran his fingers through his hair, a trait that reminded me of James. He looked at me.

"I'm sorry, Jen," he said softly and my heart ached a little at his words. "Everything's such a mess. I know, I know," he said, as I raised my eyebrows. "It's all my own fault. I deserve everything I get. Isn't that what you're thinking?"

"I'm thinking," I began, flabbergasted, "that you have a beautiful baby daughter upstairs sleeping in our guest room and a...a..." I couldn't find the right words for Sarah. "A very distressed partner sleeping right next to her. In OUR guest room, at her wits end, I might add. What on earth happened, Simon? How could you have let it get this bad?"

I watched in silence as he held his head in his hands and sobbed. He cried like I'd never seen him cry before. I wanted to reach out and hold him, but I didn't. I couldn't. I just sat there and let him get it all out, he'd obviously been holding on to all of this for a long time. I listened for movements from upstairs and kept an eye on the glass doors that led into the hallway.

The thought of Louise, Simon, Sarah and myself all coming together in the same place at the same time, filled me with horror. Unfortunately, it was inevitable. We were going to be together, in the family home, a now broken family.

Finally, I gave in to my gut instinct and moved closer to Simon and held him in my arms, hoping that neither Lou or Sarah came in at this moment. He gave into me too and tucked his head into my neck. We hadn't been so intimate in such a long time that something inside me stirred, but it wasn't lust or passion, it was pity.

Eventually, totally exhausted, he stopped crying.

"I'm so sorry for what I've done to you, Jen. I hope that one day you can forgive me." He sniffed.

I gave him a comforting squeeze, slowly taking my arms away from his body and backed away from him. He glanced at me as if he were a small boy being abandoned. Wiping his eyes, he sat back in the sofa, completely spent.

"Lou," he said, noticing our eldest daughter standing there watching us.

"Hello, Dad," she said softly, a sad expression on her face.

"Mum, about last night, the things I said…" she looked almost ashamed.

"Darling, it's okay," I said, getting up to hug her and so relieved she had calmed down after a good night's sleep. "I'm sure Sarah understands."

'I don't mean what I said to her," she began, hugging me back for just a second. "I'm sorry for what I said to you. I didn't mean any of it."

"Hey, come on, it's alright. Sit down and I'll make you a cup of tea. This is a very difficult situation. For all of us."

"It's all my fault," Simon said, as Lou plonked herself next to him. "I promise you, Lou, I will spend every day trying to make it up to you. To you all."

I stood back, busying myself in the kitchen, whilst Simon held on to Louise. I set the table for four of us and made scrambled eggs on toast.

When it was ready, Simon and Louise helped themselves and I went upstairs. I found it incredible to think that Simon hadn't once attempted to see his daughter or Sarah, instead chatting to Louise and eating breakfast.

I certainly didn't feel it was my place to tell him he probably should have – no, he would have to make his own mistakes now. At least he was making a huge effort with our daughter, something he should have done in the beginning.

I knocked on the bedroom door where Sarah was sleeping. Slowly, I opened the door. She was on her side facing Sophia, fast asleep. The baby was on her back, awake and gurgling away to herself.

"Sarah," I whispered, almost not wanting to wake her from such a sound sleep and she stirred a little. I sat on the edge of the bed. "Sarah…Simon's downstairs."

She opened her eyes slowly, confusion crossed them as she struggled to know where she was, before reality reminded her, and she started to sit up, rubbing her eyes.

"Okay," she said, groggily. "I'll get up now."

"Take your time, have a shower. I've made breakfast, so when you're ready…"

"Thank you, Jen. I hope we didn't disturb you too much in the night."

"No, not at all," I said, opening the curtains. "Do you feel able to get ready and see Simon?"

She nodded, a piece of hair flopping down into her eyes.

"Right then, shall I take Sophia downstairs?"

"You're so kind, yes thanks."

"Don't worry, I'll be passing her on to her Daddy." I winked, taking Sophia from her.

"I'll never forget your kindness," she said, as I closed the door behind me and went back downstairs.

Later when Sarah had joined us all in the kitchen, I insisted she eat the plate of food I'd kept warm in the oven for her. I'd made a pot of coffee, and decided to go and get showered and dressed myself. I decided it best to leave them all to it. Louise grabbed a jacket and announced she was taking the dogs for a walk. It was good that Simon could be alone with Sarah to try and sort out their problems.

As I just finished getting dressed Louise knocked on my door and popped her head in.

"Do you think they'll sort things out?" she asked me, closing the bedroom door and flopping onto my bed. She looked concerned and I guess she was worried for Sophia, who, after all was her half-sister.

"I hope so, Lou. I really hope so."

"Do you…is there…" she started to say biting her lower lip and regretting starting to ask me the question she desperately wanted the answer to.

"Go on, darling, what did you want to say?" I sat next to her on the bed.

"Is there a part of you that wants Dad back?"

I took her hands in mine and smiled. I replied as honestly as I could. "Not a single part of me, Lou. I'm sorry if that's upsetting to hear."

"God, no!" she replied in a flash. "I was worried that maybe you did and that would have killed me. I've been so worried about you, Izzie and James have too, but you've got through it all and we're so pleased. I think taking Dad back would have been a step backwards for you."

"Well, you don't need to worry about me any more, I'm absolutely fine, honestly."

"So, I think it's time I went and apologized to Sarah for last night."

"Good idea," I said, smiling at her. "Don't beat yourself up too much, I think she understands better than you might think she does."

"You think?"

I nodded and, taking a deep breath, she went off to find Sarah.

As I sat there in my bedroom wondering what to do with myself, the doorbell rang. Rushing downstairs to open the door, I felt such a relief to see the comforting, smiling face of Michael.

Simon, Sarah and Louise had locked themselves away in the living room, so I ushered Michael through the kitchen and into the garden. He sat down on the garden sofa and I made yet another pot of coffee. He listened as I explained about last night's events, sympathizing with the situation I found myself in.

We didn't talk about his situation with Louise. I knew it was something private between the two of them and I also knew it would all be okay. He was going nowhere, his love for my eldest daughter was so apparent.

As Louise opened the doors from the lounge into the family room, she saw Michael and me sitting in the garden and ran to hug him. I decided it was safe to go back inside and prepare some lunch. Keeping myself busy, doing what I did best. I was looking through the cupboards for some inspiration when the home phone rang.

"Jen!" The familiar voice of Anna cried out (I hadn't heard anything from her, and I have to admit, it took me a little by surprise).

"Oh, Anna. Hello," I said, as politely as I could.

"You're quite the dark horse aren't you?" she continued, "I've heard all about the exhibition, my invite must have got lost in the post, I suppose. Anyway, I hear it went very well." I waited for a 'congratulations' or 'well done', but none came. "I'm hosting a coffee morning this Tuesday and I thought how fabulous it would be if you came along. Bring some of your paintings along if you wish."

"I'm so sorry, Anna," I said without any hesitation whatsoever. "But I can't."

"Oh...you're sure?" she asked, clearly taken aback at my blunt refusal. "Everyone will be there."

By 'everyone' I presumed she meant 'friends' who hadn't picked up the phone once to see how I was doing, friends who I'd known and socialized with for so many years, who hadn't cared less about me.

"Actually, Anna," I said abruptly and taking great pleasure in knowing that what I was about to say, would give her enough gossip to last throughout the coffee morning and probably into next year. "I can't stay chatting, I'm extremely busy here with visitors and the baby is keeping me on my toes."

"Baby?" she gasped. "But...who's had a baby?"

I took a deep breath and great pleasure picturing her face before I informed her it was Simon's baby. "She's an absolute delight, now if you'll excuse me..." and with that, I hung up.

I couldn't resist, I jumped up and down on the spot, silently clapping my hands in sheer delight, only to turn around and discover Simon, Sarah, Michael and Louise standing watching me. They looked bemused and had obviously heard the whole thing.

"Well," I beamed, "that'll give her something to really talk about!"

We all stood there, laughing. For the moment, totally united.

Chapter 36

Michael and Louise left soon after. I'd suggested they get home and start living their lives. I felt like Oprah, putting the world to rights. Simon, Sarah and Sophia (the three S's) stayed a little while longer. I really felt as if I'd made them a little too welcome and I couldn't wait for them to leave, though I doubted if they ever would, they seemed so relaxed sitting in my kitchen at my table.

Sarah literally worshipped the ground I walked on which was completely ridiculous and I felt like a complete fraud. It was lucky she couldn't read my mind or she would know I wasn't the 'amazing' woman she thought I was. What an unusual situation this was becoming, however, it was better than the alternative, me being the hated ex-wife as was the case in most divorces.

When they finally got up to leave, Simon helped Sarah put Sophia in the car, before coming back to speak to me as I stood in the doorway.

He looked at me with such sadness and regret. "Stay here, in our house, for as long as you want. I won't push anything, Jen. Thank you, for everything."

I waved them off and closing the door behind me, I realised a year ago, I would have given anything to hear those words about the house, but deep down I knew, I wouldn't move on until I moved out.

I hadn't settled down to do anything in particular once I found myself alone again with puppies, who were sleeping, exhausted after their walk with Louise. I had planned to paint, but somehow, I just wasn't in the mood.

I made a cup of tea and cut myself a slice of chocolate cake left over from lunch. I had just taken a huge bite when the doorbell rang. I hadn't enough time to swallow it and without a clue who it could be, I opened the door.

Stood there, handsome as ever, dressed casually in a shirt and jeans, Alex smiled at me holding a bouquet of flowers and a bottle of champagne.

"Alex!" I cried out, spitting chocolate cake all over him, mortified once again as he brushed crumbs from his crisp white shirt.

"Hello," he said, handing me the flowers and pretending the cake incident hadn't just happened.

"Gosh, thank you, they're beautiful. Come in, come in," I said, stepping back to allow him in. "Well, I have to say this is a surprise, a nice one, but a surprise nonetheless."

"I know. Look, I saw your Aunt Rose last week and she explained that you've had a lot going on this past year…"

"Nooo…." I squirmed, imagining Aunt Rose filling him in on all aspects of my life. "I'm sorry about that." I checked my teeth in the hall mirror and ran my tongue along them in the hopes of ridding any traces of chocolate sponge.

"No, don't be. She's an absolute delight, and then, when I saw that the cottage was sold, I thought I'd pop round and help you celebrate." He jokingly showed me the champagne as if he were a waiter in a restaurant.

"It's sold?" I asked, disappointment written all over my face, even though I hadn't expected to be buying it now after all.

"Well yes," he continued, placing the bottle on the kitchen table. "I just presumed…" his voice trailed off, sounding as disappointed as I felt.

"Oh well. Never mind. It just wasn't meant to be." I pulled myself together and offered him a coffee instead. "Anyway, I'm glad someone's going to restore it."

Over coffee he told me how he was an architect and that he'd already started drawing up plans for the cottage, thinking I was the new owner. He described his ideas and I felt as if salt was being rubbed into my wounds, though this wasn't his intention.

I apologized to him for my disgraceful behaviour at the exhibition, but much like with the chocolate cake, he brushed it off, explaining that Aunt Rose had told him how ashamed I had felt.

Apparently, she had paid him a visit a few days earlier at his home and at the end of her visit he was convinced we'd be neighbours. It was clear he was very downhearted that we wouldn't be.

We chatted away and I felt so comfortable in his company. He told me all about his wife, Christina. She had died three years ago during a difficult labour and he lost the baby, a little boy, also. My heart went out to him and I couldn't imagine the pain and heartache he must have gone through.

He went on to say that it had taken a long time, but that the day he had met me in the woods was the first time he had laughed so much since Christina had passed away.

"And then I went on that stupid date. A blind date I might add, set up by a friend of a friend of a friend! I kept looking out for you in the park, but I never saw you again, so I agreed to go along." He paused and looked straight into my eyes, a long intensive look that made my stomach flip. "And then, there you were." He grinned. "I took that as a sign."

It was the most perfect moment for the most perfect kiss, and we lingered in the moment for some time, but unfortunately, this was the same moment that Max and Millie had woken up and jumped all over Alex, ruining any chance of a romantic tryst. I knew he probably wasn't the type who believed in 'signs' and I also knew there would be other moments like these and that there was no rush. The fact that the puppies appeared to adore him, just made me want him more.

Two coffees later he had to go, but we made arrangements to see each other the next evening at his place. He was going to cook for me and I wanted to jump for joy, but I felt I'd done enough jumping for one day.

"Oh, here, don't forget your champagne," I said as he was leaving.

"You know what," he suggested, kissing me goodbye on my cheek. "Keep it. Wait until you have something special to celebrate."

Once Alex had gone, I called Aunt Rose to thank her for taking the time to go and talk with him. There was no reply and it went immediately to the answer machine. I was in the middle of leaving her a message when the doorbell rang. I wondered if it was Alex coming back.

I left her a rushed message and opened the front door.

"Afternoon, my dear," Aunt Rose said, cheerfully and kissing me on the cheek. "What a beautiful day."

"I just tried to call you. I wanted to say thank you."

"What for, dear?" she asked, taking off a pale pink linen jacket and heading for the hub of the house, my kitchen.

"Alex has just left." I nodded at her as she raised her eyebrows in surprise. "Whatever you said to him, it worked."

"Of course it did," she remarked, matter-of-factly. She sat down at the table and put a small, rectangular box tied with a silky silver ribbon in front of her. "Come and sit down, I've something I want to give you." I looked at the box and wondered what it could be. "I want you to have this," and she pushed the box towards me. "You've been more like a daughter to me than a niece, Jennifer. I'm sorry your parents haven't been around for you more, to share in your life events, but I hope I've somehow made up for it."

"Aunt Rose, you know you have. I couldn't wish for a better mother figure in my life. Because of you, I've never felt like I've missed out on anything…not one single thing. You've always been there for me and for the children. It's me who should be giving you a gift. Now, what's inside this box anyway?"

"Open it and see!" she said, her eyes lighting up and removing any trace of the tears that had filled them seconds ago.

I started to slowly untie the bow. I wondered if it was some heirloom she'd been waiting to give me when the time was right, a necklace perhaps or earrings?

When I opened it up and saw what was inside, I was a little confused. It wasn't what I had expected. It wasn't some ancient piece of jewellery, but a key. I picked it up and studied it more closely. I looked at Aunt Rose, frowning.

"It's the key to 'Churchview Cottage'," she announced.

"What? But...I thought it was sold..." suddenly everything fell into place. When she'd visited Alex the other day she must have got the key from the agents and thought she'd surprise me with a viewing. "Oh, you're so kind, but it's been sold. Alex told me today. He thought I'd bought it."

She didn't say a word. She just sat there and waited, waited for the penny to drop. It took a few minutes. My mouth fell open as I tried to comprehend what she'd done. I started to object, telling her it was ridiculous, totally over the top and that I couldn't possibly accept it.

"Well you'd better! It's of no use to me."

Apparently she had contacted the Estate Agents after her visit to the cottages and met with the family. She'd put an offer in then and there, and they had accepted immediately. She said there was no point in leaving the money in the bank passing it on to me when she'd died. She wanted to see my enjoyment and she knew that the cottage was where I belonged. Not to mention how lovely my new neighbour-to-be was.

There were no words, just hugs and kisses and a lifetime of love and memories that would bond us together forever.

The next evening I got ready for dinner at my new neighbour's house. As I left, I grabbed the bottle of champagne he had left behind yesterday and I couldn't wait to start celebrating.

One year later…Saturday 3 June 2012

The sun shone in through my bedroom window and I slowly opened my eyes. I stretched out and turned to face Alex, who was still sleeping soundly. I watched him for a moment and smiled.

He stayed over at mine most nights since I'd moved into the cottage, and last night, over a romantic dinner at the restaurant where we'd bumped into each other last year, he proposed. I checked my left hand immediately just to make sure I hadn't dreamt it. But I hadn't. There on my left finger was the platinum diamond solitaire engagement ring, sparkling back at me.

I crept out of bed and grabbed my dressing gown from the back of the bedroom door. I loved waking up next to Alex, but I'd got used to that first cup of coffee on my own in the morning, contemplating the world and I now treasured these few moments I did get alone.

I stood at the top of the stairs and admired the view from the landing window of the fields and the church in the distance. I never thought it was possible to fall in love with another house, but I had.

Alex had helped me plan it all, from the spacious hallway to the beautiful cream coloured kitchen with a sunny orangey opening, up to the eating and seating area. We sat in there most times, admiring the pretty English walled garden. The main living room to the front had a cosy open fire and it was perfect for the dark winter evenings when you just wanted to be warm.

Max and Millie greeted me when I went into the kitchen. I let them out into the garden and they bounced around, happy as always. I made myself a hot cup of coffee and sat there, more content than ever.

Everyone was due here this afternoon to help celebrate my birthday, little did they know there was an engagement to celebrate too. I had invited Simon, Sarah and Sophia, who turned one today and had just started walking.

Life had sorted itself out rather well.

Louise had settled her differences with Sarah and was a huge part of Sophia's life. Michael and her had set a date for the wedding and we were all very busy with the planning.

Isobelle had started dating John, Anna and Tim's youngest son, and James was too busy enjoying university life to have a girlfriend, just the one, anyway. Aunt Rose had returned from her annual cruise and was still living life to the full.

My dear parents had still not managed to make it back home, despite their good intentions, but I didn't mind. They lived for each other and they were happy.

My divorce to Simon had come through at the end of last year and the house sold just three weeks later to a charming family with three small boys. He and Sarah had bought a perfectly nice house just outside town. I'd visited a couple of times at Sarah's request, but it still felt a little odd, the two of us chatting over a cup of tea. She often popped in here though with Sophia and my heart melted each time I saw her. And that was that, we'd all managed to move on with our lives and I sometimes think Sophia was the glue that held us all together.

As I sat there, I remembered how all this had seemed so out of reach. I had come to appreciate that through each of those dark days and nights of being alone, I had finally found me. The 'me' that had been hiding behind motherhood and a husband with high ambitions, leaving the old me so very far behind.

I wouldn't change a thing now. Not the heartache, not the pain and the tears. It's hard to imagine, but sometimes out of all that fear, we learn to grow and become stronger than we ever thought possible.

Disturbing my thoughts, Alex stood over me, blocking the sunlight and casting a shadow.

"Good morning, the future Mrs Stone and Happy Birthday."

"Morning," I replied, as he kissed me on the lips, a long, lingering kiss.

****

One by one they arrived. The weather was picture perfect and we all sat outside, cheering Sophia on as she walked between us all, Max and Millie watching from a safe distance, panting in the shade.

Sophia and I opened our gifts and blew out the candles on our cakes, mine with considerably more than her single one.

"Hey," Louise called out, as I was admiring a picture frame Sarah had given me for my birthday. "What's that on your finger?"

"That, my dear Louise," Alex announced taking my hand and making me stand beside him, "is an engagement ring. I asked your mum to marry me last night and I'm pleased to tell you all, she said yes!"

Everyone cheered and started hugging and kissing me, then shaking Alex's hand.

"Congratulations," Michael, our master of ceremonies announced. "You're a lucky, lucky man!"

"And don't I know it," Alex agreed, squeezing me tightly.

When everything and everyone had calmed down, Alex started the barbecue, assisted by a grumpy looking Simon.

I brought the champagne and glasses out and as the steaks sizzled, Aunt Rose held my hand tightly. We smiled at each other as we surveyed the family chatting with each other and she squeezed my hand before leaving me to take another glass of champagne.

I stood by myself on the patio, watching them all enjoying the day. Sarah spotted me alone and walked over to me.

"Lovely party, Jen," she said as enthusiastically as ever.

"Thank you," I said, sipping my champagne.

"I'm so happy for you. Not sure I can say the same for Simon." She laughed and nudged me as we both looked over at him assisting Alex with the cooking and begrudgingly taking orders. "It's just a perfect day, Jen, isn't it?"

I studied her, all fresh-faced and young. She had lost her baby weight and was back to her normal slim state. She smiled at me and before I could allow any jealous feelings towards her youthful appearance to creep in, the sun shone directly onto her smooth, pretty, perfect face.

"Yes, it is," I agreed, noticing the sparkling little whiskers of hair growing on her top lip. "It really is!"

THE END